D1880909

SIMRAN-A NOVEL

SIMRAN
A Novel

RAJESH TALWAR

PUBLICATIONS

KALPAZ PUBLICATIONS

DELHI-110052

Simran - A Novel

Rs. 230

© Rajesh Talwar

ISBN: 81-7835-563-9

All rights reserved. No Part of this book may be reproduced in any manner without written permission.

Published in 2007 in India by
Kalpaz Publications
C-30, Satyawati Nagar,
Delhi-110052
E-mail: kalpaz@hotmail.com
Phone : 9212729499

Lasser Type Setting by : Rudra Computer Graphics, Delhi
Printed at : Salasar Imaging System, Delhi

In memory of
Anuj Ahuja and
Neera Joharey

Contents

Acknowledgements 11

Prologue 13

1. A Letter from the Past 19
2. Banarsi Das Estate 21
3. A Visitor 28
4. Sonia 32
5. The Iraqi Embassy 37
6. The Welfare Ministry 40
7. Delhi University 43
8. A Lost Chapter 47
9. An Introduction to Modern Art 62
10. Kumari 77
11. Settling Accounts 82
12. Train to the Himalayas 85

13. The Ridge 94

14. Bununda in Shimla 98

15. Summerhill 102

16. Ganahatti 108

17. Simran 113

18. King Puppet 116

19. Komal and Bahadur 121

20. Naming and Shaming 125

21. The Rain 133

22. Speeches, Speeches 144

23. Stoned on *Hindutva* 156

24. Absent-minded Professor 168

25. Diamond's Story 172

26. A Strange Resemblance 182

27. Breakthrough 185

28. Simiran Simran 189

29. A Sudden Departure 197

30. Lost Jobs, People and Causes 203

31. The Quest for Beauty 211

32. Poonam's story 219

33. Courtroom Drama 229

34. Dreaming the Past 236

35. Photofinish to the Airport 239

36. The Denouement 246

Epilogue 256

Acknowledgements

I would like to express sincere thanks to writer-friends Fernando da Cruz, Sabitri Devi and Lorna V for their advice, support and encouragement. I cannot thank my editor Loulou Brown enough for the close attention she gave to the manuscript and for her feedback on many important issues.

Prologue

I'm not a particularly good-looking person, but I have a nice smile. Or, to be more accurate perhaps, I *had* a nice smile. Maybe I still have it. I don't know. It's important for me to tell you this because, many years ago, my destiny was decided by a smile. My own smile.

'*Do you know what the most beautiful thing is in the world*?' Eliot had asked me this question some thirty years ago. I shook my head.

'*It's the smile on a child's face*,' *he said.*

He laughed when he saw my expression of disbelief.

'*You don't agree*?' *he said.* '*Perhaps it's too early for you to appreciate my point of view, but a day will come when you will.*'

I'm going to tell you, dear reader, a story that will be unlike any you have read before. Do I promise too much? Perhaps.

You will ask: what's so special about this story?

There are at least three special things about it. First and foremost, it is a true story. It is in fact truer than many true stories you may have read or heard about. Ah, you didn't know that stories could be 'truer'? You thought they were true or false. Well, there, you see, you are already learning.

Secondly, the unique thing about this story is the way it's been written. This is a novel and, as you may be aware, two of the most common ways in which novels are written are in the thriller and literary genres. So which is this? Neither. Or both. You are going to read a curious mix of a thriller and a literary novel, which will be something quite unique – even if it happens to be very badly written. This is quite literally a literary thriller. Why have I chosen to write like this? You'll understand this by and by.

Finally, it may make you see the world slightly differently. Even if it shifts your vision by a fraction of a millimetre, my purpose will have been served. I am going to try and make you see the human face differently, you see. It's not an easy task.

When I look at my face in the mirror, sometimes I see my face and sometimes I don't. Sometimes I see a few lines, some squiggles and a lumpy mass of flesh that does not tell me who I am. And sometimes I see Eliot laughing behind me in the mirror.

We returned from Gangotri two days previously, a journey that was supposed to have taken place many years ago. Soon after that she developed this skin condition.

Today, in the morning, I helped her to take a bath. You see, she has these scabs all over her body, which will go by and by, and for the medicine to work properly – so the doctor says – she has to have a bath three times a day. It's not easy for her to take a bath by herself. So I help. But everything will soon be 'right as rain'. Isn't that the expression the kind-looking dermatologist with the round glasses used? Everything *will* be right as rain in a few weeks. God, how I worry.

But I am getting ahead of myself. This happens quite often to people who read too much philosophy and I do read a fair amount of it, for I teach it you see. Or used to, at any rate. This is not the beginning of my story. It is not even the end. To tell you this story properly, I must start from that morning two months before the trip to Gangotri...

The shrill sound of the bell ringing woke me up. I searched under the pillow for the fancy children's watch smuggled in from China or Taiwan, a thirty-rupee turquoise-coloured bargain. The pavement shopkeeper who had sold it to me had confessed, when pressed, that it could go bust in a few hours, but had given strenuous assurances that there was a far greater possibility it would last out the better part of a year, and those had been good enough odds for me given my current financial situation. It was seven in the morning, past my normal waking time, over which I exercised little option. It was unlikely in the extreme, I reflected, that the human alarm system that woke me up each day had become dysfunctional. The greater possibility was that the saki consumed the previous night at Sonia's had knocked me out cold. She had bundled me into a taxi, and in the slumberous sleep that had followed the drunken stupor I had fallen into, my dulled senses had not yet been sufficiently blunted to ignore Haha's harsh early morning shouts of 'Milan! Milan!'

The bell for the first floor was ringing, a piercing, high-pitched sound that screamed through my brain; it usually meant someone for me, though there were sometimes mistaken callers. My landlord bolted the staircase door from the inside at night. I stepped out on to the balcony to see who it was, and saw a tall, young man dressed sharply in the typical get-up of the up-and-coming corporate executive, holding a shiny suitcase in his hands. Only his shoulders were sagging, suggesting the tired weariness of a traveller. When he looked up, I saw that it was Salim; unmistakeably so, despite a recently grown Frenchie. I shuffled down the staircase in my pyjamas and let him in.

'It's been a crazy trip,' said Salim, collapsing into an armchair. 'You can't imagine the trouble I've had reaching Delhi. Engine trouble on the way from Calcutta, and the anxiety of a crash apart, we had to wait eight hours at Patna airport to get it fixed.' He shook his head. 'And then, just getting here from the airport...'

'What's with these multinational companies? Can't they pay the taxi fare for their jet-set executives?'

It turned out that all taxi and auto rickshaw unions had declared a lightning strike. Petrol prices had gone up two weeks previously and they understandably wanted meters revised –though not so legitimately – a meter revision far beyond the hike. Salim had been lucky enough to get a lift from the university's registrar who'd been on the same flight.

Still feeling drowsy I stepped into the kitchen to make coffee.

'Guess what?' said Salim, after I'd poured him a cup. 'I met your friend.'

'Friends? I have no friends.'

'Don't quote Socrates at me, or should I say Mr Confusion?' said Salim. 'This one is a friend. Perhaps even more than one. You can't not call her a friend after spending four weeks with her.'

'Did you meet **her**?'

'The jewel-cutter herself.'

Sometimes I think it's true what they say about there being only five thousand people on the planet. I had spent hours searching the city's hotels for a sign of the 'jewel-cutter', as Salim called her, without any success. The absurd coincidence of having discovered her on the verge of her departure rattled every bone in my body.

You tell me, what were the chances of Salim having bumped into her like that?

I said, 'Make yourself comfortable.'

Salim stared.

'The airport.'

'You won't reach in time. You're forgetting...'

I was already out of the room before he had finished his sentence. Half-walking, half-sprinting down Lucknow Road, I had reached the main road when I understood what Salim had meant. In the urgency of that moment I had completely forgotten about the strike. It would take far too long by public transport, even if I did manage to catch a bus immediately.

I stood on the Ring Road for some length of time, waving down all manner of vehicle. Nobody stopped; it obviously wasn't my day. Had I been a university chick, especially one of the long-haired, short-skirted kind, I could easily have managed a lift, but with a receding hairline and nearly middle-aged I wouldn't have particularly attracted either sex. To make matters worse, I wasn't looking exactly respectable in an unwashed *kurta*-pyjama and a two-day stubble. Perhaps, though, I consoled myself, I looked scholarly and learned – not that it seemed to be helping much.

*****

A black Ambassador drew up next to me. *Eliot used to say that your luck could change a thousand times in a single day.*

The driver was seeking information. 'Where is Delhi University?' he hollered, unnecessarily.

There were some possibilities here.

'Where are you coming from?' I asked.

'From Karnal,' he replied. 'How do we reach Delhi University?'

'It's quite a distance.' I threw in the statement cautiously, watching the driver's expression. No sign of any suspicion.

I peered inside and saw an elderly couple on the back seat of the car. Putting on my kindest expression, I said, 'I teach at the university and need to go there myself. If you like, I can guide you to it.'

They accepted gratefully. I climbed into the front side of the car, alongside the driver, and began to give him directions to the airport. What had Salim said? She was looking 'lost and dejected'. I thought back to the day I had returned to my flat from Karim's and had found that letter.

1

A Letter from the Past

That night I had eaten an early dinner with Kumari. After a discussion at her little shanty or *jhuggi* near Ajmeri Gate, we had strolled down the labyrinthine network of lanes in that part of Old Delhi, towards Jama Masjid, where, with her insisting, we had shared a plate of delicious mutton stew with giant-sized crispy *naans* at Karim's.

Back in the flat, I spotted the brown envelope on the table as soon as I entered the study. The writing on the envelope caught my attention. *No, it couldn't be.* I withdrew a sheaf of paper from it and slowly read a cryptic message in the same handwriting.

'Dear John,

'I came to meet you in connection with your PhD thesis. I will be here again tomorrow morning at eight.

'Diamond.'

The letter perplexed me; there were several mysteries here.

Mystery number one. How did the author of the letter enter a locked room and put the letter on my table?

That was an easy one. The only other person who had a duplicate key to my flat at the time was Salim. Dissatisfied with his job in Lucknow, he had come to Delhi for a job interview with a multinational, and had been staying with me for two days now; in all likelihood he had been in the flat when this person arrived.

Mystery number two. How could two handwritings be so similar? Only a single possibility: sheer coincidence!

Mystery number three. Who was Diamond? Was it a he or a she?

On consideration, I decided in favour of a 'he'. There was a reason to infer that the letter writer was a woman: this was the resemblance it bore to Simran's handwriting. Wasn't there something like a feminine handwriting? While conceding this, I nevertheless felt that a more persuasive argument existed for supposing that this person was a man. Anyone with a name as unusual as Diamond was probably from the '91 class; there were thirty-odd students, myself included, who had received similar names in a christening ceremony held in Professor Srinivasan's class. There was certainly no girl with that name or I would have remembered. It could have been the name of one of the less regular students who occasionally attended the philosophy class as a subsidiary subject.

This was a letter from the past. That much was certain. No one in Delhi University even knew that I had registered for a PhD thesis. It seemed a long while ago that I had been pursuing a thesis. Summerhill, Shimla.

I put away the letter in a table drawer and slammed it shut wearily. I felt too tired to wait up for Salim. Before dozing off, I briefly considered the possibility that Diamond was a real name. It seemed unlikely.

2

Banarsi Das Estate

Professor Haha's shouting woke me up the next morning. 'Milan,' he yelled, 'Come on, Milan. Let's go.'

Why couldn't they let other people sleep?

The person being summoned was my landlord's son – a dutiful member of the local exercise group. His wife, Mala, used to come up to my flat for lessons in English. A pleasant, smiling lady, she was forever asking about my family. I had invented one for her: not a wife, but brothers, sisters and parents. Her husband had stopped her visits six months ago, even before relations had turned sour between his father and me. It was a pity because I had enjoyed her company.

My landlord's name was Ram Lok Uncle. Everybody called him that, from the washerwoman to the milkman, myself included. In his early sixties, he was greying, of middling size, brisk and humorous looking. Unlike most owner-residents of the colony who belonged to the trading classes he wasn't in business – except landlord business – having retired from government service years ago. His wife, Sheela *behn*, was a crotchety old woman whose sari was perpetually in disorder and, like a dysfunctional pressure cooker or someone hard of hearing, she kept shouting her head off at somebody or other for one reason or another. They lived with their son, daughter-in-law and one grandchild on the ground floor of the building.

The house, Forty-Five, Lucknow Road, Banarsi Das Estate, was a double-storey, concrete structure, light grey in colour, on a biggish plot of land. This area itself was one of the older residential quarters of the city, built a quarter of a century before the posh South Delhi colonies had sprung up.

There were tenants in many of the houses, a large number of them students, who could not be accommodated in any of the several university hostels nearby. Rents were high and the students – especially those from the poorer Indian states – compensated by sharing two-room tenements between four, five or even six of them. Furnishings were basic and minimal, and landlords didn't worry themselves overmuch about damage to the fittings and fixtures as they were concerned mainly with the recovery of rent.

I rubbed my eyes open. It was still fairly dark, not yet dawn. I pressed a tiny switch on my new acquisition and the instrument still working shone a green light into the darkness showing the time to be five-thirty. I slipped out of bed and stumbled across to the kitchen.

As was my general routine, I put the kettle on to boil and climbed into the bath. By the time I came out, the kettle was boiling with previously measured water, enough for six cups of tea and a shave. I stepped out of the flat, brought in a steel container of milk left outside by the milkman, poured the white liquid into a pan for boiling, and took out enough water from the kettle for a shave. By the time I had shaved, the milk was boiling. Combining all these various mini-tasks took the dull edge off them for me, and although the time saved was not much, I indulged myself in the self-delusion that this was time management of a sort. I took off the pan with the boiling liquid, put it back, let the milk rise up once again, and then took it off to cool.

Finally I made tea and poured most of it into a steel thermos. Picking up the newspaper from the balcony, I carried it with my early morning cuppa back to the bedroom; it was actually a cheap quality lined glass through which I could better judge the amount of milk that gave the tea the colour I liked and better to savour the last few sips.

I leant back on the grandfather's chair. It was one of Eliot's few possessions that I had inherited: a huge, black, rosewood, rocking chair. I skimmed through the paper's headlines without bothering about the rest.

I heard a grunt. It was Salim, waking up. '*Arre,* brother,' he yawned, 'Can a fellow get some tea?'

'Help yourself. There's plenty in the thermos.'

When he got back, I told him about the previous day's incident with the landlord, who had been getting increasingly hostile over the issue of rent. For some time now I had been without any income, owing to a university decision that ad hoc lecturers not be paid any salary for the summer holidays, and practically all my savings had been exhausted. The consequence was that I hadn't paid my rent for the past three months.

There was, however, yet another reason why Ram Lok and his family were upset with me, and this was because of Kumari who came over to meet me sometimes on Sunday. They certainly wondered about our association, and may have debated within their family if their defaulting tenant was truly conducting research on the community Kumari represented – or could it be that I was a sex-starved bachelor, or worse still a weirdo who resorted to kinky sex?

The previous day the landlord had come up to the flat to claim the arrears. I had woken late with a hangover and was frantically putting together my lecture notes and reading lists in order, so as to reach the university in time for an eight-thirty class.

He came straight in, without bothering to knock. I heard him out and explained that I didn't have the money right then.

'In that case,' my landlord had said, 'give me one rupee.'

'Don't joke, Ram Lok Uncle. You will get the money.'

'No,' he insisted. 'Give me one rupee. You see, if you give me one rupee today, it means that tomorrow you can give me fifty thousand rupees.'

I wasn't happy to have the sincerity of my motives tested in this fashion. Besides, I was running late.

'Look here,' I said heatedly, 'I'm in a terrific rush right now, so if you will excuse me, I am going to have a bath. We can discuss this later. In any case I don't have one rupee in change.'

The old man grimaced, picked up a paperweight from the table, and spoke slowly and with great deliberation, 'If you don't give me one rupee, I will have to take something else.'

'Do as you please,' I said, walking into the bathroom. 'Don't trouble me at this time of day. That's all I ask of you.'

When I came out a little later, he had gone.

The paperweight was still there.

Salim was concerned. 'Do you need any cash? How many months has it been?'

'You make it sound like a pregnancy. Thanks but no thanks. I'm expecting some money any time.'

'Buy him a copy of the Rent Control Act and read him through the sections on rent control and rights of tenants. That will tell him where he gets off.'

'Thanks for unsolicited advice,' I said. 'Incidentally, who is this fellow with this strange name – Diamond? Was he with us in college?'

'It's a woman,' he said sardonically, moving out of the bedroom.

A little while later he returned, carrying a shaving glass filled with steaming water. Placing it on the windowsill he brought out a pocket mirror and shaving kit from his briefcase.

'Do you think I should grow a beard?' Positioning the mirror at an angle he began to lather his face.

'A Frenchie might suit you.'

Who could this woman be? Before I had a chance to question him further on the subject, several things happened in quick succession. The shaving glass fell off the window. I heard a chink, followed by a loud scream.

We looked below and saw the smashed glass on the cemented floor downstairs. 'Murderers!' the landlady screamed, as she shook her arms frenziedly. 'They are trying to kill me.'

'Quick,' said Salim, 'Let's lock the flat and go up to the roof.'

'There's no need. Let them come up.'

'No,' he insisted. 'Let's go up.'

Climbing up the stairs against my will, I said, 'It was an accident. Nobody was hurt. What the hell?'

From the terrace, we heard a babble of voices below. Milan's voice was raised, doubtlessly energised after the morning's work-out. I pulled out a couple of broken chairs kept on the roof for repair, and we sat there watching the pigeons for the better part of an hour. In the last five years the pigeon population in the area had swelled and I felt that this could not have been possible just by breeding alone; there must have been migrations from areas less up-market in pigeon speak, whatever that meant. Salim smiled when he heard my observations.

We had eventually decided to go down when we heard a loud siren. I moved to the parapet to investigate. A police jeep was approaching the house, its red emergency light flashing. It pulled up alongside the house, and an inspector and two constables jumped out.

'I'm going down to talk to them,' I said. 'You get dressed and rush off for your interview.'

'You sure?'

'Yeah, I'm sure. There's no problem.'

They had all surrounded the inspector: Ram Lok Uncle, his son Milan, his old lady Sheela *behn*, her sari billowing in the wind, and even the grandchild. The boy stared at me malevolently.

The inspector recognised me at once. I had met him with his superior, the station house officer, only recently, when I had accompanied a colleague from the department to the Kingsway Camp police station to get a couple of drunken students released. The station house officer who turned out to be a former student had extended his full co-operation.

'*Namaste*, Professor Sahib,' he said. 'What seems to be the problem?'

'There is no problem at all,' I said, feeling disgusted. 'How is the SHO Sahib keeping these days?'

After the exchange of some more pleasantries I told the inspector about the morning's incident.

The policeman laughed uproariously when he heard what had happened. Milan and Ram Lok Uncle tried to say something, but he interrupted them harshly, switching off his charm. Rather sternly, he warned them of the consequences of making false complaints against respectable citizens.

Milan made the mistake of protesting, and presented half-baked arguments in support of his case. His good temper already fragile, the policeman became incensed at what he saw as a sly attempt to manipulate his intelligence, and he began shouting at Milan and Ram Lok Uncle at the top of his voice, threatening them with the dire consequences that befell those who prosecuted maliciously.

Out of concern for the old man, and fearing he might have a stroke, I took the Inspector aside and attempted to pacify him.

'You were levelling extremely serious changes against the professor.' He addressed them in a more subdued tone after he walked back to the assembled group. 'Next time you press false charges I will put you in the lock up. Is that understood?'

It appeared that in the telephone conversation Milan had had with the inspector, he had made out that it was a case where a dangerous glass object had first been aimed and then hurled with force in a deliberate attempt to try and kill the old lady. Attempt to murder! Seizing upon my magnanimity in asking him to tone down the tenor of his questioning as further proof of my innocence and decency, the inspector lectured the assembled family members some more. Eventually winding up, he turned to me and asked if there was any message for his superior. 'No, nothing,' I said. 'Just give him my *namaste*.' The inspector climbed back into the jeep, and sped off.

I heard muted mutterings. Ignoring them, I climbed up the stairs back to my flat.

3

A Visitor

The door was ajar. I stepped in and saw a dark, young girl wearing a blue T shirt and jeans sitting on the grandfather's chair, a cigarette dangling between her lips. She kept rocking the chair back and forth with deliberation, completely oblivious to my presence, sucked deeply at the cigarette, and in the manner of an unpractised smoker blew a clumsy smoke ring into the air.

I was momentarily thrown off balance by what seemed to be something that had all the elements of a magical apparition. I wondered if she was a former student who had somehow managed to find out where I lived, despite my best efforts at concealment. My status as a recluse seemed to be under attack.

'Excuse me,' I said, a little sharply.

'Oh, hullo,' she said, sounding quite startled. She stood up then and stretched out a hand.

'Nice meeting you.' I shook her hand.

'Did you get my message?' She gave an uncertain smile. 'My name is Diamond.'

I walked past her to open the window more fully, making my displeasure evident.

She stubbed out her cigarette on the waste paper basket. 'If you're worried about cigarette smoke, you can relax. On average I smoke only one cigarette a week.'

'Even that's too much, given the state of pollution in the city. You don't even have the excuse of addiction.' I sounded sanctimonious, even to myself. 'Would you like some tea?'

'I suppose you're right,' she said a little tensely. 'Yes, I think I will have a cup of tea.'

When I got back from the kitchen, she was reading the newspaper. Seeing me, she put it aside. 'That's quick service.'

'I drink too much tea to keep making it all the time,' I explained. 'I couldn't really understand the note you left behind yesterday. Are you from Shimla?'

'No.' She shook her head. 'I was visiting last week and met Professor Srinivasan who suggested I meet you. He thought we could exchange notes.'

I was zapped, as one of my students might have said. She might have had some suspicion of what I was thinking, for she took out a letter from her handbag and gave it to me.

'*Dear Confusion,*

'(*I hope I can call you that without causing offence.*)

'*I am sending this note with a young friend who happens to be a research scholar at the Southern Methodist University, Texas. Her topic is more or less on the same lines as that submitted by you for your PhD. As she was leaving for Delhi, I suggested she meet you.*

'*The university will shortly be advertising two permanent vacancies in the philosophy department. If your thesis is approved, you might be considered for a position at the Faculty.*

'*I hope you have a rewarding discussion with Ms. Diamond.*

'*PROF. A. K. SRINIVASAN*'

I read the letter again and returned it to her. It had been a while since someone had used that term while addressing me.

'What's your topic?' I said.

'The aesthetics of the human form,' she said, sipping the tea. 'So far, though, I've only been collecting material and scribbling notes. I haven't started writing it out seriously.'

'Neither have I.'

'What do you mean?' She looked surprised. 'According to the professor, the university might consider awarding you your PhD purely on the basis of what you have already handed in. He believes there are original, creative ideas in what you have submitted, even though it needs to be put into academic language, instead of the way its been written up.'

There was clearly some confusion here. I was aware of being unfair to the woman in front of me, but nevertheless felt my temper rising. I had given the university a bare proposal and there had been absolutely no work done on it.

'This has been a waste of time for you, I'm afraid,' I said, trying to get a grip on myself. 'You have been misinformed. I haven't done any writing on the subject.'

She continued to sit as if she hadn't noticed the tone of my voice. Her next words belied that conclusion.

'You don't have to get upset,' she said quietly. 'Perhaps you've forgotten. As a matter of fact, I'm carrying a copy of your first chapter with me.' She rummaged in her bag and took out a large, white envelope from which she extracted a bunch of crumpled papers.

Rather careless in the way of keeping papers, I couldn't help thinking, if she truly thought it to be the first chapter of a thesis. I knew, though, that it wasn't anything remotely connected with the PhD, because I was certain that despite all the preparations and energy that had been put into the research topic, in the end there wasn't any chapter, first or last, or even a preface. Still, prompted by a vestigial curiosity to see where the confusion lay, I took the sheaf of papers from her and glanced through them. I didn't need to read more than a few paragraphs. *How could this be*? I closed my eyes.

'Why don't you leave your contact number and address with me?' I said, controlling my emotions. 'I'll get in touch with you if any collaboration is possible.'

'Okay,' she said, standing up. Her eyes were alert with the knowledge that something was amiss and that she had overstayed her welcome. She took out a piece of paper from her bag, scribbled something on it, and gave it to me. 'This is my address and phone number.'

At the door she turned. 'I'm here for another week or so before returning to Shimla. If you decide to contact me, do so before I leave.'

I had already decided not to contact her, but didn't want to hurt her feelings unnecessarily.

'I'll remember that,' I said.

4

Sonia

1

My mind on fire, I telephoned the Iraqi embassy to postpone my meeting with the ambassador, as I felt in no condition to deal with anyone on a professional basis. The next call was to Sonia to let her know I was coming over.

'Is everything okay?' she wanted to know.

'Why shouldn't it be?'

I stuck a note for Salim on the door, and caught an auto-rickshaw to Saket in the afternoon, stopping briefly at a wayside liquor shop to pick up a bottle of Old Monk rum.

Sonia's flat was a compact, independent unit on the ground floor of a three-storey structure. Pale yellow from the outside, white walls within, it was one of the smaller dwelling units constructed by the development authority.

Finding the door ajar, I stepped in to find her sewing in the workroom. The second, equally undersized, room in her flat functioned as her bedroom at night, but it was where she received guests and clients during the day.

The furnishings were simple, ethnic and close to the floor. Instead of beds there were mattresses spread on the floor with bright-coloured cushions to lend support or provide a headrest. The sparse – or rather lack of – furniture in her apartment made it seem larger than it actually was. Tall, leafy plants that somehow survived the Delhi heat stood in silent dignity in cooler, shadowy corners of the flat.

Sonia believed deep down that she was an artist, and that her true worth had yet to be recognised. Too refined to say so directly, she expressed her commitment to her art and craft by arranging all manner of fabric so that it fell from the walls like superfluous curtains. It touched the visitor with its perceived softness and created, within the limited possibilities the small space afforded her, a strange, exotic but essentially soothing ambience about the place.

After some time she stopped work on the garments laid out on the floor and we crossed over to the other room where she ferreted out some snacks and crisps from inside a table drawer. I unscrewed the bottle I had brought with me and mixed both of us a large rum and coke. We sat down on mattresses opposite a low, chic and ethnic-looking cane table.

A wheatish complexioned, lean, bony, tall and attractive woman, Sonia was in her mid-thirties and lived by herself. Although a dress designer by profession, she didn't employ tailors, cutters or a staff, preferring to work alone. She catered to an exclusive, affluent clientele.

I had first met her at a diplomatic party at Chanakyapuri; I had gone at the behest of the Syrian first secretary, while a senior woman diplomat attached to the Dutch embassy had invited Sonia. At the party, she stood out as another Indian – most of the guests were either European or distinctly Arab – but we didn't get an opportunity to introduce ourselves. Later as I was leaving, near the parking lot I had heard voices raised in anger, and as I moved in the general direction of the sound I encountered a middle-aged official from the French Embassy foisting his unwanted attentions on her. Together we cooled off some of his ardour.

'You son of a *haraami.*' She had got out of the black sedan angrily.

'Can I drop you somewhere?' I had offered, after the drunken Frenchman had beaten a diplomatic retreat, still muttering to himself.

'Okay,' she said, cautiously. 'I live in Saket.'

The Syrian diplomat had temporarily loaned me the use of his car and as I escorted her to the gleaming air-conditioned chauffeur-driven Buick standing nearby, I could see her alert eyes contrasting it with my general homespun attire.

'Are you a diplomat?' she asked, en route to her house.

I shook my head.

'So what do you do?' she persisted.

'I teach philosophy.'

'Is that so?' She gave a surprised laugh. When I dropped her off at her house, she gave me her visiting card, a rather elongated artistic one.

'Drop by, sometime.'

'I will.'

I don't remember the details of our discussion during the half-hour drive to her home, but I had been entertained and impressed by her blunt, honest style of speech, so that two weeks later when I had the use of the car yet again I paid her the promised visit. Afterwards I spent many nights in her tiny flat at Saket, yet the relationship never assumed the form of a romantic liaison or even that of a friend-lover. I never desired such a relationship with her, despite the fact that Sonia was very attractive by any standards – even though she tried to hide her feminine charms by wearing loose garments. I told her many times to give up wearing baggy clothes but she wouldn't change, despite being a dress designer who successfully attempted to make her clients look sexy. It was an extreme step, I thought, even while accepting the truth of her claim that drabness provided protection to single women in Delhi who couldn't afford to look too attractive.

We ordered Chinese food from a nearby restaurant, two different combo meals targeted at a new breed of company executives eating alone, and resumed drinking; this time it was some Scotch she had managed to procure through her diplomatic connections.

'I've run out of patience,' she said at half past twelve. 'Why don't you tell me? What's wrong?'

I said, 'The fundamentalists are getting active again.'

'Which ones? The Hindus or the Muslims?'

'The Christians this time,' I said.

'Be serious,' she said. 'Is that's what's bothering you?'

'Yeah.'

'Really?'

'These bastards are screwing up everybody's happiness.'

'Listen, you're supposed to be a lecturer. You're talking like a student.'

'What's wrong with that?' I said disagreeably. Regardless of what we spoke about, talking to Sonia always had a soothing effect on me. I felt that an electrical current that had seized my body had been switched off and once more I felt composed.

'I think you should go to sleep.'

'Funny, I had the same brilliant idea.'

I pushed one of the space-saving mattresses next to the wall, and fell asleep as soon as my head touched the cushion.

2

The next morning I woke up feeling fresh and relaxed, the anguish of the previous evening washed away by some magic. Human emotions were strange things, I mused. Sonia took one look at me and made out that it was now all right for her to laugh.

'You were like a real kid last night,' she smiled. 'You'll never say what's really troubling you, will you?'

'Just talking to you makes me feel better, Sonia. What does it matter what we talk about?'

'Fair enough,' she said. 'If that's the case, I should become a therapist. God knows I could do with the money.'

'How are the negotiations getting along?'

'He's a real dog,' she said, referring to her husband. 'He is offering five hundred thousand for the divorce.'

'That's something.'

'Listen, five hundred thousand isn't enough to buy me burial space in New Delhi. I need a house. I'm tired of living in rented accommodation.'

'He will pay,' I said reassuringly. 'You just have to outwait him, that's all.'

'I know, but I'm getting tired. This guy's a millionaire. A small flat in South Delhi is peanuts for him.'

'You forget that people get to be millionaires by sticking to every *naya paise* they've got.'

'What a dog,' she said sullenly, the bitter edge to her personality surfacing briefly. 'Shall we eat?'

It was late morning, a working day, and both of us had appointments in the city, so we didn't linger over breakfast as we usually did during the Sunday mornings I woke up in her flat.

'Where are you going?' she asked, at the door. 'Can I drop you somewhere?'

Sonia had recently bought a blue Fiat, which she had got dirt cheap from the wife of a Romanian diplomat for whose children she had designed some clothes.

'Iraqi Embassy,' I said, 'if you're going that way.'

'It's on my way,' she said. 'Whom are you meeting?'

'The ambassador.'

'You have yourself a good deal, 'she grinned. 'I should also get into this racket.'

'Why don't you?' I said, picking up my briefcase. 'It'll give me some healthy competition.'

'It's not creative,' she said, getting into the car.

'Yeah?' I said trying to sound nasty. 'Dress designing is more creative than doing a PhD?'

5

The Iraqi Embassy

Sonia dropped me off outside the main entrance to the embassy at Chanakyapuri. The name of the area translated literally into 'diplomatic enclave', and was a green, up-market part of the city where most of the embassies had their offices. Several of these had residences for senior-level diplomats that adjoined the embassy building. The Iraqi Embassy was a huge, ochre-coloured bungalow, with a large, well-tended lawn.

The ambassador, a short, balding man with a bristly moustache in his late forties, received me in his office, a plush wood-panelled, modern-looking affair. He had arrived barely a month earlier.

After the fall of Saddam Hussein's government and the takeover of the country by the Coalition forces, in a public relations exercise Iraq's newly installed National Transitional Government had ordered the transfer of a hundred ambassadors across the globe.

'Please take a seat, professor,' he said, gesturing at two large beige-coloured sofas kept in a corner of his air-conditioned office. He spoke a few words in Arabic to his assistant, a sallow- complexioned youth. It sounded like gibberish, but I understood it to mean that he desired privacy and would not welcome any intrusions. It was no secret that in the modern outsourcing world PhDs could be ghost written if the price was right, but by their very nature these arrangements were highly confidential and secrecy was of paramount importance. He barked out another order of a simpler kind and came and sat opposite me.

'Would you care for a cigar?' He opened a case.

'No, thank you, ambassador.'

'It's very hot outside, isn't it?' he said, lighting a cigar.

A red uniformed waiter appeared, carrying two tall glasses of lemon juice and a plate of roasted cashew and pistachio nuts on a silver tray.

'I find this is the only thing which helps in this weather,' he said as he took a sip of the pale liquid. 'Those American soft drinks are no good at all.'

'This is very cooling,' I agreed, 'and you can be sure there is no fertilizer in it.'

'Of course there is that advantage, too.' The diplomat permitted himself a small smile, having understood my allusion to the episode in which the Indian Parliament had banned certain soft drinks following investigations by an environmental group.

I munched cashew nuts and waited for him to continue.

'You know my problem, professor,' he said, puffing at the cigar. 'I'm much too preoccupied with affairs of state. I can't take time out for studies.'

'Don't worry, ambassador.' I sipped my drink. 'You just leave everything to me.'

'I know I can trust you.' He tipped the cigar ash into an onyx bowl. 'You have been highly recommended by the Mauritian first secretary.'

'You know the terms.' I finished my drink.

'They are acceptable to me. If you can finish earlier, I can pay you more.'

I said dryly, 'That's not possible. These things take time.'

'I know, I know,' he said, in an appeasing tone. Putting his hand into his coat pocket, he withdrew a thick, manila envelope. 'This is the advance. Fifty thousand, you said.'

'That's correct.' I took the envelope from him and stood up.

'I will be in touch with you,' said the ambassador.

We shook hands. The diplomat came to the door to see me off.

*****

Outside the embassy gates, I didn't bother to count the money. The currency would be clean and crisp, and it would be the correct amount, I knew. The balance of two hundred thousand rupees was to be paid on completion of the project. This did not include money spent on photocopying, typing and purchase of books and journals, for which I would submit separate receipts. The time limit was set at six months from the date of the contract. It was all verbally arranged without a signed contract, for in this line of business the parties operated mostly on trust.

6

The Welfare Ministry

Shastri Bhawan lay in the spacious bureaucratic heart of the city and housed the offices of the welfare ministry. A large, pink building with Victorian-style embellishments, its architecture suggested modernity as well as an imperial past. From the outside it gave an impression – entirely erroneous I was to discover- of strength and purpose.

In order to meet Mr Roshan Lal, the joint secretary, I had to follow the usual, tedious bureaucratic procedure. This meant crowding around the reception with half a dozen other people, each one trying to catch the attention of the solitary clerk sitting behind the semicircular wooden table. When your turn came, the official would pick up the telephone and ring whoever it was you wanted to meet, to confirm whether or not you would be permitted entry. Often the person would not be there and the applicant would have to wander off for ten to fifteen minutes before coming back to make another attempt.

At length, I managed to reach the bureaucrat's office, only to be asked to wait by his private secretary. It was an hour before I managed to see him, in spite of a prior appointment. While waiting inside the dingy, box-like reception room, I recalled Eliot telling a latecomer in the English Literature class, 'Punctuality, my friend, is the politeness of kings.'

The bearded joint secretary was lean and hungry-looking. Possibly ambitious, too, I thought, being reminded yet again of Eliot in class, describing Cassius in Julius Caesar. The office was bright and cool. In the corner an air-conditioner hummed. The bureaucrat himself sat behind a large, glass-topped wooden table.

'Sorry to have kept you waiting, professor,' he drawled. 'Some urgent matters to be attended to, you know.'

'Yes, I know,' I said, sitting down on one of the leather chairs facing him.

'I believe you are working with minorities,' he said crisply. 'What can I do to help?'

I described some of the problems faced by *hijras*. Living together in clusters, they were treated as worse than outcastes, with even ordinary poor people refusing to live with them. They led an extremely insecure and hard life; most took to begging together in small bands.

'We have various schemes for the rehabilitation of under-privileged groups,' said the Joint Secretary, after hearing me out. 'There are travel concessions by train or air, concessions in postage and income tax. Some jobs in public sector banks have been reserved for them. Banks have also been instructed to provide them with loans and advances at low interest rates.'

'That's exactly the point, Mr Lal. All these schemes you have mentioned are either caste- based job reservations or schemes applicable only to blind persons, those who are disabled or who are affected with leprosy. The *hijras* have nothing.'

'I agree with you,' he nodded regretfully. 'To be honest with you, I don't think the government is even contemplating taking any rehabilitative measures for this particular section of people. Perhaps you could meet the Deputy Secretary, Mr M. M. Gupta. He may be able to suggest something. Before you see him, though, I suggest you draft out your recommendations in the form of a petition.'

That was all that he could advise. It wasn't very much, but then I hadn't been expecting very much from the meeting.

7

Delhi University

'*Artsfac*', as the large red-bricked, Faculty of Arts building was popularly referred to by students, was a ten-minute walk from where I lived. It was a major convenience in a city teeming with vehicles transporting hundreds of thousands of commuters the large distances they needed to traverse to get to work through increasingly chaotic traffic conditions. At the request of students that day I had agreed to take a special class to discuss any specific queries related to Greek philosophy, so that they could prepare for the examinations due in a month's time.

Later, I was sitting on one of the hardbacked wooden chairs inside the staff room, fielding questions, soothing anxieties and giving attendance to pleading latecomers, when a tall, handsome man in his late forties, with the build of a wrestler, stepped into the room. It was Professor J. P. Mahan, dressed in his spotless white *kurta*-pyjama as usual. A month previously he had become the head of department and was now to a considerable extent in control of my affairs.

'Hullo, hullo,' Mahan boomed, taking the chair next to me. 'How are you?'

'I'm all right,' I said. 'Let me offer you my congratulations.'

'This is just by rotation,' he grinned, visibly pleased. 'Nothing to congratulate, really.'

'Do something for us, professor,' I said. 'We're tired of being ad hoc.'

'Have patience,' he said. 'The department is shortly due to announce two permanent vacancies.'

'I'm not concerned for myself only, professor. I've been teaching for just a few years. There are lecturers in the university in different departments who have been teaching for fifteen, twenty years, who are still ad hoc. It's shameful that this should continue.'

'Just because they have been teaching for a long time doesn't mean that they should be made permanent.'

'Come on, professor,' I said angrily. 'Who is deserving? Some of the permanent appointments made recently are those of fresh postgraduates with barely a year's teaching experience. Ad hoc lecturers with twenty years experience have to queue up for interviews, together with those who were their students till recently. It's embarrassing, even for the students.'

'I know, I know,' he said, 'but this has been happening for many years.' Flexing his newly acquired muscles, he added in a mildly threatening tone, 'I haven't seen you for some time. Have you been taking classes regularly?'

'Of course I have,' I said evenly. 'Today happens to be an extra class.'

'You are an intelligent fellow, you know,' he said, switching tactics. 'Not like these bloody communists.'

'Nothing very bloody about them any more I should say. There are worse people around nowadays.'

'We must have a proper discussion one of these days,' he said, ignoring my comment. He paused, as if to think. 'What about tonight? Come and have dinner at my house.'

'I'm terribly sorry,' I said, 'but I have a guest staying with me these days.'

'Bring him along,' he offered generously.

'And we have to go to this wedding,' I added hastily, standing up.

'Oh, I see,' Mahan said, a little suspiciously. 'In that case come by some other time. I will call Professor Saha from the sociology department. Do you know him?'

'Yes,' I admitted. Professer Saha, nicknamed Haha by the students, woke up Milan for their early-morning workouts. 'I see him in the morning sometimes.'

'He is an early riser,' he acknowledged. 'Goes for exercise.'

'I know,' I said. 'Good for him. Excuse me now.'

*****

Walking back home on the now darkened roads, I reflected on how there couldn't have been a worse choice for the position of Head of Department. I had been studiously avoiding Mahan for the previous few days, because for some reason he had got it into his thick head that I was a potential recruit and one who could be showcased, as I was perceived to be from the Christian community. He wouldn't hesitate to use his newly acquired clout to aid that process of enlistment. Sometime during that hypothetical dinner he would have dropped a hint that, if I could be persuaded to accept his line of thinking, he would provide his dedicated support not only for a renewal of my lecturer status (this sounded better, but was actually worse than a car licence renewal) but also for a permanent post. There were other groups in the university that were left wing but they were little better in this respect and indulged in the same kind of nepotism and lobbying.

Inside the flat, I found and read a note from Salim on the table.

'*Dear John,*

'*I have got the job*!

'*They were in a hurry to recruit and let me know there and then. I'm expected to report for work in two week's time.*

'*The job is based in Calcutta, but I shall need to come to Delhi every now and then. Since they haven't given me much time to start, I am leaving at once for Lucknow. I'll try and catch the afternoon express.*

'Where were you last night?

'See you,
Salim'

8

A Lost Chapter

The flat seemed empty after Salim left. I felt guilty for not having been able to spend more time with him. My eye fell on the sheaf of papers lying on the table. I picked them up and dragged a chair to the balcony.

My mind flew back to when I had first met Simran. I started reading.

THE FIRST CHAPTER

It was late evening by the time they reached Haridwar, the gateway of the gods. At the *ghats*, they watched pilgrims bathe, saw devotees place little fiery earthen candles in the river which, balanced on small leafy carriers, made their way across the shimmering waters.

As they strolled alongside the riverbank towards a more secluded spot, night fell and the stars came out in all their glory. At the spot where they sat down next to the river they could hear no sound except the gentle lapping sound of the waters. They were quiet for a long while. Finally, Affection spoke.

AFFECTION: What do you think of beauty, Confusion?

CONFUSION: Beauty in what? Do you mean in nature, such as this river flowing past us, or the blue mountains on the other side? There might be beauty in the architecture of buildings, say the Taj Mahal, or beauty in poetry, painting, or sculpture. Some might see beauty in mathematics and others may talk of beautiful feelings or emotions. Surely it is necessary for you to specify exactly in which context you are speaking of beauty?

AFFECTION: Is that necessary, Confusion? Isn't there a common thread running through all human perception of beauty, whether a beautiful essay, beautiful house or even a beautiful conversation?

CONFUSION: I don't really think so, Affection. You are talking of beauty in general. Socrates tried to find a common thread – that which you just mentioned – and in his dialogue reported by Plato in *Hippias Major* he concludes that the common thread is usefulness. I suppose that's how a logician or rationalist would perceive beauty, but such a view would make very little sense when considered with regard to the human face or form, for example, and has in fact been ridiculed. While it is doubtless true that a developed and healthy physique is useful to the possessor of such a body, and is also aesthetically appealing, can we say, for example, that wide, inflated nostrils – to breathe better – are more attractive? Larger ears to hear better?

AFFECTION: It is extremely doubtful, Confusion, that wide nostrils and large ears provide better breathing and hearing. You have been reading some medieval medical literature. I assure you, your assumptions are baseless.

CONFUSION: I was just joking, Affection. I was merely quoting the manner in which a Greek contemporary of Socrates, who was perhaps a little jealous of him, parodied his views. You will surely agree that a large nose or ears are not, at any rate, less useful in any way. A Greek god does not have a 'face pattern' that is more useful than one as ugly as Lucifer. In this sense, Socrates was rightly ridiculed by the commentator, who pointed out that while his views might hold good with respect to houses and horses, the same would only lead to absurd results if applied to the human form.

AFFECTION: Do you then, Confusion, have any views on beauty with regard to any particular or specific area? In relation to the human form itself, for example?

CONFUSION: As I just mentioned, that would be difficult and improper to conclude with regard to beauty, generally speaking. In relation to the human form, I believe that beauty doesn't actually exist. It is our human consciousness that determines what constitutes a beautiful human body.

AFFECTION: Confusion, it appears that you are getting into a general discussion about whether the universe exists, or whether it is only our consciousness that exists. Your argument seems to be that we know that the universe and beauty (which is a part of it) exist only because of our consciousness.

CONFUSION: No, Affection. I don't mean that at all. I feel sure that the universe exists – as well as human consciousness. Perhaps even beauty exists in some form. Without getting into a discussion on that aspect of the matter right now, I do believe that beauty in relation to the human form does not exist. What exists is only a human perception or consciousness of it, and behind this consciousness there lie certain clearly identifiable causes that govern and define this perception. The reasons why human beings perceive beauty with regard to the human form in a particular manner can be rationally comprehended and understood.

AFFECTION: Let's hear about these identifiable factors.

CONFUSION: I think several factors may influence our perception of beauty. The most important and central factor, to my mind, is our concept of normality. The notion of normality dominates and prejudices our perceptions. Thus any individual feature on the face should not be in excess in shape and size in either direction, for example, small mouths and large noses! This concept of normality has a curiously democratic character to it. If we were to pause for an instant and imagine an absurd situation in an imaginary society where the prevailing majority opinion was that large noses were the most attractive, the logical corollary to this would be a corresponding opinion that small noses were terribly repulsive. A similar situation would arise in the case of any other feature of the human form. If we make such an assumption, the consequences of such an assumption immediately demonstrate the very impossibility and falsity of such an assumption. In our existing human society, therefore, it would be impossible for long noses to be regarded as more attractive. The consequences of an absurd assumption have shown us its impossibility, and also suggest the actual dominant assumptions in our society. You see, largeness or smallness is relative. In order to preserve the interests of persons having small noses, etc., who themselves form a substantial minority, it is important that largeness of any human feature must not be considered beautiful. Thus medium-sized ears, noses, lips, and so forth, are the only solution that is acceptable to the majority population. What we call a very long nose can be regarded as such only in the context of the length of most of our noses. Therefore, we find a substantial minority, maybe forty per cent of the population, with larger than average noses and a substantial minority, another forty per cent, with smaller than average noses. The presence of these substantial minorities on both sides of the spectrum itself gives rise to our notion of what is average, what is normal, and hence what is beautiful. Our talk of pygmies and giants is also in the context of a normal human size – the 'normal' signifying the points at which most of us tend to converge. Many notions of size and distance also begin from a consideration of our own size as the normal and natural size. This is so in the case of most objects used by humans. A small table is relative to our physical size, and so also are what we consider to be a small room or a small house. If the human species were a hundred times smaller than our present size, then our entire descriptive vocabulary dealing with size, measurement and distance would change. (Here, Confusion points at a small tree on the other side of the riverbank.) That would be a very tall tree and a eucalyptus would be a super skyscraper in terms of trees.

AFFECTION: It appears you are suggesting that it is general human narcissism that makes us believe that humankind is the norm and that all measurements must begin with humans – and within humankind, too, the average becomes the starting point from which even aesthetic attributes get measured. Don't you think that even objectively, however, we are more attractive as a species?

CONFUSION: That is absurd, Affection. It would be far too much of a coincidence for it to be so. After all, during our long evolutionary history, if you accept Darwin, we have possessed so many different outward physical characteristics (not to speak inner mental capacities). Isn't it surprising that we should have suddenly reached an aesthetic high?

AFFECTION: Coincidences occur only too often. I see some contradictions in what you have just said. You will admit that we talk of beautiful horses, dogs, deer, and ugly frogs, cockroaches and lizards. Drunk in our narcissism, why do we even bother to classify the other species aesthetically? We could simply ignore them and regard them all as equally attractive – or ugly for that matter – at an inferior level, of course.

CONFUSION: (slowly) The reasons behind the aesthetic classification of other species and how it is done – for example beautiful birds and slimy worms – does not admit of any easy explanation. It does appear clear, however, that we classify them as beautiful only if in their outward appearance we do not sense any counter-posing elements in their appearance. I do not mean by this that they should be similar in appearance to the human species – the subject is more complex than that. Certain species are possibly evocative of symbols that are regarded for historical reasons as ugly in the collective memory of mankind. Perhaps snails, lizards, frogs and worms are deemed to be ugly because they resemble human faeces. You will ask, 'Why are human faeces regarded as ugly?' Freud has said something about this. All this is, of course, a grey area and largely guesswork. How these various and diverse symbols become combined in a particular form might make all the difference. The best illustration with regard to this in modern times comes in cartoon strips for children, where we have green- and yellow-coloured monsters with huge, distorted eyes, ears and noses. Similarly, in our mythology, we have descriptions of demons and witches who possess greatly exaggerated physical elements, which become representative of ugliness.

AFFECTION: Let me check if I've understood you, Confusion. First, you are saying that as a species we possess a collective narcissistic content that makes us believe we are the most beautiful species on this planet. Secondly, you are also suggesting that within us 'normality' or 'average' in the human form is an aesthetic ideal.

CONFUSION: No, Affection. You've got me wrong. I am not suggesting that normality is the aesthetic ideal – there are so many other factors to consider. Generally speaking, however, only those human forms and features that are within a certain 'normal' framework can be considered attractive. The notion of normality is aesthetically significant, even with regard to the inter feature spacing – you will forgive me if I use these expressions, won't you? – in a face. You see, each individual feature in a face might be normal and aesthetically satisfying. Nevertheless, if this inter feature spacing – the distance between two features, say, the nose and the lips or the eyes and the eyebrows – crosses a certain threshold of normality, (which is, of course, impossible to quantify), the overall or collective aesthetic impact might be very displeasing and produce a sense of disgust in the primitive human viewer. For a person to look good, as the expression goes, all individual features have to be harmoniously placed on the facial map (sorry once again). The positioning on the face of individual features and their relative distance must be within a certain normal range.

AFFECTION: You don't have to apologise. You have just said that these notions of normality exert an important influence on our perception of beauty, but that there are several other factors that have an important bearing on the shaping of this perception. What are these other factors?

CONFUSION: Yes, as I said, our notions of normality are the most important influence on aesthetic perception, but normality itself is like one of those legal provisions which has several modifications and qualifications expressed in its sub clauses, with possibly even a couple of exceptions at the very end. This is because each feature possesses a certain individuality of its own. Let me make my meaning clearer. Take, for example, the forehead. Now the forehead expresses emotions, thought and feeling, primarily by means of lines and furrows that appear on it – of course, in conjunction with other features, and facial and body movements, etc.

The lines that appear on the forehead are indicative of many different emotions and shades of feeling – happiness, surprise, shock, anger, etc. Although occasionally they may be expressive of a happy sentiment, generally speaking they convey negative emotions. If you made a mathematical calculation (which, of course, is not possible) you would discover that most of the emotions or feelings that tend to be conveyed are negative.

Now the impact of these lines is stronger on a smaller forehead, where they would stand out, than on a larger one, where they would appear to be less significant. This might be the reason why, in certain regions, a larger forehead is preferred to a smaller one. In places like this, another explanation commonly offered is that a large forehead is indicative of more 'brain'. In such a situation the aesthetic ideal would shift from normal to somewhat larger than normal (not too much larger, of course – it would have to remain below a certain threshold). What the actual reason operating on the human consciousness would be might be difficult to ascertain. I am only putting forward likely possibilities or suggesting a hypothesis, which, given the subject matter, is very difficult, if not impossible, to test. The point I am making here is that it is not important to be accurate – it is sufficient to establish that there must be reasons of this kind that affect aesthetic sensibilities.

Take another example: the human eye. The eye is believed to be the most beautiful feature in the face, possibly because of its ability to express thoughts and feelings more than any other feature. Generally speaking, the greater the eye's expressive potential, the more beautiful it is. (This is subject to certain other factors that we shall discuss presently.) Its particularity lies in its ability to express emotions. Like a boat being rocked on a river – at times calm, at times turbulent – the narrowing and widening of the eye, together with the movement of the pupil, are suggestive of a thousand different emotions.

AFFECTION: Would I be correct in summing up what you have just said if I were to say that you consider that human aesthetic values are shaped primarily by certain notions of normality, and that they are also influenced by certain 'individual' aspects of particular features, such as the eyes and the forehead?

CONFUSION: No, Affection. You have obviously never studied law; there are many more sub- clauses to come. The matter is more complex. The aspect of male female sexuality is another important influence. To illustrate what I mean, I will ask you to consider a hypothetical situation where men and women are externally more similar than they are at present. Let us imagine that they are so similar that it is not be easy to differentiate the sexes. What would be the consequences of this if it were somehow to 'happen' tomorrow? Since man's instinctive behaviour is diluted by his rational behaviour, one logical fall out, *ceteris paribus*, would be that there would then, perhaps, be a far greater tendency towards homosexuality, both amongst men and women. This would happen, even if existing differences were reduced, say, to a difference in their genitalia only. If women did not possess breasts, there was no facial or body hair for the male, no difference in voices and body structure, then, given our present state of clothing, on what basis would they distinguish, and be distinguished from, each other?

We have therefore to consider sexual attraction as being based substantially on an exhibition (I do not mean exhibitionist) and exploitation (not in the feminist sense) of existing physical differences between the male and female. Certain physical aspects more commonly found with men – say, a greater presence of hair on the face or body – would be regarded as repulsive if found on a woman, and vice versa.

Apart from physical differences, which exist naturally, such as breasts in women, and male female differences in genitalia, many differences between the sexes have been introduced in most societies to enhance the differences in physical appearance. Long hair is considered more representative of a female form. Similarly, differences in dress for men and women have been introduced in most societies. Women use make up, creams, oils, etc. We don't need to discuss these issues in detail; as far as hair styles, make-up and dressing styles are concerned, however, I believe that a general statement can be made (there could, of course, be exceptions) that, at a hypothetical starting point, most societies exhibited a preference to have their women appear more beautiful than the men. They therefore elected to hand over the more 'beautifying' or beauty-enhancing styles to the women.

Let me provide an illustration to explain what I mean here. Consider the hair. Now, in styling it, you will agree that a centre parting is more harmonious, since it divides the face in two at its (epi) centre. The symmetry achieved consequently enhances the aesthetic appeal of the face – this would be less so in the case of a side parting. Similarly, the length of the hair; long hair will provide a better background. It is with this idea of sexual differentiation that lips are painted, nails coloured and shaped, and muscularity sought or avoided.

AFFECTION: But is this desirable? Don't you think it's excessive?

CONFUSION: That's a separate issue. I agree with you that it's excessive – but right now we are discussing the reasons for our aesthetic preferences. I was about to mention that in most societies, probably even amongst Amazon tribes, women have been perceived as the gentler sex. This may have something to do with their nurturing role as mothers. For this reason, I find that as far as women are concerned this 'gentleness' attribute becomes an aesthetic plus. A kinship has also developed between weakness and gentleness as physically weak persons cannot very often be rough; this is not only true in psychological terms but is valid in an aesthetic context. Thus, as far as faces are concerned, a certain shape might symbolise gentleness and femininity and therefore be an aesthetic plus. So, you would observe that a certain kind of 'thinner' face, with gently sloping curves, is considered attractive in a woman, but not so in a man. Even the neck: a woman's neck is considered elegant (an aesthetic plus) if it is a little thinner and more shapely than normal, perhaps, but this is not the case with a man's neck, where such a neck would be considered an aesthetic minus.

AFFECTION: Is there anything else? We began with how notions of normality determine aesthetic preferences, and then went on to discuss how individual peculiarities, or characteristics, of a particular feature might cause deviations from this aesthetic norm. Now we have just discussed male female differentiation, where you point out that sexual differentiation takes place with the more beautifying styles generally being adopted by women. Are there any other factors that influence our aesthetic perceptions?

CONFUSION: You do like to pin people down to what they have said in a precise manner, don't you Affection? Anyhow that's an admirable trait, although it makes me fear you will suddenly point out such a major contradiction in what

I have said that it will leave me totally devastated. To come back to your question: is there anything else? Yes, of course!

Racial characteristics cause considerable shift in aesthetic perceptions. No race of people likes to think of itself as ugly, or in any way inferior to another race. Thus in Thailand, smallness and delicacy in a woman is regarded as aesthetically very appealing; in Egypt, however, the heavy build of an Egyptian belly-dancer is seen to be more attractive. Similarly, to a Westerner the enormous bulk of a Japanese Sumo wrestler is regarded as flab and an aesthetic minus, but in Japan most Japanese would admire such a build. In these illustrations, racial variations, along with societal differences, combine to create differences in aesthetic perceptions. They also indicate how aesthetic perceptions are not a priori but 'shaped'. But more of that later.

The sexual and cultural mores prevalent in a society at any particular point of time also exert an enormous influence on the shaping of this aesthetic perception. Thus, in a given society, a subdued 'passive' beauty (for women) might be preferable to a more vigorous and athletic kind of beauty. The reverse of this might equally be true.

The class composition of society or the level of violence at a given point of time might significantly affect aesthetic preferences. Thus a 'soft' male face might be regarded as not only indicative of the possessor belonging to a 'good' family, but might also, at a given point of time, be an individual, class, or even general, criterion of beauty.

Next, we come to an individual's preferences, that is, his or her personal prejudices and subjective values. Here, various factors about the individual are important: the face and body structure, the individual's views and perception of what they are, his or her sexuality, the individual's early association in childhood with certain people, childhood impressions of certain people, and how those people happened to look. For example, I might have had a hawk-nosed teacher who tyrannised me at school, and thus I might grow up with a prejudice against such a feature. As a consequence of all these factors pertaining to the individual (which are impossible to determine completely) a particular person's aesthetic preferences might be at considerable variance from the 'general' public opinion, whatever that means – you know what I mean, don't you? It's what's given birth to the adage 'beauty lies in the eye of the beholder'.

AFFECTION: Thank you for ending on a cliché. You have truly carried out your promise of making it all seem like a complex legal provision. I now understand why they call you Confusion. It is not so much because you yourself are confused, though that, of course, might also turn out to be the case, but because you have succeeded in confusing others. Now, if you have finished with all your fancy reasoning, will you let me know if there are any exceptions to the rules that you have just enumerated?

CONFUSION: You are really very intuitive, Affection – I wonder if that has any thing to do with your name. You are right: an exception is bound to exist which, by virtue of its existence, will prove the rule. (Here is another cliché for you.) There might be an exception to all that has been discussed about the importance of human notions of 'normality'. For example, a harmoniously constructed individual who is of larger size than normal and perfectly proportionate might well be considered attractive, even superior or godlike.

AFFECTION: Are you perhaps talking about tall men?

CONFUSION: (doubtfully) I am not sure if that's what I mean, exactly. Tallness in men would possibly have something to do with the male-female differentiation that we have just discussed. I was talking more in the sense of largeness, not height. By the way, I might mention here that I personally knew two very tall Indian sisters, whose tallness made people comment – the feature was regarded as unattractive and an aesthetic minus. This, of course, has something to do with sexual differences, where the male is expected to be the taller of the two. Also, of course, this particular perception of the sisters' unattractiveness was related to a rigidity of social attitude and was within a particular racial context. One of these women – a rather thin person – is today a highly paid model in Paris, where her height is regarded as an aesthetic plus and is considered to be an advantage.

AFFECTION: You know, Confusion, there are some contradictions that you have not dealt with. If aesthetic perception is not a priori (that is, unshaped), how would you explain that all over the world youth is regarded as aesthetically more attractive than old age? Surely this is an indication that youth is a priori, and universally, more appealing?

CONFUSION: (musing). Youth and age? What if physical changes were actually to follow a reverse cycle in the human form? What would be the consequences? Let us consider a hypothetical situation, where physical changes consequent upon ageing take place the other way round. What I mean to suggest is that the disappearance (and not appearance as is now the case) of wrinkles would attend the process of ageing. Children would have wrinkled skin that would become increasingly smooth with the process of ageing. In such a situation there would be a huge shift in our aesthetic perceptions. We would then perceive wrinkles as enhancing beauty. Of course wrinkles are actually only one of the many symbols of the process of ageing. The perception of all the other attendant changes, such as body slackness, coarsening, drying up and hardening of the skin, balding, etc, would also change. All the various physiological changes that occur with age are by no means inherently ugly.

The End

I read the chapter several times before I turned off the light.

The whole thing was incomprehensible. From Delhi, we had boarded a train to Haridwar where we stayed for five days, and had then travelled by bus to Rishikesh. We were enjoying the purer, sharper air, the view of the Himalayas and bathing in the clear, unpolluted waters of the Ganges, when a telephone call had disrupted all our plans. She left for Gurdaspur the very next day, and had insisted on going alone. 'You carry on,' she had said. I hadn't bothered to consider her suggestion; it was meaningless for me to go to Gangotri alone.

She had been extremely quiet that evening after the phone call. After dinner, she didn't want to come with me to the riverfront as she had some writing to do. As she was leaving early morning the next day, it bothered me a little. When I came back, she was still writing. After a shower I decided to sleep. In the morning when I awoke she was still bent over the desk.

'What's wrong with you?' I said. 'What on earth are you writing?'

'I have finished.' She gave a wan, apologetic smile. 'It was a letter.'

'You should have left something for next time.'

'Next time will be even longer.'

Replaying events in my mind over and over again, it was still incomprehensible how Srinivasan could have received the chapter. Could it be that she had been writing to him that night? There was no earthly reason for her to have done so surreptitiously. The other thing was that the photocopy brought over by Diamond showed that the original had been typed out on a computer. Could she have got the material typed out on a computer while in Rishikesh? When did she have the time? We had been having discussions till the day before she left. We had been forced to abandon our plans to travel ahead to Gangotri, the last stop of our journey, as she had to leave for Gurdaspur immediately. The morning she was leaving I had been with her throughout, and had in fact put her on to the bus. Could she have somehow managed to have got the whole thing typed out after leaving Rishikesh?

Where? In Gurdaspur? It still didn't make sense. What was the urgency? Hadn't we agreed not to discuss our progress with anyone until we had firmed up some of the conclusions? No, it was just not possible. Quite apart from the fact that she would almost certainly have discussed the matter with me beforehand, according to the version of events I had received, Simran never really managed to ever reach Gurdaspur.

9

An Introduction to Modern Art

1

I was at home listening to Indian classical music when I found my mind drifting away from the soothing strains of the sitar and turning to my encounter the other day with the research scholar from the American University.

What must she have thought and felt about coming here? Reconstructing the sequence of events in my mind, I realised that she had come up and entered the flat in the interval between the time Salim and I had gone up to the terrace and the arrival of the police. She would have at first rung the bell, and when it failed to elicit a response must have climbed the staircase, noticed the door to the flat ajar and stepped inside. Whilst waiting in the room, she would have heard the commotion and possibly have even witnessed the human drama carrying on downstairs from the window.

Seeing the police gathered below, she would have become tense and decided to light a cigarette. Hadn't she left behind her address and telephone number on a slip of paper? I looked around, but couldn't find it anywhere. Eventually, I emptied the table drawer and found it. Her name was clearly written in a strong, firm handwriting, and there was the address of a guest house in Defence Colony underneath it, together with a neatly printed phone number.

The writing once more caught my eye. Deciding to clear any doubts in my mind, once for all, I pulled out an old steel trunk kept under the bed and dug out some of the letters that I had kept together in a yellow plastic box. I compared the two scripts: they were different, although there was a distinct resemblance.

When I called the guest house, a man answered. For a reception desk at a lodging house in a fairly upmarket area, it was an unusually rough, abrasive voice. In what I thought was a fairly uncouth tone, the voice demanded to know who was calling. I was provoked into ignoring the question and responding with equal aggression.

'I want to speak with a lady by the name of Diamond who is staying in your guest house,' I said, injecting a dismissive and patronising note to his request.

The voice went off the line to confer hurriedly with another voice. I heard him say quite distinctly, 'Is there a new girl by the name of Diamond? Has she been sent anywhere?'

It was a woman he addressed, for she said something in reply. It was indistinct and unintelligible over the line, and I couldn't make out what had been said.

Several minutes later, Diamond came on the line.

'Hi!' Her voice sounded cool and breezy. 'I was thinking you weren't going to call.'

'I've been busy,' I said. 'Where's a good place to meet?'

'How about Connaught Place?' she suggested.

We decided to meet the following day opposite the Coffee Home near the emporia on Baba Kharak Singh Marg in Connaught Place.

2

As I was early for the meeting, I sat under the small shade afforded by an Ashoka tree on the *Jantar Mantar* lawns, and waited. My eyes dwelt on the red stone structures, one of the five eighteenth-century observatories established by a North Indian ruler with an interest in astronomy. The observatory had been preserved; the possibilities of observing diminished by the multitude of high-rise buildings that had arisen all around it in the centuries that had followed its original construction.

Near the time of our meeting, I started walking towards the emporia. The city is turning hellish, I thought, as I waited opposite the *Rivoli* cinema for a passage through the endless stream of smoke-belching vehicles that would allow me to cross the road.

A split-second gap in the flow of traffic and I surged forward, taking care to muzzle my nose with a handkerchief that needed washing every time I journeyed outside the confines of the university's greenery.

I stepped inside the coffee house.

The large hall full of tables and chairs was packed to capacity. The sounds of traffic from the streets penetrated the thin walls of the cafeteria, compelling those inside to speak louder than normal, and this cacophony of many voices yelling at the same time created a vicious cycle of shouting to be heard. It was definitely not a place to sit inside and talk.

I waited near the telephone booths outside. She was right on time, but I didn't realise it was her.

'Don't you recognise me?' She came near, an amused expression on her face.

'Sorry,' I said. 'I wasn't focused. Now, where would you like to go?'

'I don't know. You decide.'

There were numerous cafés and restaurants in Connaught Place, only yards away. Even so, I had found that during recent visits, despite the remnants of a lost grandeur suggested by statuesque white pillars that circled the entire shopping area, its original reputation as a spacious and elegant commercial centre had suffered from increasing congestion created by cars and shoppers. The cafeterias were either loud, noisy Macdonald types, or expensive restaurants intended for family lunches and dinners.

'If you don't mind walking a bit, we can go to a café in a quieter area,' I suggested.

'Wherever.'

On the way to Triveni Kala Sangam, which contained a small, quaint café, I realised I hadn't recognised her because she was looking different. She had come to my flat wearing a T shirt and jeans, looking like a student. Today, she was dressed in a white cotton sari with an embroidered floral arrangement.

I took a close look at her walking by my side. She was short and darkish, with clear features. A little plump perhaps, but she moved with grace and was on the whole not bad looking. She had thick, black hair, cut medium length that fell over her shoulders. Her face and arms had a reddish tinge to them; there was something fresh and young about her skin.

'So who are you going to be voting for?' she said. 'I hear that it's going to be neck to neck.'

'I wish I didn't have a vote.'

'Now you are being irresponsible,' she smiled. 'It's a simple choice. Can't you decide between horse shit and bullshit?'

'It's more complicated than that. If it were simply a matter between horse shit and bullshit, I would know what to choose.'

'And that would be?'

'Bullshit any day. Don't forget you can cook food over bullshit in India.'

'That's cow shit, actually,' she laughed.

'In this case it's like having to choose between gangsters in Bombay and those in Delhi. I'd vote for the goons in Bombay because they don't have any hidden agenda. They are motivated by pure greed, unlike the hoods in Delhi who want to make profit but have a hidden agenda as well.'

We took a short cut through the Central Park. As usual, there were many people squatting on the lawns, mostly office types, some foreign tourists enjoying the sun in their T shirts and shorts, a few boy girl couples, and a family or two. A couple of tall, dark women passed us balancing baskets full of bananas on their heads. Their postures erect and stately, they created a curiously dignified vision in the banality of their surroundings. They rarely, if ever, solicited potential customers seated on the grass, but kept walking around the park in a mock posture exercise, silently waiting to be beckoned.

We avoided the main streets and followed the narrower, less crowded, lanes I was familiar with. I reckoned we would reach Triveni in the same time it would have taken in a taxi. We walked at a fairly brisk pace. On the way, I questioned Diamond about her life in a foreign land and her family.

'We are from Bengal,' she said, in response to a query. 'Both my parents originally hailed from Calcutta.'

'Where do they live?'

A shadow fell over her face.

'They both died two years ago. Within months of each other, actually.'

'I'm sorry.'

'These things happen. What can anyone do?' I sensed waves of emotion flooding through her, but she rapidly took control of herself.

'How did you meet the professor?' I changed the subject.

'Sheer chance. Six months ago, there was an international conference at Michigan on 'The Family and the Juvenile Delinquent'. Dr Rehana Vaishali, who teaches psychology at Himachal University, was one of the participants from the Asian region. At the conference I found that we shared many interests in common. Before coming to India, I wrote to her. She wrote back and insisted that while I was in India I should visit Ganahatti, a small village near Shimla. Rehana took me around the university and introduced me to professors from various faculties. That's how I met

Professor Srinivasan. During the course of my conversation with him, he mentioned the work you had done on the same subject.'

Triveni Kala Sangam was an oblong building with green, manicured lawns, an arts centre of sorts. It was famous for its canteen, which served excellent food, smelling of home. A radical political outfit held its weekly meetings there.

Inside, she paused by the art gallery to look at a poster pasted on the aluminium door.

'Can we take a peep inside?' she asked.

'Yeah, sure.'

I followed her, masking my disinterest. There were mostly abstract paintings hung on the walls; including a particularly gruesome artwork that looked like a mountain of greyish human skulls. Paintings had never interested me, especially modern art.

I was insensitive to colours. I could never remember the colour of clothes people were wearing, or even the colour of birds, books, walls, flowers – anything I might have seen, even recently. It was not as though I was colour-blind, for I could identify colours as easily as the next person; it was just that colours simply didn't make any impression on me. I sometimes wondered if this had something to do with the years that I had spent at the orphanage.

She didn't spend too much time over the exhibits. When we came out she said, as if explaining her interest, 'Before I got on to research, I used to be a painter.'

'That's interesting,' I said.

Inside the canteen, a few down-and-out artists were sitting on low ethnic stools around small black tables. The placid, middle-aged woman, who managed the café, watched us behind thick glasses. A cat slunk past our table. There were always a couple of cats at Triveni. We ordered Tasty Toast, a local speciality, and coffee.

'What were your impressions of the paintings we just saw?'

'I'm the wrong person to ask as I have almost no idea about painting,' I said. 'To be honest with you, I believe most of the so-called symbolism in art is sheer nonsense. At any rate, it's too absurd or subtle for me. Let me give you an example of what I mean. I remember reading somewhere about a Picasso painting, which showed a pair of white pigeons without feet. The reviewers and art critics saw much symbolism in the missing feet – till finally a journalist met the great man himself and asked him the reason. Picasso's explanation was simple. As a child, his father would often paint pigeons and ask the young Picasso to do the feet. He just got so tired of painting pigeon feet...'

'Many people tend to react to modern art in this way.' Diamond gave a little laugh, a pleasant, tinkling sound. 'Probably their number is much larger than those who are genuinely enthusiastic about modern art. But people often hesitate to speak out openly on the subject. My own interest in this particular PhD topic – the aesthetics of the human form – came about because I had similar misgivings over the use of symbolism in modern art. Before going to the US I had never been to art school, but I used to enjoy painting flowers, landscapes, animals, and also quite often the human form. In the States I got myself enrolled in an art school where I came across different schools of painting: impressionism, cubism, modern art, and so on. Here, the artists were no longer painting 'reality', but were representing aspects of reality through the symbolic use of colour and form. In the beginning I didn't appreciate modern art because it made no sense to me. I had many heated arguments on the subject with my professors; it was only after several months that I began to realise that I had been prejudiced in my approach.'

'How did you come to philosophy?'

'Before the end of the semester, we had to submit a written paper – something like a mini-thesis – on any subject relating to art. Because of the arguments I used to get into with classmates and even the teaching staff, they asked me to prepare a paper on the historical development and use of symbols in modern art.'

'How did you do that? You mean you related the use of symbols to increasing modern-day concerns, frustrations, obsessions, radicalisation...?'

'Not exactly. Let me ask you a question. What do you think distinguishes painters from other 'lesser mortals'?'

'Nothing at all, I would imagine. At least nothing really tangible or concrete.'

'I tried hard to pinpoint some difference. Of course, it's true that they are generally less conservative in their life and views, but that wasn't a very satisfying conclusion. I kept on telling myself that from a psychological point of view there had to be some other distinguishing factor, otherwise why would they paint?' She looked at me earnestly. 'Why not others?'

I shrugged my shoulders. She seemed to be really bright.

'It struck me then,' she resumed, 'that painters are different from other people because they are obsessed with the form and colour of the environment they perceive. Quite naturally, therefore, the paintings will change once the environment changes. Now, aesthetically speaking, what distinguishes our present-day environments from, say, earlier agricultural environments? One aspect that stands out is the presence of a greater geometry and regularity of shapes. Especially in cities, but even in towns, most of the perceivable environment is just so much geometry.'

'Is that really so?' I said. 'Wasn't there a lot of geometry even in earlier times – in the architecture of buildings, in roads, vehicles, or even furniture, such as tables, chairs and cupboards?'

'It was far less. You forget that in handicraft industries there was greater scope for innovative shaping. But that is another matter. Consider the proliferation of geometrically shaped consumer goods – toothpaste, toothbrush, records, cassettes, soaps, matchboxes, cigarettes, ad infinitum. You spend your day in a city visiting round swimming pools, sitting in geometric parks, or travelling in geometric vehicles on geometric roads, seeing all around you geometrically shaped buildings that make up the city. What will you paint? Or rather, a better question would be, what could you paint? The only language one learns is geometry.'

'Aren't you exaggerating?' I said. 'The environment hasn't been altered to that extent. If you travel even a few hundred miles out of a city you will start to see mountains, lakes, trees..."Yes,' she said, 'but in Europe, many artists grew up in cities. All art centres, galleries and schools were located in the city. In any case, people also continued to paint in traditional forms. Drastic changes took place in the architecture and physical environment of cities, however, which generated new trends in painting and other art forms. Increasing urbanisation and modern technology heralded, in aesthetic terms, a tremendous increase in the geometry of environments, and modern art, aptly named, emerged. The fascination of the artist with form and colour persisted, but with the change of environment it was now geared to 'half-shape geometry ' – since one cannot paint a modern day family watching television, as they are as the television set has too regular a shape. In an earlier century, however, one could have painted a woman eating grapes. For a person brought up in the city, an occasional trip to the countryside might not make much difference. The lakes, mountains and trees you are speaking of, do not dominate an artist's overall visual experience in terms of, scientifically speaking, length of exposure. In the cities, therefore, a new art form had to emerge. These new artists even drew men and women geometrically, just as they would also paint their depressions and feelings.'

I didn't understand what she meant by 'half-shape geometry', but guessed that it was probably some form of intellectual shorthand.

'What about colours?'

'Even so with colours,' she said. 'A tree, for example, is a fantastic creation shape-wise, with its endless twists and turns – there is a complete lack of predictability. It also has endless shades and hues of green. Now you could get the walls in your house painted a particular shade of green, but essentially the colours of a city are cement-like, that is, particular shades of grey, brown, etc. You will find those colours coming on to canvasses ever more often – that's modern art for you. It's not only geometry – it's a hundred other things connected with the modern environment. Speed, for example. Speed can create an impressionistic perception of reality, which can be related to the blurring of objects. Inside the train, the landscape rushes past me. Buildings, trees and fields are racing away from me faster than ever before. Tired of the monotony of stereotyped regular shapes, speed gives me the necessary illusions of freedom, imperceptibility, and intangibility... Thus modern art in all its forms is rooted in the modern-day physical environment, although it has become immensely psychological and symbolic. In fact, it has been helped in this, or pushed in this direction, by the changed physical environment. Could impressionistic paintings have predated the arrival of the steam engine?'

In the midst of what was clearly a rhetorical question, the Tasty Toasts arrived with the coffee. Throughout the discussion on modern art, Diamond had been quite serious and earnest. Now, pouring the coffee, the serious expression flitted out of her eyes and she said brightly, almost laughing, 'Once you look at art like this, you cease to see such exhibitions as excessively subtle, or even as a way of hoodwinking a gullible public. You won't be so disinterested any more.'

'I'm already more interested,' I said sincerely.

'You haven't told me anything about yourself,' she said quietly.

'You haven't yet finished telling me about how you left art school and turned to philosophy. Professor Srinivasan must have already told you about me.'

'Still...' she insisted.

'There's nothing much to tell. I was working on the PhD at Summerhill on this particular topic, the same one as yours, apparently. For certain reasons, I abandoned it and left Shimla to join Delhi University as a lecturer in the Department of Philosophy.'

'The professor told me something about the circumstances in which you decided to leave Shimla,' she said. 'He had no idea that you had decided not to complete the thesis.'

'As you know the circumstances, you can understand why I did that.'

'No,' she said, looking shocked. 'It had never occurred to the professor or to me that you would abandon the project.' A wave of sympathy flooded her face. She leaned across the table and said quite gently, 'It's quite understandable that you didn't want to stay on in Shimla, but it's difficult for me to see why you should have abandoned the dissertation halfway through. It would have been a tribute to her memory.'

I was dumbstruck. I felt physically winded. It felt as though somebody had given me a hard blow on the solar plexus. I didn't know what to say. Nobody had so clearly and directly voiced my own doubts about my decision to cease work on the project.

'I suppose it's actually none of my business.' She abruptly changed the topic of conversation. 'You were asking me how I turned to philosophy. It happened like this. I had submitted my paper on the genesis and development of symbols and forms in modern art, which created a bit of a stir. The head of the faculty, Professor Brian Fowley, who was taking our classes, called me to his office one day. It was a turning point in my life, although at the time I'd thought that it was some routine matter. I spent almost two hours with him inside his office. He wanted to know why I was doing the course. I explained that I liked painting flowers and landscapes. I didn't have any illusions about ever becoming a famous artist or painter. Painting was something I could do moderately well, and my idea was that the degree at art school would turn out to be very useful when I started a small business of selling fabric painting, batik, etc., which is what I intended to do after finishing art school. At that stage in my life, it was very important for me that I somehow learnt to stand on my own feet. The professor heard me out, and then he said something very strange. He said that if I did the arts course it would be a waste. I wasn't cut out to be a painter or an artist, because I was only moderately talented. In his opinion, I was also not cut out for undertaking any kind of business, and that even if I did go into business I would not find it satisfying. He had seen hundreds of students at the School of Arts, some of them now very accomplished painters in their own right, but none had ever put forward such an original point of view as myself. It was, of course, an unresearched effort, and would require a year or more of painstaking research to substantiate some of its conclusions. But he felt that even that would not be worthwhile since it was an arts school and not a department of philosophy or psychology. He instead suggested that seeing that I had a natural aptitude for philosophy and psychology I should go in for a master's in either of these two subjects at the university.

'It seemed a terribly rash assessment. I wasn't at all sure I had the aptitude that the professor spoke of. It's true that I'd always had an interest in subjects that were philosophical or psychological, but they were more like private hobbies or interests, and I'd never really contemplated a career in teaching or research. For two weeks I couldn't sleep. There was, of course, another problem, in that I needed to pay fees all over again. Professor Fowley said that he knew some senior professors at the university, and that he would try and wangle an Assistantship for me, because he genuinely believed that I had potential. Finally, after two weeks of the most painful indecision and soul-searching, I decided to go in for a Masters in Philosophy at the Southern Methodist University. So that, sir, is my story of how I came to philosophy.'

I threw the last remaining piece of the Tasty Toast at the cat that had slunk back into the café, and received an approving smile from the manageress who was watching us closely, having decided that we were the most interesting couple in the café. I ordered another round of coffee.

We were silent, both of us, thinking our own thoughts. I reckoned she wasn't entirely relaxed. When I pushed back my chair to make myself more comfortable, I noticed her right leg shaking under her sari. Nevertheless, her face didn't betray any emotion.

Professor Fowley had accurately assessed her aptitude for philosophy. She was gifted with an extraordinary imagination and ability to think analytically.

What was it she had said just now? It would have been a tribute to her. The past was always so close at hand. She was right. Equally, I mused, it would have been a tribute to Eliot, for whom originally it had been intended. The project should never have been abandoned.

It struck me how the woman sitting across the table had travelled maybe five thousand miles to the mother country with no intention whatsoever of meeting a person like me. Nevertheless, through a chain of circumstances, she was now sitting here discussing philosophy, and had just succeeded in convincing me that I had made a mistake in abandoning a certain venture. In five minutes' time, would we walk out of the café and she return to her orbit and I to mine?

I came out of my reverie. She was addressing me.

'What I found interesting was the use of the Socratic method. Why did you decide to write it out in dialogue form?'

'Our plan was to write out the research initially in the form of a dialogue, so that it would make interesting reading even for a lay person.' I spoke lightly, trying to keep my voice neutral. 'We had the idea of trying to get the dialogue published in popular book form. Once we had written it out in the form of a conversation, we were going to convert it into academic dissertations by using the necessary technical language and references. I still have the notes and photocopied material on the subject with me. You are free to use them in any manner you like.'

'I'd be grateful,' she said slowly, 'but don't you think it would be better if we could somehow get together and discuss everything? Isn't that how you had originally planned out the research process? I promise that, when I get back to the States, I'll try and get all this published in book form.' She appeared to have thought of something for she was quiet for a moment, then she said, 'You wouldn't mind my name appearing as co author would you?'

'No, of course not,' I said. 'It would be a collaborative effort, after all, and might even get some international attention because of your involvement. By the way, weren't you supposed to be in Shimla right now?'

'My programme got delayed. I've come to India with a friend from the States. We are staying together at this guest house. She was to leave for the US earlier, but she extended her stay and I decided to stay on till she left.'

'When is she leaving?'

'In four days' time. Once she leaves, I do have to leave for Shimla, most definitely.'

I made a quick mental calculation. The course set for the examination had been completed. I needed to tie up some loose ends at the university, collect material for the Iraqi's thesis, and have a meeting with Kumari, who had to be briefed on the charter of demands to be prepared.

'Why don't we do it like this?' I said. 'After four days, you could leave for Shimla as planned. I could go there, but would require at least a week to wind up all my affairs in Delhi. After one week, I could meet you there. I think that in Shimla, we would be able to work better and faster.'

'It sounds like a very good idea. It will also be cooler there.' She paused. 'If it's a matter of only one or two days, we could travel together.'

'In that case let's catch the Himalayan Queen. It leaves rather early, though. Six in the morning.'

'That won't be any problem.'

The canteen was getting ready to close. The lady sitting at the counter with the kindly expression picked up a small bell from the table and began waving it about.

Outside, Diamond said she wanted to buy some sweets. Barely fifty yards from Triveni lay Bengali Market, known for its sweets and confectionery. She bought a kilo of *gulab jamun*, a classic Indian dessert of fried cheese balls in golden syrup.

'Are these for your American friend?'

'No,' she smiled. 'These are for me.'

10

Kumari

When I got back to my flat, I found a message on the pad hanging outside. The note was from Kumari, asking me to see her as soon as was convenient.

The following evening I went to see her. She lived in a crowded slum near Ajmeri Gate with fifty other *hijras*. A gutter filled with greenish slime served as a cut-off point and separated them from the others in the slum.

I walked across the narrow lane, past the sari-clad *hijras*. A few sitting outside their *hutments* on string beds gave me a wave of recognition. They appeared relaxed in their own homes, without the cheap jewellery and lewd jokes their public begging necessitated.

Kumari, her neighbour said, had gone to see a film at Delite cinema, but had left a message asking me to wait. I didn't mind waiting but was a trifle surprised as in her note she had said that the matter was urgent.

Her ramshackle plastic tenement held up by short bamboos stood at the edge of the slum; it was fortunately on the other side of the gutter end. She shared it with a young, polite darkish-looking *hijra*, but she too was missing.

The neighbour, who had left me the message, took three small cane chairs out into the open. I sat down in one of these; they were so small they appeared to have been made for a child, although I supposed they were the right size to store inside the small tenement.

'I don't suppose everybody can fit into these,' I said.

'No,' she smiled, exposing big, blackened teeth with gaps between them. 'If you are too fat, you can't fit. We picked them up from the Sunday market last week.' Her name was Roopa. Her dark face, half-male, half-female, was lined and tired-looking, the hair tied in a single, thick plait.

'Where are you from?' I said.

'Tamil Nadu.'

'That's a long way off.'

'I heard that conditions were better in Delhi. The *hijras* were better organised, earned more, lived better, and were less persecuted.'

'Is that the reason you moved to Delhi?'

'That's correct.' After a pause she added, 'There was another reason. A year ago I was arrested in Madras by the police and charged under the Penal Code for soliciting business and committing sodomy.' At that moment, she broke off from her narrative to shout at someone I couldn't see. 'Poonam, bring two teas.' Turning to me she continued, 'I spent eight months in Madras central jail as a detainee. That's what I mean when I say they are poorly organised in Madras.'

'Did the court finally acquit you?'

'No.' She laughed bitterly. 'The trial had barely started. I was released on bail through the intervention of a friend. Someone from my village agreed to stand surety. The entire experience was so humiliating I decided to jump bail and leave Yerravada for Delhi.'

I nodded sympathetically.

'It was terrible,' she said. 'People think that because we are *hijras* we have no feelings.'

'What about the surety?'

'He was a rich man. The amount of bail was only three thousand. He would've had to have paid that sum, that's all.'

I was reminded of Ram Lok Uncle and the unpaid rent.

'What about the police?' I said. 'Didn't they try to trace you?'

'Not a chance,' she laughed. 'That's an advantage we do have. Most of us have hardly any family connections. Normal people don't like to associate with us, so it becomes rather difficult to find us.' She added, as if as an afterthought, 'And there are other reasons why the police hesitate to meddle in our affairs.'

A small, dark bright-eyed girl came forward hesitantly, holding two cups of tea.

'Who is she?' I asked.

'Poonam,' she said, with some emphasis. The girl smiled, again hesitantly. She patted her on the head, and she went away slowly as if a bit dazed.

'Kumari brought her,' she elaborated. 'She now lives with her in her *hutment*. I know that for all practical purposes she is an orphan without any family. Kumari knows the details.'

Roopa was explaining the differences in city culture between Madras and Delhi when Kumari arrived.

Unlike Roopa, Kumari's features were less obtrusive. Dark and thin, the male-female divide was not very apparent in her. She was, moreover, quite flat chested.

Roopa said, 'I have to go somewhere, *bhai*. Please excuse me.'

'We will continue our discussion on the next occasion we meet.'

'Of course.'

After she had gone I asked Kumari, 'How was the film?'

'Excellent.' She winked. 'Some good dances, *babu*. You would have enjoyed it. We can go and see it some other time.'

'What was the cast?'

'Bipasha was in it,' she laughed. 'The rest are not important.'

'What happened? You said there was an emergency.'

'Yes, *babu*. There was an emergency,' she replied dourly. 'Three of our friends got arrested last night under S 92 93 of the Delhi Police Act.'

'What do these sections stand for?' My tone was impatient. Kumari would recognise the offence and the punishment, I knew. She'd been in and out of prisons so often that, if it were not for her handicap, she could have become a successful criminal lawyer.

'Vagrancy,' she said. 'It's described as loitering around public places in late hours without purpose.' Her voice became agitated. 'It was nothing, *babu*! They were just picked up at five in the evening. Is that late? The reason: one of the local cops wanted to fuck.'

'Then?' I said, feeling disturbed.

'They spent the night in the lock up, because they refused to co operate. By the time I came to know about this, it was six o'clock. At the police station the cops told me to get lost, otherwise they would have me booked as well. I didn't know under what provisions they were arrested, so I was a little worried. It could have been anything. The police could have planted a couple of knives on them and framed them under the Arms Act. If they were arrested for this or for stealing, they would need to be bailed out. It occurred to me that perhaps you could help. That's why I left the message on the pad last night. I thought it was better to call you in the evening today, in case matters got sorted out by themselves earlier in the day, as in fact they did. Today, in the afternoon, they were produced before a magistrate's court. A petty fine had to be paid. Once it was paid, they were free. After they were released we went to this film.'

'Did the magistrate say anything?'

'Nothing. Nothing at all. There was no point in telling him it was a frame up. He wouldn't have believed us. He glanced at us and asked if we had the money to pay the fine. It was thirty rupees. Then he dismissed us and called out the next case. It could not have taken more than thirty seconds.'

There were several matters I needed to discuss with Kumari.

I told her of my meeting with the Welfare Ministry bureaucrat and my imminent visit to Shimla. Could she draft out a charter of demands on behalf of the association?

Kumari pressed me to stay. 'Have some tea, *babu*.'

'No thanks. I just drank some with your neighbour. Let me get back from Shimla and we will make another trip to Karim's.'

'You liked the food?'

'It was fantastic.'

'See this Bipasha film if you can.'

'What's it called?'

'*Omkara*,' she said. 'It's a new film and likely to be showing in many places. If you don't find it running in Shimla, let's see it on video when you return.'

'We could do that,' I agreed. 'That is, if you don't mind seeing it again.'

'I don't.'

When I reached home, I thought of the little girl Poonam, and remembered I had meant to ask Kumari about her.

11

Settling Accounts

The next few days were hectic. I called the YMCA in Shimla and spoke to Prakash, an old friend who was a manager there. 'Accommodation is no problem, my friend,' he said. 'If you like you can stay with me.'

I visited several libraries in the city, got several books issued and photocopied relevant pages from various journals. I wanted to get the entire material ready, so that I could begin work on the Iraqi's thesis as soon as I got back.

The day before my scheduled departure I went downstairs to meet Ram Lok Uncle. There was no need for me to ring the bell; he was outside on the veranda playing with his grandchild. Seeing me approach, the boy rushed inside.

He must have understood at once that I had come to give him the money for the rent, because he ushered me inside with great courtesy, as if I was some maharajah come to visit a lowly chieftain. I was shown into the living room and asked to sit down on the sofa opposite him. The family came out from various parts of the house to see the action as though this was some historic meeting that was taking place between two monarchs, and that very shortly some kind of grand theatre would take place.

It was only Ram Lok Uncle who was all amiability, perhaps owing to his greater experience. Milan stood next to him, arms folded across his chest and striking a morally righteous pose. With Ram Lok Uncle around he was a dutiful son who didn't speak out of turn.

Somewhere, I could hear the muted mutterings of the attempt to murder victim, whom the grandchild would have informed of my arrival. Sheela *behn* stood in the doorway leading into the kitchen, looking at me with bloodshot eyes (her eyes were always bloodshot). Her grandchild clutched the edge of her sari, staring at me as if I was some kind of monster. Did they think I was going to take out a knife?

Milan's wife stood in another doorway, watching me with a much more sane and reasonable expression. It may have been the memory of the student-teacher relationship.

I sat quietly and looked at all of them coldly. 'Guptaji,' I said in a formal tone, 'I have come to give you the cheque.'

He realised I was waiting for an apology. 'Milan got carried away the other day,' he said gently.

'There was no need to have called the police.' I curtly handed over the cheque. 'This is for arrears and for the coming three months.'

'*Arre*, Professor sahib,' he said, 'I knew you would give me the money. I have to run a household, you see. If I were a bachelor like you, I would have no problems.'

He was lying through his teeth. Several thousand rupees came in every month as the rent for a commercial flat that he owned in the north of the city, and there was the rent being paid by the tenant on the second floor of the house. The remark about my being a bachelor was typical. If a man was above a certain age in India without having married, conservative mainstream society held it against him, concluding that it indicated either deviance or saintliness. The latter was not a likely epithet to be chosen for me.

He carried on in this vein, talking of escalating prices and the rising cost of living, and would have probably continued with further talk of family responsibilities. In the process, he was trying to shame me and acquire a moral ascendancy. Pre-empting this I said, 'Do you know, Mr Gupta, no one at the university has received a salary for the past six months. Not even the vice chancellor. The University Grants Commission hasn't sent the money.'

He looked stunned, as I had thought he would be. 'Is that so?' he said.

'You've been a salaried man yourself and your son also has a job with the government,' I continued. 'You know how difficult it is to manage if you don't receive a salary for even a single month. I received payment only yesterday, and have immediately come to pay you your dues.'

He looked suitably chastised. In a low voice he said, 'I didn't know...'

By this time the family members had lost interest in the proceedings and had gone back to their respective early-morning chores. He offered me tea, which I refused, as I didn't want him to get the impression that I took their calling over the police lightly and that all was forgiven.

'I'm in a hurry.' I stood up. 'Just send me a receipt through your servant.'

'Yes, yes, there is no problem.'

'Make sure it's stamped,' I added dismissively.

12

Train to the Himalayas

I reached the New Delhi railway station shortly before the train was due to depart. There had been a bad mix up. The previous evening I had instructed an *auto*-driver to reach the house early in the morning.

I had set the alarm, but it wasn't its ringing which woke me. The previous night I had slept late after consuming close to a quarter-bottle of cheap liquor. It was something quite horrible, akin to pure spirit, which I had purchased in the lean period before receiving the advance money from the Iraqi. These days if I took a couple of extra drinks at night, I woke up the next day well before sunrise.

I heard the sound of an *auto-rickshaw* and, throwing off the bed-sheet, strode across to the balcony to confirm its arrival. Its black exteriors blending into the night, the yellow plastic flap at the back of the vehicle and the fluorescent numberplate were clearly visible under the streetlight. I unzipped my bags and felt through various package sizes for a last minute check to make sure I hadn't forgotten anything. When I reached the entrance to the house with my baggage, however, the yellow-black contraption had vanished like a giant mosquito into the silent night. A peacock screeched.

I looked around, but could see no signs of it anywhere. The road was deserted. The driver could have gone round the corner, or back to his house to get something he had forgotten. In vain I waited for him to return. Finally I was left with no option but to take a cab from the taxi stand. The taxi driver, a lean, wiry fellow, drove fast; there was skeletal traffic on the roads and we made it to the station in record time.

At the ticket counter, I found Diamond leaning against one of the grey pillars, wearing a brown T shirt with grey corduroy trousers, looking very relaxed. She gave me a smile of recognition.

This was no time to be so cool, with only minutes left for the train to leave. I saw a long queue at the ticket counter.

'Have you bought the tickets?' I said.

'Yes, I have,' she grinned. 'Don't look so hassled. The train starts from platform 1, just next to the entrance.'

'Yeah, I remember that,' I said. 'Also, the compartments are interconnected. We can get on anywhere.'

We walked through the entrance quickly, shrugging off the red-shirted porters hustling about. The Himalayan Queen was half empty at this its starting point, but it would soon fill up en route.

We settled down in a section of a large, almost empty, second-class compartment. It had hard, though adequately comfortable, seats: wooden planks with a blue plastic cover over negligible cushioning.

My need for tea surfaced. Did she want a cup? She pulled out an orange thermos flask from inside her bag for me to fill with some cool water. There was a water cooler machine nearby on the platform from which I hurriedly filled the flask and walked further to the stall nearest to our compartment. The vendor gave me two cups of tea in white plastic cups. As I received the change, I caught sight of Milan standing inside the adjoining compartment's doorway, staring at me. A moment later he had disappeared.

Strange things were happening: first, the incident in the morning when I thought I had seen the *auto-rickshaw* and now seeing Milan or his lookalike.

I returned to the compartment. As soon as I sat down on the berth opposite Diamond, the train started moving as if by some prearranged signal.

'The last time I travelled in a train in India, they used to serve tea in those lovely brown earthen cups.' She made a face as she took the thin plastic cup.

So the lady was an environmentalist. Like me.

'Must have been a while ago,' I said. 'Plastic has taken over for some time now.'

She had an old issue of *Time* magazine in her hands. This one had the nuclear tests carried out by India and Pakistan as its cover story. She saw me glance at it.

'So what did you think of the nuclear tests?' she said.

'I thought they were a real blast.'

'What exactly is that supposed to mean?' She sounded angry, even offended.

'I'm opposed to nuclear testing, but I'm also opposed to superpowers such as the US telling other smaller powers that they can't test.'

'What does that mean? In a nutshell, do you support the tests, or are you against them?'

'That's like Bush,' I said dryly. 'Are you against the war or do you support us? I may not support nuclear testing, but I wouldn't join in a demonstration against them.'

'How can you say that,' she said heatedly. 'It's such a major diversion of resources. What our people need is food and education, not nuclear capability.'

'Maybe we need both. Just tell me one thing. Would the US have bombed Hiroshima and Nagasaki if they'd thought that Japan possessed nuclear capability?'

'Those times were different.'

'Were they really? Don't forget that a necklace of nuclear weapons surrounds us.'

'You're just being paranoid.'

'I'm not; I'm being realistic. You are being naive.'

'That's not true,' she retorted. 'I think when Gandhiji spoke of *ahimsa* he was being extremely practical. If you followed the principle of an eye for an eye, in no time at all the world would be destroyed.'

'I'm no Gandhian,' I said.

'Look, don't you realise that nuclear weapons are unacceptable? If there is ever a nuclear war, it will mean the end of the human race.'

'I somehow don't think that's such a bad idea,' I replied. 'It would give Mother Earth a break from all of us.'

'You're not being serious,' she said, sounding annoyed. 'Let me get back to my reading.'

I propped up the carry bag against the window to use as a pillow and lay down on the berth. She took out a book from inside her bag and began reading. I glanced at the title. It was a play, entitled *A Most Unsuitable Girl*. Oh, oh. A feminist as well.

I slept for a couple of hours and woke up feeling refreshed but sweaty. The sun had come up and it was a little warm inside. I turned on several switches, but the small black fans on the white- painted roof refused to move.

We reached Chandigarh by eleven, having spoken very little to each other. She was very absorbed in the play. A large number of people boarded the train at this point, fewer got off, and our privacy of the previous four hours was shattered. All the seats were now occupied.

The train started again and the fans above our head began moving frenziedly, the one above hers with a loud *tak tak* sound. As the train picked up speed, the noise changed to a more complicated rhythm and finally disappeared altogether.

'Tell me something,' she said, putting her book aside. 'How did you and your friend manage to undertake research together? Do the Himachal University rules permit two researchers to work on the same topic simultaneously?'

'We decided to submit apparently differing research projects, which would in fact be intimately related. My topic was "The Reasons for Certain Aesthetic Classifications of the Human Form" and her choice was "The Development of

Prejudice Based on Differences in the Physical Appearance of Individuals". We wrote separate proposals as required by university regulations and were cleared by the committee without many problems. The only person who knew about this small trick we had played on the university was Professor Srinivasan; he made sure he wasn't a member of the committee.'

Caught up in giving explanations, I didn't notice the time spent in the journey from Chandigarh to Kalka. The train was running behind schedule, but we didn't have to worry; the hill train would wait for the Himalayan Queen to arrive before it left.

At Kalka there was a scramble. People were anxious to get out of the train and obtain seats in the hill train standing slightly ahead on an adjacent track. We hurried, but even so were too slow. By the time we had reached the toy train, all the seats had already been occupied.

While rushing past the compartments in search of a vacant seat, once again I was sure I saw Milan, but when I went back to look, he had gone.

Half an hour later, when the hill train chugged its way out of the station, we were sitting quite comfortably on our luggage, which we had placed beside the closed exit door near the toilet. A Bengali tourist party, comprising some nine or ten families, was travelling in the same compartment, and they had organised a communal meal for themselves. As a result there were two large containers and one basket, containing food placed between the berths in the compartment. A young man with long, curly hair began shovelling food on to steel plates that were passed around.

It was now that I mentioned to Diamond that I'd seen Milan or his lookalike on the train. 'I'm hallucinating,' I said. 'I'd better be careful.'

She chewed on my statement for a while. 'This fits in with this morning's incident,' she said. 'My first assignment: the case of the disappearing auto-rickshaw. The simple and obvious explanation, my dear Watson, is that your landlord's son was also planning to leave today by the same train. In the morning he must have seen the scooter-rickshaw and asked him to take him to the station. The driver must have assumed that you had left the message with him for Milan's benefit. You didn't tell him that you yourself would be catching the *auto*, did you?'

I mulled over her statement. In hindsight, it was the only possible explanation that fitted the facts.

'Well done, Sherlock Homes. This, of course, introduces another mystery. Why is my landlord's son following me?'

'You are completely paranoid.'

*****

The Bengali party finished their meals. One by one they kept coming to the toilet to wash up, and this was a lengthy and time-consuming operation for each person. Every now and then I had to move my legs back and forth and twist them at strange angles for the passing human traffic.

'They are washing their hands very thoroughly,' she observed.

'It's the *haldi*.'

'*Haldi*? I don't understand.'

'Turmeric. Bengalis add a great deal of turmeric to their food, don't they? It needs a lot of scrubbing to get the yellowness out. But why am I telling you all this? You are a Bengali yourself. A synthetic one, apparently.'

'I don't think that's true of all Bengalis,' she said defensively. 'In our family we never used excessive turmeric in the food.'

'I suggest we shift our position to save ourselves from the threat of a water deluge.' I pointed to a growing puddle of water that was slowly but surely making its way towards us.

We shifted to the other end of the carriage and pushed the large steel exit door open. We sat on the floor at her suggestion, my legs placed on the steps that led up to the carriage and hers dangling in the air. The train was now climbing with greater speed, although it was still possible for an agile person to hop off the train, run alongside, and then jump back.

I said, 'Is your real name Diamond?'

She unzipped her leather bag, dug out a newish-looking passport and passed it over to me. The holder's first name was, as she had claimed: Diamond.

'I don't know anyone else with such a name,' I said.

Her face clouded over as if there was something she didn't want to remember.

'Do you believe in rebirth?' she asked, after a long silence.

'Probably not.'

'I do.'

'That's interesting,' I said. 'What were you in your previous life?'

'I was married,' she said shortly.

'I see,' I said, waiting for her to continue.

'My marriage broke up three years ago,' she said. 'I was reborn then.'

'I'm sorry...'

'Don't be,' she said. 'It was the best thing to happen to me in a long while. Let me explain.' Her expression turned bitter. 'After the break-up, I did a complete revaluation of my life: everything I had over done, the way I used to think, everything. At the time I wanted to destroy everything even remotely connected to my marriage; the experience had been so terrible. I saw that my name was a symbol of enslavement.' She took a deep breath, and gathering her feelings continued, 'When I was born, a relative asked my mother on the phone, "Is it a boy?" and she had replied, as well as she could, "*Hira hai*. It is a diamond."' She laughed. 'That's how I came to be called Diamond. I was called by this name till I was thirteen, when it was changed to a name people felt was more suitable. As a child I had resented having my name changed. At the time of my marriage, my in laws changed it once again to Shobha, which is the custom, as you know. I joined my husband in the States a few months after marriage, with my new name on my passport.' She paused reflectively. 'After my divorce, I wanted to make a complete break with the past. I decided to drop the name given to me by my in laws. I made up my mind once more to adopt the name I had first been given, to go back to my childhood years, those years when I was treated more like a person.'

The train gave a jerk and stopped. A signpost indicated that we were at Solan, an important industrial town and district centre. Several passengers disembarked, and we managed to get window seats in a compartment.

'Was it a problem changing your name?' I asked, pushing up the window.

'There were so many formalities.' She threw up her hands. 'I had to put an advertisement in the newspaper and prepare so many affidavits sworn before a notary public. It wasn't easy because, apart from the legalities, there was an element of public ridicule as well, from fellow classmates and professors. Finally, my name got changed everywhere: at the banks, at the university, and at all the various government departments.'

We had crossed the halfway mark from Kalka. Pine trees were now predominant, with smaller tracts covered with firs and deodars. Twice we had a glimpse of a hill train coming on parallel tracks from Shimla, and then the two trains crossed each other. Not so far away, we could see the glittering lights of Shimla. The train reached Jutogh, from where Diamond would get a bus to Ganahatti.

'Would you like me to come with you?' I asked.

'No,' she said, with a knot in her brow. 'That wouldn't really serve any purpose, would it, unless you were planning to stay overnight?'. Gesturing to her luggage, she added, 'Would you take care of my bag for a few minutes?' She got off the train.

The halt at Jutogh was longer than at most stations. It was getting chilly now. I pulled out a jacket from my suitcase.

She returned, looking fresh in a light brown cotton sari, a black shawl wrapped around her, with a *bindi* on her forehead.

I said, 'Was that necessary?'

'Yes, I think so.'

I helped move her luggage on to the platform. We shook hands briefly. I returned to my seat.

The train lurched forward, stopped and then took off again.

13

The Ridge

The toy train trundled along, reaching Shimla shortly afterwards. The station was clean and tidy, free from beggars, porters and the usual chaos that usually accompanied such venues. It was only the Himalayan Queen that ventured back and forth from the town, and stalls and eateries did only moderate business there.

Families were organising rapid exits from the train, with parents issuing instructions to children to stick close. There were sounds of youthful cries of enthusiasm that their destination had been reached and that the holidays had begun. I was painfully aware that my own feelings were vastly different.

I walked past the trolleys of books and magazines, and vendors selling tea or coffee, on to the dark railway tracks. These continued ahead of the station towards the bus terminus, from where I would ascend, by means of an electronically operated lift, to the Mall.

From the tracks, Shimla loomed majestically. The Ridge, close to the summit of the town, sparkled with white light, resembling a crown or tiara to be placed on the head of a goddess. This was not, perhaps, inappropriate as the town was, after all, named after the hill Goddess Shamli. It was brighter than the maze of *bazaar* lanes below it, which also shone with more subdued yellow lighting.

Night had descended on the town by the time I reached the YMCA, a tall, red-coloured, old building, with two towers on each flank that had been inaugurated by the governor general Lord Irwin in 1930.

The reception confirmed there was a reservation in my name.

I checked into a large room on the second floor with simple, though adequate, furnishings. There was one bed, one table, one sitting chair, one armchair, one cupboard, one jug and **two** glasses – why this luxury?

From the suitcase I took out a bottle of Black Knight whisky and made myself a drink. Half way through the second drink I heard a knock on the door. It was Prakash, the same as ever, still sporting his wafer-thin moustache. Only his hair had grown thinner, otherwise he had added a few pounds.

'Welcome, dear friend,' I greeted him. 'I was just wondering what this extra glass was doing in my room. Can I make you a drink?'

'No, thanks,' he said, sitting down on the armchair. 'It's against the rules for staff to drink with guests in their rooms.'

'It's against the rules for guests to drink in their rooms at all.'

'That's true,' he said. 'Everybody knows that guests will drink, however, so that rule doesn't matter.

'I thought you were the manager, Prakash,' I said, pressurising him. 'Rules don't apply to managers.'

'I'm not the manager yet. I'm only the assistant manager. The rules still apply to me.'

'Is that so?'

'Yes, unfortunately, that is so. However...'

'However?'

'However, since we are meeting after such a long time and, moreover, because I'm leaving tomorrow for Chail....'

I poured him a drink.

'How is your wife?' I asked, remembering that Prakash had married within months of completing his Master's. It was the major reason he had taken up his present employment when it was offered to him.

'She's fine.' He paused before adding shyly, 'She gave birth to a baby girl last week.'

'That's great news. Please accept my congratulations.'

'Thank you.' He put a box of sweets on the table. 'Here is some *gulab jamun*.'

'It isn't necessary, Prakash.'

'I have a dozen boxes at home. Please accept it.' He sipped his drink. 'Of course, her birth has made it more difficult for me to leave this job.'

'Aren't you happy here?'

'Not really.'

'Problems with the boss?'

'No, he is all right... but still, you know, a job is after all a job.' He laughed suddenly. 'You should know. How many jobs did you have before coming to Shimla?'

'Six.'

'In that respect I'm just like you – but I am married now, with a child. I have responsibilities. I have to have a job.'

I reminded him that I, too, had a job.

'It's not the same. You have more freedom and leisure in your line of work than most other people in other jobs. Two classes in the morning and you're free for the rest of the day.'

'What would you like to do?'

'I think I could be successful as a scriptwriter in the Bombay film world. I've already written out a couple of screenplays.' He paused to sip his drink. 'I'm saving money so that I can live in Bombay for a few months and visit the studios. My wife is dead set against the idea. What do you think?' He sounded so earnest and serious that I almost laughed.

'I don't know, Prakash,' I said. 'It's really something only you can decide.'

'I'll get a script written out,' he said, 'and mail a copy to you in a month or so.'

'Do that,' I said. 'By the way, have you met Professor Srinivasan recently?'

'No.' He shook his head. 'I haven't seen him in the past couple of weeks.' He glanced at his watch. 'I had better be going now. I have a meeting with my boss.'

With my friend's departure, my temporarily uplifted mood swung. I felt tired and depressed. I made myself another drink and lay down on the bed, my back against the wall, sipping it slowly. I turned on a pocket transistor. Asha Bhonsle began singing. A sad song:

Yahi voh jagah hai
yahi voh fizaiyan
yahin par kabhi
aap humse mile they.

14

Bununda in Shimla

The dining hall at the YMCA was full of young, foreign tourists with exploration and trekking high on the agenda. I was not in a mood to fraternise, and decided to substitute the excellent breakfast it offered with a *bununda* at Tara's.

I strolled down the Mall, already overflowing with tourists, past the Shimla High Court, till I reached the café. It was called, rather plainly, 'TEA SHOP'. According to Tara, with his quaint though impeccable logic, Indians drank more tea than coffee, and therefore he insisted that there be many more tea shops and fewer coffee houses.

Tara recognised me at once and greeted me warmly. He was effusive. How was I? I must be an important person by now; so and so had become a high-ranking officer.

'I'm doing all right, Tara,' I said. 'How are you? I don't see many students around. Is it too early?'

'Students don't come here any more,' he said. 'It's because I've stopped giving credit.'

'Did you have a bad experience?'

'Some students went away from Shimla without clearing their dues,' he admitted. 'It's not the same as when you were studying here, Sahib. Those days were different.'

'Was it a large amount?'

'About six thousand rupees.'

'Six thousand rupees!' I repeated. 'That's a very large sum. Why did you give so much credit?'

'You don't know the situation here. Tell me, Sahib, do you think there should be a separation between student life and politics?'

'I'm not sure.'

'Oh **yes**, Sahib,' he said earnestly. 'There **must** be a separation. If someone wants to help people, let him. I'm not against that. Social work is fine, but politics is different. There is so much hooliganism here these days.'

'Which political party were these students affiliated to?' I asked, understanding him now. 'Was it any particular one?'

'No.' He shook his head. 'The student wings of all the political parties are just the same. There is no difference nowadays.'

'Why didn't you complain to the university authorities?'

'Don't make me open my mouth,' he said, using a colloquialism, 'but senior professors are protecting and encouraging, yes, even encouraging, these students. I can't say more, can I?' He noticed a customer beckoning him at one of the tables. 'Excuse me, please.'

I sat down at one of the tables towards the far end of the café.

A lean, proud Himachali with a caterpillar moustache, Tara had consistently refused to sell his small teashop, despite lucrative offers. During the time I had studied at Summerhill he used to give credit to the hostellers; it used to be a favourite hangout for university students whenever they came to the Mall. Then, the most popular snack, which sold more than the samosas and pakoras and was consumed by us till well past midnight, was Tara's *bununda*, a frothy omelette filled with tomatoes and onions, placed inside a bun.

'How's business?' I asked, when Tara came over with my *bununda* and tea in a glass. 'Isn't this rush unprecedented?'

'Yes,' he admitted. 'Business is exceptionally good this year.'

'Have you seen the professor lately, Tara?'

'Professor Srinivasan?'

'Yes.'

'No, I haven't seen him for a couple of weeks now.' He stroked his moustache thoughtfully. 'Go to Summerhill. I'm sure you will find him there, or else he will be at his house.'

'Do you have the address?'

'No, I don't, but there is no problem. Ask anyone in Sanjauli. Everyone knows him.'

I finished my breakfast and got up to leave. With difficulty, I managed to convince Tara to accept the money. He clasped my hand between both of his and shook it warmly.

I took the lift down to Cart Road, from where I caught a bus to Sanjauli. Inside the rickety mini- bus, which became progressively crowded, it struck me how Tara had made no mention of her. I realised on reflection that that had been deliberate, and was glad of it.

It was noon by the time I reached the suburb. As Tara had said, there was no problem in locating the professor's house. The elderly, bespectacled shopkeeper from whom I made enquiries told me that he wasn't at home. 'The professor has gone to South India,' he said.

It was a tiny cottage, freshly painted and smelling of new wood. A dark-faced woman, possibly a maid imported from the South, opened the door and showed me into the drawing room.

I sat down on a brown velvet sofa and waited. The furnishings inside were simple, though elegant. A basket chair hung by a chain falling from a wooden beam in a corner of the room, and there were other South Indian artefacts and decorative objects.

The professor's wife, a dark, fine-featured grey-haired lady, came out of an inner room. I was shocked to see how much she had aged. Always underweight, she now looked as thin as a grasshopper. She was tall, and her height, together with the thin arms and translucent glass frames that covered her mournful eyes, increased her resemblance to the insect, and gave her an almost sickly look. She had a half smile on her face and an uncertain expression, as if to say she was sorry but that she didn't really recognise me.

'I don't think you remember me, ma'am,' I said, putting her at ease. 'I'm an old student of the professor. I met you while you were staying in the university flats at Summerhill.'

'I'm sorry...' She still appeared hesitant.

'Those days I used to keep a beard,' I added, patiently.

'Oh, now I remember!' she exclaimed. 'You look quite different now.'

'I believe the professor is away.'

'Yes, that's right,' she said. 'He went to Bangalore only the day before yesterday. There has been a death in the family; it's the professor's elder sister, a favourite of his. Cardiac arrest, you know. He will be returning in two weeks' time. He has to wait for the thirteenth day.'

'I'm sorry to hear that.'

'I have not been well in recent years,' she said, by way of explanation, 'and have therefore not accompanied him.'

'I understand,' I said.

'Did you wish to see him about anything in particular?'

'There were some papers I wanted him to look at,' I said obliquely. 'I will come again.'

15

Summerhill

1

The local bus from Sanjauli dropped me off at Summerhill ahead of schedule. As I drifted past the familiar buildings, the campus seemed smaller than I remembered. The buildings were more run down compared to those at Delhi University, but the location of this hill university more than sufficiently compensated for its rather poor infrastructure. Surely, for certain subjects such as philosophy, literature and history, it made a difference if you studied your subject at a university housed in beautiful surroundings such as those that Summerhill had to offer, rather than in high- rise buildings locked inside a bustling metropolis?

Out of curiosity, and with time to kill, I looked at the notice boards in the main administration block. There were the usual timetables and examination schedules. A notice requested all students to be present for a seminar on 'The Relevance of Contemporary Social Science Research'.

A young, bearded man, formally dressed in a dark-coloured suit, passed me in the corridor, stopped, and then came back. The face somehow seemed familiar, but I couldn't immediately place him.

'Hi!' he exclaimed. 'You look different.'

'So do you,' I said, recognising him from his voice. His name was Jai Ahuja. He had joined the university as a student the same year I had registered for my Master's but had been studying history instead of philosophy. I remembered that he had been a pot smoker, always shabbily dressed and casual about his studies. Somehow, however, in the last crucial month he had managed to get his act together and do well in the examinations. His successful turn around and examination results had managed to get him appointed as a lecturer, and I saw that with his shining tiepin and sober grey suit his new respectable mantle did not ill-become him.

'I've grown a beard.'

'I've shaved mine off.'

'Why did you go and do that?' he said. 'Anyhow, it's great to see you. What are you doing here?'

'Just looking around,' I said. 'You're teaching, aren't you?'

'History,' he said. 'Aren't you at Delhi University?'

'That's right.' I wondered if I could detect a trace of envy in his voice. 'How are things out here these days?'

'Terrible. Going from bad to worse?'

'What's going on?'

'Right-wing conspiracy.' He looked at his watch regretfully. 'I have to rush now. I'm already late for my class. Are you coming to the seminar?'

'Possibly,' I said. I thought Jai sounded bombastic, though vague.

'Do come,' he insisted. 'It's important for all of us to be there.'

We shook hands briefly. He darted off to take his class, far more conscientious now than he had ever been as a student.

I wandered off in the general direction of the staffroom on the ground floor of the grey modern Arts Faculty building. Inside the square hall, a pale yellow carpet on its polished floor, I spotted Professor Anjali Sinha, who taught Indian philosophy, sitting on one of the cushioned chairs.

She was a fair, plump friendly Bengali with a large, open face. An attractive woman in a homely sense, her friendly nature had ensured her popularity with staff and students alike, even though her class lectures were often disorganised and poorly presented.

'Hullo, my dear,' she smiled warmly. 'It's so nice to see you. I understand you have left Shimla for better prospects in Delhi.'

'Philosophy anywhere seems to be a poor prospect, ma'am,' I said. 'You know how even within the social sciences it's an underrated subject.'

'And within philosophy, it's Indian philosophy that's the most neglected specialisation,' she said. 'What do you teach?'

'Greek.'

'You should have taken Indian philosophy,' she said reprovingly. 'It's very deep.' She glanced at her watch. 'Oops, I'm ten minutes late for a class. Excuse me, dear.'

2

There were a few students sitting in the canteen, a drab, tin-roofed structure, where Diamond and I had agreed to meet. It had not changed from the old days. I liked the sparse furniture and the equally simple food that was on offer. In Delhi University, several of my students drove expensive cars and ate in fancy restaurants. Class had entered the classroom more prominently than here. Of course, this was the reality of the world outside, and it could be argued that the sooner students were exposed to it the better. On the other hand, there was something to be said for providing a more level playing field in which student interaction took place. You did not have to be a believer in simple living to appreciate a university atmosphere in which rich and poor students interacted on more equal terms. This artificial student environment was good in a way, for a few years at least.

After a while she stepped in, dressed in a bright green cotton sari, a white shawl draped around her shoulders.

'What's happened to your double role?' I said, signalling two coffees to the canteen manager. 'Today was the day for T shirt and trousers, if I remember correctly.'

'From now on, till I'm back in Delhi, you will only see me in saris. In any case, I don't understand why you call it a 'double role'. Women keep wearing different dresses – it's nothing unusual.'

'It's just that with you the dress also somehow affects your personality.'

'Does it? I, too, feel that. It's surprising that you could sense it. I think it's because of the way I used to be. You see I haven't been able to reject everything about the past. There are so many things I still believe in.'

'Such as?'

'Such as family.' She didn't elaborate.

'Family?'

'Family, you know. Family ties, relationships...' She changed the subject. 'Were you able to meet Professor Srinivasan? You worked with him, didn't you?'

I told her briefly about the morning's visit to the professor's house.

'Oh, that's a pity,' she said. 'You'll have to wait till he returns.'

The waiter, a young lad in his early teens, put two steaming cups of coffee on the table.

'There doesn't seem to be any other option,' I said, stirring the coffee. 'How shall we co-ordinate the research? We could meet at Summerhill, or in town. In Shimla, the streets are too crowded; the atmosphere isn't right. Often there are too many people on the streets to even walk about. It doesn't seem to be as good an idea as it had first seemed.'

'All the rich people from Delhi seem to have turned up in Shimla.'

'It's mostly the middle classes. The rich go to Europe these days,' I said. 'Let's make it the university, then.'

'A slight problem has arisen. Rehana's daughter, Asma, who is studying in Chandigarh, has mumps, and it's quite bad. The school authorities telephoned her today.'

'How old is she?' I said, wondering what Diamond was getting at. 'Is her father in Chandigarh?'

'Her father lives in Dubai. Rehana and he are separated, though they haven't thought it necessary to get a divorce. Asma must be fifteen or sixteen.'

'She's old enough to take care of herself, then, and mumps isn't so serious for girls – but I guess mothers will be mothers.'

'Exactly,' she said, sipping the coffee slowly. 'So Rehana is leaving for Chandigarh in a couple of hours and will need to be there for some days. I came away because I had to meet you, but I have promised to get back early. While she's away, she's asked me take care of her weekend school at the village. Rehana suggested you came and stayed at Ganahatti. I thought you might want to spend time with the professor. Now, since he isn't there, you don't need to go to the university or to his house. Why don't you stay at Ganahatti till he gets back?'

I had planned it out differently. Knowing Srinivasan, I had thought it unlikely that he would come out with answers there and then on how and when he had received the script. It would take him time to remember, if he did remember anything at all. A highly intelligent man, he was extraordinarily lucid and fast in presenting philosophical arguments, but on more mundane matters he was slow and forgetful. I knew that I would need to keep prodding him, and had therefore decided to meet him every other day to try and shake his memory. One day the penny would drop, and he would recall what had happened.

In his absence, there was nothing for me to do in Shimla. Staying in Ganahatti would cramp my style somewhat, living as a guest in the house of a person I didn't know and in a place where I didn't know anybody, but there wasn't anyone in Shimla I really wanted to meet or spend time with. Besides, staying in Ganahatti would without a doubt improve the quality of our discussions and research. Neither of us would waste time commuting. It would also be quieter and free from tourists.

She was waiting for an answer.

'All right,' I said. 'I'll be in Ganahatti tomorrow.'

'That's settled then,' she said, looking relieved. 'I better go now. I promised to rush back.'

I strolled past the university buildings and took a narrow dirt track leading up from the main road towards a small, old Hanuman temple. It was a steep climb, and took me about an hour to reach. Situated on top of a small hillock, at this time of day it was deserted. On the way up, I noticed particular trees, rocks and even smells; everything appeared unchanged. It had been a favourite spot of ours.

Sitting on the hillock, gazing across that vast space, watching the mist descend, I experienced the strange sensation of her presence behind me sharing my vision. I felt her to be quite close, and I hoped against hope that all I had to do was to turn my head and that everything in my life would then return to me, just as before. Then all the years I'd experienced since would disappear in a flash as though they were an unusually extended nightmare. Yet I was afraid to look. I also reckoned that although she was certainly there, if I looked round, she would disappear.

I stayed on the hillock till it became dark.

16

Ganahatti

The next day I caught the twelve o'clock bus. Ganahatti was on the way to important towns such as Bilaspur and Mandi, and this particular state roadway bus, a grey, ramshackle affair, would travel en route through the village. We passed two or three villages after Jutogh (where the toy train had stopped) when the conductor nudged me to indicate that my stop was imminent.

I got off on the highway and surveyed my surroundings. Because Ganahatti was at a lower altitude than Shimla, the surrounding hills were largely covered by blackish, brittle-looking Himalayan oak. On a lower road running parallel to the highway were several shops. It was a short climb from the highway to the village. A cobbled pathway ran through the village. It seemed everybody knew Rehana,. A woman who managed an all-purpose general merchandise store in the village sent her child with me to point out her house.

It was a pukka mud house, much like others in the village, with a sloping roof tiled with slate, only it appeared to be sturdier, larger and of more recent construction. The green-painted wooden door was ajar, indicating someone was at home. I rang the bell.

A bright-eyed, *kajolled* fair hill woman in her mid thirties opened a leaf of the door.

'Are you the person who was to come from Delhi?' Her speech was a mixture of Hindi and a local dialect.

'Yes,' I said. 'I'm from Delhi.'

'Please come in,' she beamed welcomingly. 'Do sit down. Can I make a cup of tea for you?'

'Please don't bother.' I put my bags in a corner and sat down on a cane chair.

'It is no bother.' She remained standing.

'It's not needed.'

'All right, *bhai sahib*,' she said, sounding offended.

'On second thoughts,' I said, sensing that she didn't like my refusal for some reason, 'I will have a cup of tea.'

'I thought you would want one.' She looked happy. 'You must be tired from your journey.'

'What is your name?'

'Komal,' she said. 'I live close by, only a few houses away.'

She went inside the kitchen. I stood up and briefly surveyed my surroundings. I had been sitting in what was evidently the living room, and I saw there were two other rooms in the house that served as bedrooms. All three rooms had brightly coloured rugs spread on the ground. There were no fitted cupboards and few things hung on the walls; the mud walls could take only so much weight.

The bedroom towards the rear side of the house, which must have been used by Rehana's daughter, had a large number of posters pasted on the wall: Sylvester Stallone, Madonna, and Bugs Bunny amongst several others. There was a pile of comic books and music cassettes.

I heard a voice calling: '*Bhai sahab*'. I took the cup from her, sipped the tea and said something appreciative. It was a formality (there was actually too much sugar for my taste), but she was pleased.

Now that Komal had done her duty, she wanted to get away. She took me to the porch, and pointed out her house – 'the one with the green windows'. If I needed anything, I shouldn't hesitate to come and ask her. She begged to be excused. *Didi* (sister) would be returning from school in half an hour.

I was pottering about the house when Diamond arrived, carrying a big cloth bag on her back. Komal, whom she must have met on the way, was with her. A small boy accompanied them. Wearing school uniform, a satchel on his back, he must have been around seven or eight years' old.

'Hullo, there,' she said, panting a little from the climb. 'I believe you've already met Komal.'

'She has been very hospitable,' I said.

Komal simpered.

Diamond sat down on a small settee in the corner. She patted the space next to her, and her village companion joined her in the shared intimacy that only women seem to be able to participate in.

'What's you name, son?' I asked the boy.

'Kalyan,' he said. 'Are you a doctor?'

'No, I'm not a doctor. Why? Do you want to become one?'

'I asked, because you are wearing a white shirt. Doctor's wear white shirts, don't they?'

'That's correct, but I'm not one. Do you want to become a doctor when you grow up, Kalyan?'

'No, I want to be a pilot,' he said. 'I want to fly an aeroplane.'

'Are you sure you don't want to fly a rocket instead?'

'What's the difference?'

'If you want to go to London, you need an aeroplane. On the other hand, if you want to go to the moon, you need a rocket to get there.'

'I want to go to London.'

Seeing both of us fairly engrossed, Komal and Diamond left us to our own devices and started chatting to each other. I questioned the boy on what he had been taught at school that day.

'Today, our teacher told us that Gandhiji used to clean out other people's shit,' he said.

'Why did your teacher tell you this?'

'One of the boys in my class had gone to the toilet and had left it dirty.'

'Did he forget to flush?'

'The flush wasn't working. The teacher scolded him in front of the entire class, and told him he ought to have taken a bucket of water and done the job, and that Gandhiji used to clean out other peoples shit.'

'Why did Gandhiji do that?'

'It has been puzzling me,' he admitted, before adding with a smile, 'I don't know. You tell me.'

His mother, who had been listening to our discussion, interrupted.

'Don't talk dirty, Kalyan,' she said. 'Go home, now. Your father is waiting for you.'

'Bye, uncle.' He picked up his bag reluctantly and trudged off. I was sorry to see him go, carrying his heavy satchel crammed full of books.

Diamond and Komal continued to talk softly. I was happy to be excluded from their conversation. I realised that the sari Diamond wore made a huge difference to Komal's perception of her. They would have met only very recently, but were chattering away like old friends.

During a lull in their conversation, it occurred to Diamond that it was lunchtime. Komal made a move as if to leave, but Diamond insisted that she had a bite to eat before going. We spread some newspapers on the floor.

'Bahadur is at home today,' Komal said, as she got up to leave. 'He will want lunch.' She turned to me. '*Namaste, bhai sahib.*' She folded her hands and left.

'You could use Asma's bedroom,' Diamond said, after I had helped her wash the dishes. 'Would that suit you?'

'I would prefer it. It has a window. Tell me, how do the villagers react to such an arrangement?'

'What do you mean?'

'We are a fairly conservative society, aren't we?'

'Oh, they can't be bothered. Rehana is known to have many visitors. Both men and women have stayed here frequently.'

'I suppose it could get boring living here alone.'

'Perhaps,' she said, 'but she is very gregarious.'

I settled myself into the smaller bedroom. I opened the window. The view was simply breathtaking. Outside there was a thick forest of Himalayan oak, and beyond the hills a snow-capped mountain range, the rough-hewn window framing the view as if I were looking out onto a painting. The window faced west, so the days to come held out the promise of a view of glorious sunsets in the evenings.

We spent two hours inspecting each other's academic material. There were many books, photocopied articles and notes. Our plan was for me to study the material brought by her and she would do the same with my material.

'Care for some *gulab jamun*?' I offered her a box of brown, syrupy cheese balls for dessert.

'Oh, I hadn't noticed it. That's lovely.'

'I thought you might have finished the sweets from Bengali Market.'

'Oh, those got devoured ages ago. By the way, *gulab jamuns* aren't the only sweets I like.'

After we had retired to our rooms, I picked up a philosophical treatise on the principles of aesthetics to read.

I read in bed for about an hour. All of a sudden, I sensed her presence, just as I'd felt it at the temple. I climbed out of bed and gazed through the window. It was dark outside. A few lonely stars twinkled, and there was only the barest sliver of a moon. A strong wind was blowing, and I heard the pines sighing as they swayed. At a distance, lighted, cosy huts could be seen, that belonged to some far away village. I stepped into the living room, switched on the light and looked around.

There was no one there.

I returned to my room and climbed back into bed, haunted by memories of the past.

17

Simran

Her name was Simran, a common name in Sikh families. She was studying in the same year as me, although she was much younger. I had had various jobs over the previous five years, which made me the oldest student in the class.

It was Eliot's death that had made me decide to resign from my last job, when I think about it now, although I did not resign overnight. Rather, it started in me a process of questioning that ultimately culminated in my decision to quit.

After his funeral in Lucknow, when I returned to Delhi, I had continued with my job for a while, but gradually I began to become increasingly dissatisfied. It was fortunate I stayed with the job for some time after the funeral, however, because it helped me to get a grip on myself, and with time the pain lessened.

Eventually, I decided to leave both the job and the city. My savings were minuscule, but there was some money Eliot had left behind. It was not very substantial, since he had never believed in saving for a rainy day. Still, I estimated that I could survive on a student's budget for two years, and with no clear goals in mind I enrolled for a Master's degree in philosophy at Summerhill.

*****

I had noticed her in class on the very first day, but never found a chance to talk to her. The entire first semester passed without our exchanging more than an occasional greeting. Without a doubt she had a friendly disposition, but somehow an opportunity to become friendly never presented itself. I hesitated to take the initiative and approach her because I was afraid that I would stoke a fire within myself that would not find a corresponding response.

Salim, too, was in my class. We were room-mates at the hostel. He had come all the way from Kanpur. They were not having regular examinations there; the last two years had been declared 'zero' sessions. One day I casually mentioned her name to him to try and find out more details about her.

'So you've fallen for her,' he concluded at once. 'Love at first sight, is it?'

'I didn't say that. I was just asking about her out of curiosity.'

I didn't convince Salim.

'Shall I talk to Radha?' he said. Radha Chenoy, the superintendent's daughter, nicknamed SFI because of her involvement with the left wing Students Federation of India, was one of Simran's closest friends. A lean, bright-eyed intellectual, she was dedicated to the party's ideology.

'No thanks.'

'Why not?' he persisted.

'There's no point. She's out of my league.'

I meant it seriously. It wasn't that I had a low opinion of myself, but I was sure that many other students felt the same way about her. I was content to watch her from a distance and hope... despite my inaction. I couldn't stop that.

Salim was more optimistic. I swore him to secrecy and insisted that he restrain himself from attempting to advance my cause in any manner whatsoever. Remembering one of Eliot's favourite quotes, I pointed out that the way to hell lay paved with good intentions. As things turned out, Salim was to prove right in his assessment that I had underestimated the possibility of Simran ever evincing a romantic interest in me, although I could never really understand what she ever saw in me.

She couldn't have been classified as beautiful. She was fair, with a face that might almost be called handsome. It wasn't her looks that made her stand out, however, and drew people to her. Neither was it her friendliness; many people are friendly. It was her genuine affection for other people, a concern, warmth, call it what you will. Radha later said that she exemplified 'socialism with a heart'. She was concerned about everyone, from the cleaning lady to the head of department – which, of course, meant Professor Srinivasan.

Was it because of her openness that, despite their interest, she had no students approaching her romantically I wondered? It wasn't that Summerhill had particularly well-behaved students. There was a high wolf element within the male student population, which would have found anyone projecting an image of unsullied innocence too difficult to tolerate within their midst. But the men respected her. Perhaps that might not have been possible had it not been for the one flaw in her character – if it could be called that – a massive temper! When she got mad, she got **really** mad. But this generally happened for a reason, something she believed in, something she felt strongly about, or some injustice.

I once saw a religious painting in a bookstore of a child playing, with a huge black cobra poised in the background, watching and protecting the child. It reminded me of her. The snake was the temper in her that allowed Simran to preserve her child-like, good-natured innocence.

18

King Puppet

'Would you like to come and see the school?' Diamond asked during breakfast the next day.

'Where's it situated?' I said, munching some toast.

'There's a path leading downhill near the market, where the bus dropped you. It's not far.'

'I'll come for a short while.'

The walk to the school was bracing, the air fresh and clean, and a welcome change from Delhi. It was early morning with the grass still wet with dew. We walked through a narrow pathway, brushing past the occasional leafy plant and shrubbery. I felt certain she was more comfortable with trousers, but she was dressed, as usual now, in a colourful cotton sari.

'Are you allergic to synthetic material?'

'No.' Her eyes glinted with amusement. 'It's more a matter of aesthetics.'

'I notice you don't wear silk saris.'

'That's right.'

'The poor silk worms that get killed in the process?'

'How did you guess?' There was amazement in her voice.

'It wasn't so difficult.'

We were now on a grassy hillside, the grass as yet yellow and sparse, but with the rains it would turn lush green, providing fodder for the livestock. At a distance, I could see several houses; the first of these was the school. We passed by fields of mustard and wheat. There were no signs of any agricultural activity; there was, however, still time for the harvesting.

The school was really just one large, square room, fifteen feet by fifteen feet, not big enough to be called a hall. It was empty inside without even the usually inevitable blackboard, and bereft of tables, chairs or, indeed, any furniture. Simply a huge, grey jute carpet spread on the floor.

Two fresh-faced *Pahari* girls, both in their late teens, were inside waiting for her. Diamond and the two girls hugged each other in turn. The girls noticed me, and became slightly self-conscious. I sat on the carpet in a corner of the room and tried to look as unobtrusive as possible.

Gradually, the students started filtering in, one by one. There were around nine or ten students in all, belonging to different age groups, probably between seven to twelve years old.

Diamond took out various things from her bag: strips of cloth, cotton wool, coloured pieces of paper, needle, thread and small round pieces of wood. 'We will make a king puppet today,' she announced. There was clapping and cheering. The two older girls began distributing the tool kits to the children.

The class commenced. Diamond began by initially explaining the procedure. The two older girls then went around and periodically checked on how the children were coping. If they became stuck they explained the correct method. Occasionally they would come back to Diamond for clarification. With young children you need enormous patience, and I saw that she possessed that quality.

I stayed for an hour, watching her and the children busy in their work, and then left quietly.

On the way back I thought of Eliot and the French-named public school, where he had taught English literature. Two incidents, which occurred in my first year at the school, firmly established my faith in, and respect for, my foster parent. In those days we were staying in the residence within the school complex provided by the authorities. I was six years old, and had only recently come away from the home with this tall, dark man with a deep voice.

The first incident. I was in the second standard. As centre forward I had scored a winning goal during a football match in school, and had run back to the house triumphantly in search of Eliot – who wasn't there. I eventually found him, book in hand, sitting on the steps of the wide terrace at the front of the school, by the Oude cannon cast by General Claude Martin, colonial founder of the school.

'Guess who won?' I had asked excitedly.

'Your team won.' His eyes twinkled as he put aside the book he had been reading. 'Did you score the winning goal?'

'How did you guess?' I said, astounded by the assurance with which he made the statement.

'You wouldn't be looking so happy otherwise, or have bothered to find me.'

I was deeply impressed. It was my first lesson in logic.

The second incident. I was older. On that day I had come back from school, and Eliot had casually asked me what I had studied. We had in fact studied icebergs in the geography class, and there was to be a class test the following day. This was one of the rare occasions when Eliot asked me to bring him my book on geography. He found the chapter on icebergs and asked me to read it. I spent two hours memorising its contents and came back to him, eager to be questioned. But Eliot threw me off balance by asking a simple question – which tested my understanding, not my memory. I couldn't answer correctly. 'Read it once again,' my foster parent had said. 'I don't want to spoon-feed you.' I came back to him after an hour, this time convinced I could answer any question accurately. He asked me a single question – which

I did manage to answer correctly. That satisfied Eliot, and I wasn't asked anything further, much to my disappointment.

After so many years I still remembered what had been written in that chapter on icebergs. It was as if it had become imprinted on my brain.

There was a rumour spread at school that *hijra* prostitutes were frequent visitors at our house, and that sex orgies used to take place. The first part of the story was true, the second a fabrication on the part of over-imaginative students and possibly some of the members of staff. There was some circumstantial evidence that supported their theory, for the purpose behind the visits by these outcastes, these dregs of society, was not known to anyone except Eliot himself. What was clear to everyone, however, was that the *hijras* did visit fairly frequently and Eliot was known to have given them money – a neighbour had watched him do so from her house – and several of them may indeed have been prostitutes. I thought of the painful confrontation I had had with Eliot.

*****

In the house, I took an armchair out on to the verandah, and resumed my reading of a book on plastic surgery. It was a medical textbook belonging to Diamond. I read for an hour and then, as I turned the page, something fell on to the floor. I picked it up. It was a photograph of someone sitting upright in what appeared to be a hospital bed. It was obviously a woman, a fact that could be determined by the shape of the body, not from the face, which was completely swathed in bandages. At the bottom of the photograph, 'Berne, Switzerland, '02' was written in ink.

There was a knock on the door. I replaced the photo inside the book, put it aside and went to open the door. It was Diamond returning from school.

'You're a woman of many talents,' I said. 'Where did you learn to make puppets?'

'At Art School there was a course on puppetry that I joined.'

'It's interesting for children.'

'Yes, it is,' she said. 'At first I was worried about what I would teach. I was reassured that the place wasn't meant to be an alternative to the regular school, since in any case practically all the children go to the government school in the village. It was designed more to fill the gaps, for developing a child's interests and imagination. Teaching them to do interesting things with their hands is one way of doing this.'

'How do the villagers feel about the school?'

'They are happy about it. Most villagers hold Rehana in high esteem, and are glad that their children are learning new things. Some parents don't send their children because of the presence of low-caste children, but there are enough students who do come.'

'Yes, there were quite a few, although I didn't spot Kalyan there.'

'Kalyan goes to a public school in Shimla. He's the only boy from the village to study there.'

'His father must be spending a packet.'

'I guess so. I don't think he can afford it, really. That reminds me, I've accepted a dinner invitation for both of us at Komal's house tomorrow. I hope you are okay with that.'

'That's fine,' I said.

19

Komal and Bahadur

The following day we went to Komal's house for dinner around eight o' clock. Komal greeted us at the door with a welcoming smile. Inside we met Bahadur, her husband, a stocky person with a crew cut, in his late thirties.

'Hullo, madam. Hullo, sir.' He greeted us with folded hands.

'Hullo, Bahadurji.' I shook hands with him.

Diamond made a *namaste*.

The room we entered ran the width of the house. It was well furnished. A portable black and white television set stood on top of one of the smaller tables in the corner.

Bahadur and I sat down on white-painted armchairs around a Formica-topped table. Diamond followed Komal into the kitchen.

'Diamond tells me you are a brilliant carpenter,' I said.

'He is a very good carpenter, *bhai sahab*.' Komal came into the room carrying a tray with mugs of tea and fried snacks. 'He has made every single piece of furniture in the house. Down to the very chair you are sitting on.'

'Is that so?' I said, impressed. The furniture in the room was skilfully crafted, suggesting a more than ordinary passion for carpentry.

'It's not a big deal,' said Bahadur. 'It's just an ordinary skill that can be developed with practice.'

'He is being modest.' Komal put the tray on the table and swept out of the room.

'I believe you work for a furniture factory in Solan,' I said. 'Why don't you start your own business?'

'Wood is frightfully expensive these days. Besides, I have no aptitude for business. I can only do a job like my present one. It would have been different had I been educated.'

'Are you making something at the moment?' I spotted planks of wood, a hacksaw and a drill on the floor of the adjoining room.

'A shelf for Kalyan to keep his books in.' Something was troubling Bahadur because his face had turned grey and he appeared tense.

Kalyan rushed in from outside. He slowed down when he saw there were visitors, but his face lit up when he saw me.

'Hi, there.' I was glad to see him.

'Now Kalyan can become someone important if he studies hard,' said Bahadur, rather too seriously. 'Perhaps he could become an officer in the army.'

'Join the army? I wouldn't want to do that.' Kalyan screwed up his face. 'I'm going to be a pilot. Isn't that right, uncle?' He looked at me for support.

'That's correct,' I said.

In a while, Diamond joined us and Komal began serving dinner.

'I told Komal that she should prepare something very simple,' said Diamond, 'but actually she has made a feast for us.'

The food was delicious: lamb curry, lentils, kidney beans and white curd. From time to time, Komal brought hot fresh chapattis from the kitchen.

We didn't stay long after dinner. Bahadur seemed to be relieved to see us go, though he was perfectly courteous and did his best to hide it.

Back in the house, I made coffee. We talked for a while in the living room.

'Did you notice anything unusual?' she said.

'Not particularly, although Bahadur seemed rather withdrawn.'

'That's what I meant.' She was quiet, as if thinking. 'You know, Komal has been having problems with Bahadur. He is ill treating her.'

'Komal seems completely devoted to Bahadur. What's his problem?'

'He blames her for not being educated. She can't read or write, and therefore can't help Kalyan at school. Recently, the boy's results have been very poor. He nearly failed. It was a big blow for Bahadur. He loves Kalyan dearly, so thankfully he isn't haranguing him, but he is taking it out on his wife. He himself is not educated, but that doesn't seem to matter to him.'

'Perhaps it'll just blow over soon. How long has this been going on?'

'Since Kalyan's results came out ten days' ago.'

I was silent. It explained why Kalyan had also appeared to be out of sorts.

'What makes it worse is that for the past couple of days he has started hitting her. She comes here and cries all the time. Komal can't imagine ever leaving the man; she was brought up to regard it as a sin even to think on those lines. I don't know what to do. She won't let me speak to Bahadur.'

'She probably thinks it would make him even angrier. Let me speak to him, after a day or so. It won't make things worse for her, I can assure you.'

'I feel so helpless. I don't know what to do.'

'I know,' I said. 'It's a problem.'

*****

As I lay in bed later that night watching the shadows cast on the mud roof by the hanging light, I thought of how the same problem had been presented to us years ago in the philosophy class. It was also the reason for our initial acquaintance and how I had eventually come to know her.

20

Naming and Shaming

1

It was the start of the second semester, and Professor Srinivasan had been taking a class in ethics. Unlike most other subjects, philosophy is not easy to teach within fixed time slots. This is because the subjects discussed are without any defined borders. You can stretch the discussion as much as you like. For this reason, those who teach philosophy sometimes cannot keep up with the syllabus. This is part of the very nature of the subject; anyone who wishes to be a philosophy student would be well advised to understand this before embarking on a course of study. The best teachers of philosophy pepper their lectures with concrete examples or illustrations taken from everyday life. And Professor Srinivasan was one of the best. There was no doubt about that.

On that particular day he was lecturing on subjective morality and relativistic ethics.

'So we find that what was considered moral or right conduct during one period in history was regarded as highly improper and immoral at another stage,' said the professor, concluding his lecture. 'Even someone like Socrates, with all his wisdom, upheld the institution of slavery. Are there any questions?'

Several voices piped in with comments and questions. It was wrong, many felt, to say that ethics were relative to time and space. A strident Radha, already known for her communist views, and a less vocal but equally firm Simran, were ranged on one side together, arguing that there were objective standards which could be applied to questions of morality and ethical conduct. Weren't human rights universal and timeless? Other students disagreed.

'Kindly end this shouting match.' The professor held up his hands to silence the class. 'We will have a discussion during the next period.' He thought for a few minutes. 'We will take a specific situation. All students will be called upon to advise a person faced with a particular problem on the proper course of action for her to take.'

The problem he described to the class concerned a married woman who was being badly treated by her husband. On a couple of occasions the husband had beaten her up. The reasons for what had happened were unspecified.

'Now,' said the professor shrewdly, 'you are not being asked to evaluate the husband's conduct. The problem being posed is: What is the morally correct course of action for the woman?'

'What's the class background of this woman?' asked Radha.

'Lower middle class and uneducated,' he smiled. 'No further information now.'

There was an excited buzz in the classroom.

'In the next class,' the professor announced, 'every student will be expected to give a brief presentation on what, according to him or her, is the proper course of action for a woman in such a situation.'

2

On the day of the presentations there was a good turnout, and many students spoke. There were many shades of opinion expressed about what the hapless woman should do.

'Now, according to our sacred scriptures,' commented Jaspal Singh, a dark, athletic young man, who played basketball for the university, 'it is the duty of the woman to take care of her husband's needs, and she should bear in mind that he must have hit her for some reason. She might have neglected some of her duties. She should reform herself accordingly.'

There were screeches and loud hooting from the girls in class, and Jaspal Singh had to beat a hasty retreat as he was warming up to the theme of a devoted wife in various scriptures.

It was then the turn for a plump, round-faced woman called Sangeeta to speak. Her approach was Gandhian, though she did not refer to Gandhi in her speech. 'This woman must be patient with her husband,' she maintained, 'and make him realise that what he has been doing is very wrong. She should lodge a silent but effective protest. By her sacrifices and through her behaviour, she can succeed in reforming even the most uncouth and ill-mannered of husbands.'

Radha, who came next, was unequivocal in her approach. 'There is no question but that the woman should seek a divorce,' she said firmly. 'It's part of the women's struggle against a male- dominated society. She must stand up and fight for her rights. That's the only way in which eventually our society will become transformed.'

Simran's presentation was brief and to the point. 'Ordinarily, I would have agreed with Sangeeta,' she said, 'that a sincere attempt should be made to save a marriage from collapsing, but physical assault is something too contemptible and disgusting to accept. Such a man is not worth living with under any circumstances. The lady in question would do well to file for a divorce.'

I was the last speaker and spoke at length.

'Let's speculate about what this woman can do, and the possible fallout or consequences of her actions,' I said. 'Two possibilities exist. In the first case – let's call it situation A – the woman succumbs to pressure and beatings from her husband and learns to 'adjust' and compromise. She has also been advised to do so by her parents and friends. She somehow 'adjusts'; the marriage continues to subsist; the arguments and fights lessen; maybe she has children; a family emerges. Ten years later, when she is reviewing her life and the decision made at that particular point in time, she is thankful that she made the 'right' decision by listening to the advice of her parents, etc. Her husband has mellowed by then, and has become more accommodating. She is happy with her decision.

'In the second situation – situation B – it is the same woman, but her situation is somewhat different. Here, her parents have been advising her to try and adjust, but she has a different set of friends, maybe people like Simran and Radha who give her emotional support and tell her to break out of the arrangement. Owing to their support and encouragement, she leaves her husband, files for divorce and begins to search for a job that will provide her with an income to support herself.

'She does get a job, and then she goes in for some vocational training course in the evening, gets another, better job, and ten years' later is doing a job that is equivalent, if not better, than the job her erstwhile husband worked at. She may even form a new friendship with another, more liberal, male, and might even get married to him.

'Ten years later, when this woman, who is now a different person, reviews her decision, she is glad she broke out of the marriage and is thankful to her friends for their support and encouragement during a crucial period in her life.

'In both these situations, the woman took different decisions but later in life was satisfied that she had made the right choice. It might well be otherwise. She might live to regret her decision, ten years later. If she had decided to stay with her husband, ten years on she might regret it and reckon that her situation is now much worse. She is now too old to think of starting her life all over again. On the other hand, if she had left her husband having taken the advice of friends, she might not have subsequently got a job, and might have been forced to stay with her parents who were unhappy with her decision. Ten years later, she might deeply regret her decision. She might even come to the conclusion that her wicked, unmarried spinster friends had given her bad advice and had got her to walk out of her marriage so that she would be miserable like them.

'All these different possibilities exist. In life, anything can happen. I don't know enough to be able to speculate about what possibility is more likely to occur in her life. Therefore I am really not in a position to give her any advice. It's a question that requires more intimate knowledge about the woman and her situation.'

There was muted applause at the end of my talk. The women were dissatisfied. As I made my way back to my seat, I heard mutterings and expressions such as 'vague' and 'confused'.

The professor was pleased with the overall class response.

'Let me sum up today's discussion for you,' he said. 'As the divergent views might indicate, human affairs are often far too complex for easy decisions to be taken. Today's discussion has demonstrated, I hope, the difficulties in creating a universal ethic to determine the right or proper course of action for a person in a given situation, since each situation has its own unique angles and dynamic.'

3

Two weeks after the debate, barely a month was left for the academic year to conclude and examinations to begin, yet with Professor Srinivasan we were only half way through the philosophy course. This created a degree of consternation and anxiety amongst the students. In class there were discussions about the course still to be covered; many students were worried about the lack of progress from the point of view of the examination.

When Professor Srinivasan entered the class the next day, he found a drawing of a tortoise in chalk on the blackboard. Underneath the sketch some bright spark had written the name of the animal in Hindi: *kacchua*.

Professor Srinivasan was not easily provoked, neither did he often fly into a rage. As he wiped the blackboard clean with a duster, his brow was creased and his lips determinedly pursed. Temperamentally a mild and gentle soul, he hated to shout or to become angry. While teaching, he would often speak emphatically, but without raising his voice.

'I wish to make it clear to all of you,' he announced, with the barest hint of anger in his voice, 'that no question outside of what has been taught in class will be asked in the examination.'

There was an audible sigh of relief. A few 'Thank you, sirs' and 'Sorry sirs' were heard.

'It appears to me,' he continued, 'that there is much creative talent in the class that is trying to find expression. Therefore, today we shall have a naming session in which the class shall collectively give every student a name other than his or her usual name. Suggestions can be written out on a piece of paper and given to me. I will read out the suggested names, and the correct choice will be decided by vote of voice.'

The competition got underway. At first students were hesitant, but when they saw that the professor was relaxed, they became increasingly enthusiastic.

Many students were given names that subsequently stuck to them for the rest of their stay at the university, including Radha, Salim, Simran, and I.

It became an occasion for general hilarity. Radha was already known as SFI by everyone because of her political leanings and association with the left-wing Students Federation of India. When four separate slips were sent up to the professor, each with SFI written on it, and he read out the same name again and again, there were loud cheers and clapping.

'Stubborn' was selected as the most appropriate name for Jaspal Singh, not the brightest student in the class, having secured admission into the philosophy course on the basis of his performance on the playing field rather than on account of his academic grades. (Other suggestions were 'Solid' and 'Dense', but it was 'Stubborn' that carried the day.)

A number of different names for me were suggested; several were unflattering or comic and a couple almost insulting. I looked the oldest student in class, and therefore there were names such as 'Uncle' or the Hindi equivalent, '*Mamaji*'. There was also 'Philosopher King', proposed by Salim.

Simran sent up a slip and eventually it was her choice that was chosen. This was 'Confusion'. There was general amusement and loud laughter, partly because of the resemblance it bore to Confucius, whose doctrines we had studied in class, but more because everybody remembered my seemingly ambivalent stance during the class debate.

Salim was favoured with 'Decent', a joint contribution from the women, who out-shouted rivals who had provided more sleazy names.

No one wanted to come forward to name Simran. Her popularity might have been the reason for this. I wrote down a name; as it happened it was the only suggestion that was sent up, so it had to be chosen. My choice of 'Affection' was odd and at variance with the overall class mood. The class response was confused and lukewarm, although a couple of the women did cheer. Someone shouted: 'What a corny line, yaar!'

*****

In the weeks that followed, the name given to me became a bit of a joke, as did several others. The professor's ruse had worked: he had deflected the purpose of those who had sought to make fun of him by calling him '*kachua*' by introducing a naming and shaming ceremony for the entire class. In the classroom, sometimes a joker would wisecrack, 'Sir, don't you think we should take Mr Confusion's views on this matter?' and everyone would laugh.

Some days later I bumped into Simran in the corridor. She was wearing salwar kameez, with a green floral design against a white background. These were fairly ordinary and simple clothes, but to my mind in their very ordinariness they somehow appeared to enhance the beauty of the most luminescent and lovely woman I had ever seen in my life. My heart thudded with the delight and pain of love.

'I've been looking for you,' she said, sounding anxious. 'I wanted to ask you – I hope you didn't mind – my sending up your name as 'Confusion'. I didn't realise it would generate so much lightheartedness. I hope you aren't feeling hurt.'

I was amused by her use of the expression: 'generate so much lightheartedness'.

'Of course not.'

She had given me a name. For me, it was more of an occasion to celebrate. I didn't tell her that, of course; it would have been far too premature and crude. Instead I invited her for a coffee in the cafeteria.

It was the first time we had sat alone. I told her about myself, about the school, and the various jobs I had done. She spoke about herself: she had been at university in Chandigarh; her father was in government service with the state government; and after graduating in Chandigarh she had come up to study in Shimla because of the climate. Over the last few years she had developed a slightly asthmatic condition, and everyone agreed that the Shimla climate would be good for her. We sat together and talked for a long time that day. Subsequently she would unabashedly seek me out and we would again talk for hours at a time. But it was this first day that for me marked the beginning of our relationship.

21

The Rain

1

'Why is Affection always listening and Confusion the one who is giving bright answers? It's unfair.'

Three days' later, after dinner, we were sitting outside on the verandah and watching the rainfall. Or rather I was watching it fall: an untimely rain, though beneficial for the crops. It had been raining since the morning. Diamond had switched on the light. She was reading Lombroso on criminology and had broken off from her reading to ask me this question. She thought I hadn't heard and repeated the question.

'It's odd you should make that comment,' I said, 'for this had been my first objection to Simran's planned format. On the way to Rishikesh, we had decided that she would do the writing. It was her idea that, of the two characters, Confusion would be the more brilliant and Affection would assume a relatively passive role, cross-questioning acutely, yes, but contributing less in terms of substance. I pointed out that this might suggest to the reader that Affection was feminine and Confusion masculine. Since the dialogue was supposed to be consciousness-raising and directed against a prejudiced conception of the relationship between the sexes, it might be terribly ironic if it simultaneously reinforced prejudiced stereotypes. Simran had disagreed, maintaining that this would not happen, since we had never mentioned the sex of either of the two characters. Also, that if we prepared a script in which both Affection and Confusion contributed equally, the discussion would become less interesting. Equality surely didn't mean mechanistic equality.'

'Why did you give the characters in this dialogue your own class names?'

'It was for many reasons. It was partly out of a spirit of fun, partly an act of ego. Also, we didn't want to give them a name like Jack or Jane, or something that sounded more exotic. Another reason that weighed with us was that the human qualities of affection and confusion would have symbolic value, as they form primal elements in any search for philosophical truth.'

'Couldn't the roles have been reversed? Wouldn't it have made more sense if Confusion had been made the passive listener and Affection the one with all the answers?'

'That issue also surfaced. I'd asked Simran why it should be Confusion who gave all the answers and not Affection. "For very good reasons," she'd insisted. "Confusion represents the process of moving away from established principles. Confusion symbolically represents anti dogma, the spirit of enquiry, the unsettling of well-entrenched principles in aesthetics. It could never be Affection who had all the answers, but symbolically Affection is a necessary complement – for didn't an expounder of philosophical truth need a receptive and open-minded audience? Confusion is a name people would ordinarily laugh at – you've experienced that, haven't you? Confusion is also the underdog, the weaker name. Therefore it needs to be made the stronger intellect."'

'Both names sound bizarre when you read them for the first time,' said Diamond, 'but they do make sense. Did you have a problem convincing others?'

'Matters never reached that stage. We had, however, decided that we would stick with these names and not settle for anything else.'

Oddly, Diamond appeared to understand. She nodded her head in a gesture of total comprehension.

I reflected how most people would have thought of us to be a couple of love-struck dilettantes, which was true, of course, but only partially so. It sounded immature, but then, as Simran had so often said, 'Wasn't life crazy?!'

*****

It was a dark moonless night outside. I could see the rain bouncing off the stairs where the light fell, and heard it clattering on the roof.

After a while, Diamond put the book aside and said angrily, 'I don't understand this man, Lombroso. He appears to have been demented, even considering the times he lived in. It would have made some sense if he'd started with himself and, having completed his self examination, proclaimed that everyone with the physical characteristics he'd outlined would be bound to have criminal tendencies.'

I laughed at her indignation.

'He wasn't the only one,' I said. 'There are many such books, even nowadays. Some are even best-sellers. Books based on the ancient Chinese system of face-reading, books on physiognomy or phrenology, where the study of the shape of the skull is supposed to reveal certain characteristics, criminal or otherwise, of a person.'

'Next there will be someone who can analyse you by examining the shape of your toes, or legs.'

'Don't be surprised if you find a school of thought famous for that approach.'

'It's totally absurd.' She went back to reading her book.

I could have told her that she wasn't far wrong. I'd forgotten the name, but there was such a school of thought that came into existence some years after Lombroso, quite a lot weirder than anything to do with toes or legs. A memory was connected to that.

We were at the hotel at Rishikesh two days before she had left for Gurdaspur. I had gone to sleep, when all at once I felt a hand gripping and squeezing my buttocks. It jolted me wide awake, and I saw Simran smiling at me, with an innocent and unapologetic expression. This was highly unusual, and I wondered if her behaviour had been caused by revenge, lust or mischief. She had never done this before.

I said, 'What gives?'

'Nothing,' she said. 'I was just checking you out.'

'Checking out what? Whether I was asleep?'

She gave me a grin. 'I was examining your rump to see if you had any criminal tendencies.'

'Like Lombroso?'

'No, not like him. That was a school that came some thirty, forty years later.'

'I don't believe it.'

'Yesss,' she screeched, switching on the tubelight. She removed the quilt, jumped out of bed and came back in a trice, a bulky encyclopaedia in her hand. She showed me. 'It's here,' she said excitedly. 'Really and truly.' A school of thought some thirty years after Lombroso's death, which had carried out surveys on young boys that proved conclusively, according to the founders of the school, that the shape of the buttocks could be related to the presence of criminal tendencies.

'Isn't it wonderful?' Her eyes shone with enthusiasm. 'We must include it in the dialogue.'

*****

Diamond had finished reading the book. She said disgustedly, 'It's amazing that this fellow Lombroso, the worst kind of criminal for fomenting prejudices and persecutions, is today regarded as the father of modern criminology.'

*****

She was tired and went inside to sleep. After she had left, I continued to sit and watch the rain fall, enjoying it, though not, I thought, excitedly like a child or an Arab. In a five-star hotel I had worked for in Bombay, I had seen Arabs who, having arrived during the monsoon season, sat next to the window in their hotel room watching the rain fall. They would sit there endlessly, in excitement and wonder; it was a rare and beautiful sight for them. It wasn't, of course, an unusual sight for me, but then it wasn't the rain I was watching or thinking about, really. I was remembering another day when it had been pouring incessantly.

2

It was the day it had been decided to formalise our relationship, tie the knot and take the plunge. We managed to reach the office of the registrar of marriages before two o'clock, the scheduled time, but had got quite wet in the process. For protection against the rain, between the two of us we had only Simran's delicate ladies' umbrella. Even two full-size umbrellas would have been insufficient to protect us from the rain that, buffeted by an indecisive wind, attacked us from different directions.

The registrar's office, located near the district court building, was an ancient structure, built in the Victorian gothic style during the days the British had their summer capital in Shimla. Originally designed to house the prison administration office of those times, a perverse, or benevolent, bureaucratic gesture – one could argue either way – now arranged to bind couples in holy wedlock.

There were several other couples who had turned up that day at the marriage office. We were to appear before the marriage officer, together with our witnesses, to ensure our application for marriage was registered. The actual marriage itself could take place only after a one-month mandatory waiting period.

Simran, dressed that day in a long, peasant skirt made of some lightweight material, was attempting to look cheerful, but I sensed she was quite upset. The tension built up. Radha, who was to be a witness to the registration procedure, had arrived ahead of us, but Salim, the other witness, hadn't yet turned up. Simran's skirt swung about as she walked to and fro impatiently in the corridor outside the marriage room.

This was natural enough. No woman, no matter how blasé and tough she might think herself to be, likes to go through a marriage procedure – the marriage was still a month away – without her beloved parents being present. And she had tried her best to get both of them to be present.

She had returned from Gurdaspur two days earlier. The decision to get married had been taken long ago, but we'd postponed the event till we'd finished our degree courses. Professor Srinivasan, whom we had taken into our confidence, thought there was a fair chance that one of us might be accommodated in the department as a lecturer on an ad hoc basis.

Simran's father had retired from a government job at Chandigarh and had gone back to Gurdaspur, his home town, where he owned agricultural land. She had gone to see her parents with high hopes that they would at least agree to meet me and then decide whether or not to give their permission for the marriage.

There had been a stunned silence when she gave them the news that, despite my first name, I was not a Sikh, Hindu or Christian. My adoptive father, Eliot, had been a Christian schoolteacher, but he was now dead and I had no other family. Stunned silence gave way to shock, when, after further enquiries, they learnt that at present I was without a job and doing the worthless course of an MA in philosophy at an age when anyone with intelligence and ambition was already settled in a suitable profession.

Her father had a strong dictatorial streak in him, although like all successful despots, especially those ruling a family, he did have benevolent aspects to his personality, viewed from a conservative standpoint. The way he perceived it, Simran was taking advantage of the freedom he had allowed her. Had he not accepted Simran's wish to complete her studies before marriage? He had even allowed her to study at a university hundreds of miles away from home, and had generally tolerated (within limits it must be said) free expression of views in the house. His benevolence did not, however, extend as far as accepting his daughter's choice, even though she was the apple of his eye. He would not accept me as a son-in-law and he made this clear to Simran – loud and clear.

Simran fought back determinedly, but was unable to wring any concessions from him. He categorically refused to see me. There was high drama during her week-long stay at Gurdaspur: anger, recriminations, blame, her mother's hysterics, and her father's stony silences – but the net result was that they would not budge. The father's blood pressure went up and a doctor had to be summoned. Emotional blackmail became the name of the game. There were all the elements and trappings of a 'B' grade Bollywood production, only it was infinitely worse for Simran because she could not switch it off or walk away; the 'production' was now part of her life.

Simran finally accepted the parental diktat that she see no more of me; they would trust her to go back to Shimla and concentrate on her studies. Her father lectured her on how it was getting rather late, now that she was already in her twenties, and that she should be married. He said that she would shortly be summoned back to 'see' and be 'seen' by a non-resident Indian Sikh settled in Canada with a view to marriage. The mother explained to Simran that this NRI boy was infinitely more suitable than someone like me of unknown parentage and uncertain future.

Simran's tacit acceptance had only been a ploy to gain time and reduce her father's blood pressure, which had shot up dangerously, during the furious debates in her parents' house. It would have needed ten armies to make her change her mind.

As she explained to me later, it wasn't in her nature to practise subterfuge or deceit, but in certain situations such as this the best solution was to produce a fait accompli. The fait accompli in this case would mean us getting married and presenting her parents with a copy of the certificate issued by the marriage officer – whom we were waiting for to arrive and initiate the process.

*****

It was two o'clock and Salim had still not arrived. He might have been held up because of the rain.

Simran asked, 'How did you come here, Radha?'

'You aren't even carrying an umbrella,' I observed, 'but you are drier than we are.'

'I was actually badly drenched,' Radha said. 'Fortunately, I'd been to the dressmaker's and had collected a dress from him, which I changed into. It had remained dry inside the carry bag.'

'Where did you change?' asked Simran.

'Where else but the bridal dressing room?' she grinned. 'There's a room that's meant for the bride to put the finishing touches to her make-up.'

Seeing Simran so tense, I approached the bespectacled lady clerk to make enquiries.

'We are waiting for one of our witnesses, ma'am,' I said. 'What happens if he fails to turn up?'

'In that case you cannot get your marriage application registered today,' she said, politely but firmly. 'You will have to come another time.'

Everything now depended on Salim arriving on time.

At quarter past two, the magistrate arrived in a white Maruti. He was short and corpulent, dressed in a lawyer's black coat and tie. He sat on a table behind a wooden partition in the large hall, while the waiting couples sat on upright wooden chairs placed in a row against the wall.

The usher started calling out the names of the couples in turn. The fifth couple was sitting opposite the magistrate when Salim arrived. With his raincoat, umbrella and plastic cap he looked like a snowman.

'*Yaar*, I'm really sorry for being late,' he said. 'I'm terribly, terribly sorry, but it's not my fault.'

'What happened?' demanded Radha

'I'd gone to Solan in the morning. After I reached Solan, there was a landslide, and the road got blocked. It was cleared just an hour ago.'

'Why on earth did you go to Solan?' I said.

'Don't you know marriage witnesses are not supposed to go hither and thither?' added Simran.

We were the next couple to be called inside by the magistrate. He scrutinised our documents carefully. We had brought our school certificates in original as proof of our dates of birth, part of the unnecessary paperwork and bureaucratic procedures. I was quite clearly old enough to get married, and Simran, too, could hardly have been mistaken for a person aged under eighteen.

'I'm sorry,' said the magistrate regretfully, 'but I cannot register your marriage application today. You haven't supplied photocopies of your ration cards as proof that you are both residents of Shimla. You will have to come again and bring the ration cards with you when you do so.'

'We are students who eat at the mess,' I protested. 'We don't maintain kitchens, and therefore don't need ration cards. None of us possess one.'

'I am sorry,' he repeated. 'These are the rules. What can I do? Ration cards are essential.'

'But sir,' pleaded Radha, 'there must be another way of proving residence. Can't you have our application registered and ask the local police to verify our state of residence?'

'No, I am afraid that cannot be done, madam.' The magistrate shook his head with a gesture of finality.

The argument with the magistrate carried on for some time. Finally, Simran pushed our identity cards in front of him.

'Do you think these are forged, sir?' Simran gazed at him directly. 'Aren't these cards proof that we are bona fide, full-time students of the university and therefore reside in Shimla?'

It was like a powerful searchlight being turned on him. He mumbled something and tried to look away. Forced back inevitably to confront her frank, open gaze, he grunted awkwardly, realised he was beaten, and decided to give up.

After that he was quite amiable, even though he did once or twice glance at me suspiciously. He might have been wondering why she was marrying me. Fair enough. I would have wondered the same had I been in his place. At length the fat little man seemed satisfied and asked us to come again in a month's time for the final ceremony. 'Come again within three months,' he added, wagging his little finger at us.

From the marriage office we trooped down to Shimla's major five-star hotel, *The Oberoi's*, on the Mall for a celebration.

At the table, quoting from Asterix, Salim remarked, 'After the battle – the feast!'

'Some battle,' I said sourly. 'You nearly finished us off by coming late.'

We were all a bit excited now that the deed was done. Simran had visibly cheered up. We ordered extravagantly, despite Radha's proletarian objections: pastry, fruit salad, sandwiches, and cold coffee with ice cream. After all, even though we were not yet married, the process had been initiated and it was not every day that one registered an application to marry in court.

Later that night, we made plans for the immediate future. I was no longer staying in the hostel, and had taken up a single bachelor room accommodation at Sangti, near Summerhill. Simran couldn't move in till we were married; it would cause too much of a scandal in Shimla's conservative society.

Eventually we decided to take a working holiday. We would travel to Haridwar, Rishikesh, Pauri Garhwal, and finally Gangotri. During our journey we would work on the script.

Radha was staying in Shimla as it was her hometown. Her house was next to the disused skating rink near the Ridge. Periodically she would go to the girl's hostel to collect Simran's mail. This was necessary, as Simran's parents believed she was in the hostel, and for tactical reasons we didn't want to disabuse them of that impression. Every now and then Simran would phone Radha to check up on any developments.

Five days after the visit to the marriage office we had left for Haridwar.

*****

It wasn't raining hard any more, though there was still a slight drizzle. The clattering on the roof had become subdued. The water tank was overflowing. I could hear the steady drip, drip from one of the outlets. On the cobbled streets I saw frogs leaping about excitedly. I stepped out on to the road outside the house in the clean darkness. The village had long ago fallen asleep, evident from the absence of lights. I stood outside for some time, enjoying the feel of the cool breeze on my face, despite my sadness. She, too, had loved the rain and the mountains.

22

Speeches, Speeches

It was almost two weeks since I'd arrived in Ganahatti. The days had passed by swiftly, with most of the time spent reading, discussing, writing, cooking, washing up, and going for long walks, during which we continued to discus and argue. Occasionally we had visitors, mainly women who came to talk to Diamond. Apart from Komal, there were the two girls who dropped by, Lakshmi and Ranjana, who helped in the Sunday school, as well as several others. Usually, they would stand outside the house, and instead of pressing the bell simply yell 'Diamond *dideeee*'. It got to the point that occasionally, whenever I felt like it, I too would go out to the entrance and screech in a woman-like way: 'Diamond *dideeeee*'. Eventually, though, I stopped this as I realised I was upsetting her.

'Let me prepare the first version of the second chapter,' she said, during breakfast one day.

I had agreed that it was better that one person should work on it.

I was amazed by the enthusiasm with which Diamond worked to prepare the dialogues. We had made substantial progress. Eliot was the reason I was passionate about the subject, but Diamond, too, was involved in a manner that suggested more than simple academic curiosity. I was intrigued by the strength of her conviction that what we were doing was important.

'It's a pity about Rehana's magazine, though,' she said. 'I haven't yet been able to write the short article I had promised her for *The Psychologist*.'

'That reminds me,' I said. 'It's two weeks since I visited Professor Srinivasan's house. He might be back now. I'll go to his house and check to see if he's returned.'

'I thought we could go to Summerhill. There's a seminar today on the relevance of contemporary social science research. It might be interesting. Eminent scholars from various universities have been invited to speak.'

'I'll meet you in the canteen at lunch time,' I said.

*****

Once more the door to the professor's house was opened by his wife.

'I'm sorry,' she said. 'He is not yet back.'

'Any news as to when he is likely to be back?' I tried to hide my disappointment.

'You won't have to wait long, now. I received a telegram from him yesterday. He is scheduled to arrive the day after tomorrow, on Sunday.'

'That's good news.'

'He should be here by noon, I think. Why don't you come in and have some coffee?'

'Some other time, ma'am, if you don't mind?' I said. 'I have to rush to the university.'

'Are you going to the seminar?'

'Yes,' I said, surprised that she should know about it.

'At the university, you know...' After some hesitation she blurted out, 'I really think things are going from bad to worse.'

Jai Ahuja had used the same expression.

I nodded my head sagely, although I had no idea what on earth she was talking about.

*****

It was a quarter to two by the time I reached Summerhill. Diamond was sitting in a corner inside the canteen sipping a cola.

'Am I ever so glad to see you,' she exclaimed, as I joined her across the table.

'Have you been waiting long?' I asked solicitously, beckoning a waiter. We ordered a vegetarian fixed meal, a combination meal that provided small portions of many dishes that had survived all my years away from the university.

'It's not the waiting that's bothered me, but I have been really bugged by the peculiar people I've met this morning.'

'Whom did you come across?'

'A most obnoxious character by the name of Professor Inder Chaudhury.'

'What does he look like?'

'He would be in his late forties.' She frowned. 'How should I describe him? Short, stocky, a white moustache.'

'I don't remember him,' I shook my head. 'He must have joined after I'd left.'

'He wears half a dozen rings on his fingers,' she added.

'Is that what you didn't like? His taste in jewellery?'

'I wouldn't have minded if he wore a jewelled necklace,' she snorted. 'It's his retarded thinking that's the problem. What makes it worse is that he is currently head of department.'

I was at once reminded of another department head. Professor Chaudhury and Professor Mahan ought to get together. Someone should introduce them.

I said, 'How was the morning session?'

'Oh, it was terrible. You didn't miss anything worthwhile. Our friend Chaudhury gave a speech about cultural regeneration and restoration of lost values. A professor from Delhi gave a long, boring speech.'

'Why am I not surprised?'

The waiter arrived with our food. There was rice, lentil soup, vegetables, white yoghurt, chutney, poppadum and a sweet dish.

'Let me tell you about what happened later,' she said in between mouthfuls. 'We don't have much time right now. The post-lunch session is due to begin, so let's hurry.'

Inside the auditorium, Jai Ahuja, the thin, bearded lecturer, beckoned us. He was sitting in a corner seat on one of the last rows of the auditorium, which was rapidly filling up. As we took seats next to him, he whispered, 'Now the real show is going to begin.' He seemed preoccupied and tense, as if some extraordinary event was about to happen.

'Is this seat empty?' I heard a melodious female voice say near me. 'Can I join you?' It was Anjali Sinha, the plump Bengali lecturer.

'Please do join us.' I said.

'Thank you.' She smiled at Diamond and lowered herself into the seat next to her.

The auditorium had now filled up. At the front of the stage a few tables had been joined together, and a large white cloth placed over them. Behind the tables there were eight to ten red-cushioned chairs that gradually began to be occupied.

Diamond pointed out Professor Chaudhury, a short, beefy character with shrewd, appraising eyes. Even from this distance I could see that he wore some six or seven rings on his fingers. Walking towards the stage behind him was a large, broad-shouldered man in white *kurta*-pyjamas, who looked like a wrestler – it just didn't seem possible to elude Professor Mahan, my head of department – and right next to him, smiling happily, was my landlord's son, Milan Gupta.

The post lunch session got underway. The first speaker to be introduced by Professor Chaudhury was a Professor Thadani, professor of mathematics from Allahabad University. He had been sitting next to Milan, with whom he appeared to have struck a rapport, because even before he began to speak Milan made some clapping sounds.

Professor Thadani was a thin, frail-looking man with a reddish mark on his forehead, which made it clear that he was a man of strong religious beliefs. He spoke mainly on the need for conducting research on ancient Indian texts to relate them to modern developments. In a slow, laboured voice, he said, 'Recently, there has been a special workshop conducted by the State Council for Education Research and Training in Allahabad. One of the highlights was a detailed discussion of the Vedic principles in the context of modern mathematics. We are trying to convince the state government that in the higher classes in schools the maths syllabus should include the preliminary principles of Vedic maths dating back to 1000 BC. I hope that these changes will soon be introduced at university level as well.' He then went on to explain why he had come to Shimla. 'This seminar is on the relevance of social science research, but as a professor of mathematics I nevertheless wanted to attend it because I believe that the Vedic verses are not only applicable to mathematics, but in their philosophical interpretation may even explain the functioning of human psychology. The other reason I came was because I could not refuse my old friends Professor Chaudhury and Professor Mahan, who are great and committed scholars with whom I have had a long-standing and rewarding association spanning two decades.' At this juncture he paused and turned to look at Mahan, who gave him a dazzling smile. After some further elucidation of Vedic mathematical concepts he hobbled back to his seat.

'That makes a lot of sense,' whispered Professor Anjali Sinha. 'After all, we discovered zero, didn't we?'

'It's all right if it's introduced at the university level,' said Diamond, sounding puzzled, 'but why should you burden school children with Vedic principles?'

'The discovery of zero was crucial to the development of modern mathematics,' said the professor. 'I don't know why we have to be so defensive about our own culture.'

'It's because we are poor,' said Diamond. 'If we were richer, we would be more confident.'

The next speaker to be introduced was Manohar Kumar Joshi, the head of the Hindi department from Gorakhpur University. A middle-aged man dressed in a spotless white *kurta-dhoti*, his long, wavy hair speckled with grey gave him the appearance of a poet – and indeed it was a poem, somewhat bloody and violent, he had come to talk about. 'We are making efforts to introduce Hindi text books in schools and universities, glorifying our grand Indian past,' he said, in a sing-song tone. 'I want to make special mention of a poem written by the great poet Shyam Narayan Pande that we are trying to introduce into school syllabuses. In this poem he dwells on the bravery of Maharana Pratap in the battle of Haldighati.' He paused to recite verses from the poem and then made an immediate translation into English. Finally, he summed up in the same sing-song manner. 'As described to you, the poem begins with an invocation to Lord Ganpathi and the goddesses Chandi, Durga and Kali. It goes on to describe how, after invoking the gods and goddesses, Rana Pratap heads towards Haldighatti and camps on the Aravali hills where he plants the *kesari* flag. It describes the ferocious fighting taking place; how the Rana seeks out Man Singh, who is described as the pride of the Mughals; and how Man Singh hides in his elephant carriage before being killed.' This last bit of the poem, on how Man Singh was attempting to hide, he repeated twice, as though there was some important lesson included within it.

I recognised the poem as it had been taught in the school in Lucknow where I had been studying, though it had been taken out of the syllabus in 1975 because of its strong Hindu overtones. The clashes between the Mughals – the ruling power in India for many centuries – with certain Hindu kings could not be denied, as this was a historical fact. Nevertheless, it clearly went against the secular ideals of the country to have poems taught in schools that described such conflicts in a way that extolled the bravery of Hindu kings and contrasted this with the supposed cowardice of Muslim representatives. Twenty-five years later, attempts were being made to have such a poem reinserted into school syllabuses. Suddenly the seminar no longer appeared to be so innocuous.

After Mr Joshi had gone back to his chair, Prof.essor Chaudhury came forward to take the microphone. 'I will now ask a guest from Delhi to say a few words. The gentleman in question is deeply interested in issues relating to education. Although he is not a lecturer, he is a grass-roots worker, who I am certain will have something important to say to the younger members of this august audience.'

Milan came up to the mike slowly, grinning from ear to ear.

'I have been listening very carefully to the learned gentlemen who have spoken before me,' he began in chaste Hindi, holding the mike between his chubby fingers. 'Although I am satisfied with the contents of their speeches, especially the poem recited just now by Professor Joshi, I have one extremely serious complaint to make.' His tone turned aggressively strident. 'Most of the speeches have been in English, which is shameful, considering that it is a colonial language. The entire discussion today ought to have been conducted in Hindi. Furthermore, the medium of instruction in universities all over the Northern States should be changed to Hindi. Even in the Southern States, Hindi must replace English as the medium of instruction.' He paused momentarily before gathering steam and thumping the dais. 'Only then can we become a strong and unified nation, able to protect ourselves from enemies across the border and their agents in Kashmir and Punjab. Henceforth, all further discussion in this seminar should be carried out in Hindi. *Jai Hind...*' Having said his piece, Milan folded his hands in a *namaste* and returned to his chair.

Any pretence the seminar might have had up until then of being a genuine attempt at what Professor Chaudhury had termed 'cultural regeneration' and 'restoration of lost values' lay fully exposed.

'Who the hell is this character?' said Diamond.

'My landlord's son,' I said.

'You mean the fellow you saw at the railway station?'

'That's right. By the by, the wrestler sitting next to him is currently my head of department.'

'It's a small world,' she observed.

Meanwhile, the audience, silent until now, came to life. During Mr Joshi's recital of the Haldighati poem, the audience had started to get restless, but now audible protests could be heard from various sections of the hall.

A thin, bearded figure in a dark-coloured suit raced forward and climbed on to the stage. It was Jai, the history lecturer who had been sitting next to me; we hadn't even noticed him leave his seat.

'The previous speaker has exposed the seminar for what it is,' he said in a voice choked with emotion. 'Clearly, this is a well-thought-out conspiracy aimed at undermining the secular credentials of the university. A communal diatribe has been imposed upon a captive audience. The linguistic fanaticism of the speaker has shown beyond any doubt that an attempt is being made to communalise the atmosphere in educational institutions in this and other states.'

The expression 'linguistic fanaticism' crossed over to the audience and circled around the auditorium, bursting into a thousand fragments and piercing the hearts of every single person sitting in the hall.

At least that's how eloquently expressive it appeared to me, till I took a look at Milan to check his reaction and realised how completely mistaken I was; the young scholar's thick hide was impervious to any such criticism, and he retained a self satisfied, beatific expression on his face.

Anjali Sinha was shaking her head vigorously. 'How can they impose Hindi on us?' she said agitatedly. 'I understand only English and Bengali. What will people such as Professor Srinivasan do? He understands only Tamil and English. Are we going to turn into a fascist state?'

There was a round of applause as Jai finished his speech. Anxious that the seminar should not conclude on such a note, the expert from Delhi University instantly rushed to the mike in a bid to try to save the situation.

Mahan spoke smoothly, as though he were addressing a grumpy child. In a smooth, placatory tone, he said, 'It has been rather unfortunate that my learned brother Milan Gupta was not able to express himself more clearly and has therefore been misunderstood. What Milan was saying was the sad truth that fluency in English is nowadays often regarded as more important than fluency in one's mother tongue, whether it be Bengali, Tamil or Hindi. All speakers are free to speak in the language of their choice. There is definitely no attempt to undermine the secular credentials of the university, neither has a "communal diatribe been imposed on a captive audience", the expression used by Mr Ahuja.' In a populist bid, he added, 'I strongly protest that anyone should call members of this audience captive. To call them captive would be to insult them. I have too much respect for the people sitting here to call them captive. Now, in the Open Session, any member of the audience is most welcome to give his or her views.' He carried on in this vein, and about how there were certain 'young, immature people in the audience' – this remark was targeted at Jai – who suffered from 'overactive' imaginations and did not bother to listen carefully to what was being said.

While he was speaking like this, Anjali Sinha and Jai, who had now returned to his seat, were pushing me to go up to the stage. 'Someone else must go now,' said Jai, sounding anxious. 'In the original programme there was to be no Open Session. He has been forced to have one now. Someone must go and blast them.'

I walked up to the stage and took the mike.

The audience listened attentively as I spoke about how terrorism and secessionist movements in Punjab had been practically eliminated, but how they continued to fester in Kashmir and the northeastern states. I linked this to the progress made by certain political elements that sought to reduce the diversity of the country by imposing a single ruling ideology.

'Perhaps Professor Mahan is trying to suggest,' I said, towards the end of my speech, 'that we place greater emphasis on Hindu victories with the aim of refurbishing a sagging Hindu morale, if, indeed, it is at all sagging, which I doubt very much. Is Hindu morale to be built up by the recounting of Hindu bravado and prowess in battlefields? What about Muslim and Christian morale?' At this juncture I paused, for there was a splattering of applause. 'Once a pro-Hindu position is taken,' I continued, 'it will be impossible to fix any limit, and we will be irrevocably pushed in the direction of greater and greater fanaticism.'

Throughout my speech, I had sometimes briefly turned to look at the faces of the various speakers sitting behind me, particularly when I referred to statements made in their individual speeches. I could see them becoming more and more embarrassed, but they were helpless and I was in no mood to stop.

Mahan's face in particular had turned a dark shade of purple. His eyes were blazing with rage, but he was powerless to stop me – who, after all, was speaking at his own invitation.

Inder Chaudhury looked as if he was going to have a fit, there and then. For him, months of planning and preparation had come to nothing. Clearly, Professor Chaudhury and other like-minded individuals had hatched a conspiracy with the agreement of the new vice chancellor to have syllabuses redrafted. The printing of new textbooks on the basis of the revised syllabuses would be the next step.

The audience lapped up my speech. As I finished, a wave of applause swept through the hall. Now several other would-be speakers had emerged, having gathered downstage.

I returned to my seat feeling light-headed and giddy. 'Welcome back, Demosthenes,' said Anjali Sinha. Diamond gave me a mock salute. Jai was at ease. The tension had drained out of his face and he looked almost joyful.

The next speaker, a bespectacled middle-aged gentleman, had barely uttered a few sentences when a dark-complexioned, burly young man in white *kurta-pyjama* rudely snatched the mike from his hands. The latter, who was in his early twenties and appeared to be a student leader, announced hurriedly: 'Seminar is over! Seminar is over!'

There was pandemonium in the hall. Another prospective speaker, a slender young man with a cloth bag hung across his shoulder, angrily snatched the mike back from the politico after he had made this announcement. Before he could say more than a few words, however, someone disconnected the electricity. From a corner of the hall, a clamour of voices could be heard. A fight began between two groups of students.

Professor Chaudhury walked off the stage, and as if on cue the other speakers also abandoned the red-cushioned chairs on stage and began drifting out through the side entrance. It was a signal that the seminar was concluded. By now the audience had lost interest in any further proceedings and started streaming out of the hall.

'Bye, bye, all of you,' said Professor Sinha outside the hall in the corridor. 'I would like to have stayed to have a chat, but my car is giving me trouble and I want to stop at the garage on my way home.'

'I suggest we have a coffee,' said Jai.

'In the staff room?' I asked.

'It's better to avoid the staffroom,' he said. 'Professor Chaudhury will be there with his professorial coterie.'

'And his students,' added Diamond.

I said, 'Let's go to the canteen then.'

By the time we reached the canteen it was already packed with students, and there were no chairs to sit on. Around several tables, intense discussions were taking place. We were immediately surrounded and became the focus of attention.

'We are really glad you spoke out, sir, and your friend too.' A tall, lanky student addressed Jai.

'Please sit down sir.' A few students offered us their chairs.

Coffee arrived shortly. An excited discussion took place about the seminar and related developments in the university.

The students sitting with us were a determined lot, who insisted they would not allow Chaudhury and his friends to have their way.

'I have a splitting headache,' Diamond leant across and whispered in my ear.

'We have to be going, Jai,' I said, finishing my coffee.

'Drop by sometime, Jai,' said Diamond.

We left for Ganahatti immediately.

Back in the house, after dinner she went to her room to rest. I took a notepad and, sitting opposite the rosewood study table in my room, started to write a short story. It was past midnight by the time I had finished.

23

Stoned on *Hindutva*

1

The next day, a Saturday, Diamond was to leave for the school in the morning. I walked down with her to the market. She was unusually silent and pensive. From the market, she carried on ahead towards the school while I waited on the highway for a bus to St James School in Shimla.

The day after we had had dinner at Komal's house and had discussed her problems, I met Bahadur in the evening and had spoken to him in private.

'*Didi* tells me you are worried about Kalyan's school results,' I said. 'Would you like me to speak to his class teacher?'

'If you can do that, sir, I will be greatly obliged.' He folded his hands in an embarrassingly grateful gesture. 'It's all the fault of the new teacher. Kalyan's grades in earlier examinations were consistently high. For many days now, I have wanted to speak to the teacher, but I cannot summon up the courage. The truth is that I feel quite out of place in that institution.'

'In that case, I will talk to her,' I said, 'and try to find out what's going on.' I could understand his diffidence in speaking to any of the smart ladies who taught Kalyan.

'Please do that, sir,' he said, in an emotionally choked voice.

The rickety state roadways bus I boarded dropped me off at Chotta Shimla. It took an hour of brisk walking to reach the school.

The school campus was large and impressive. Two tall, brick-coloured buildings stood out. These were the senior and junior school blocks.

Inside the junior school building, I managed to locate Leela Swaminathan without much effort in the teacher's staff room. It was a large room with wooden armchairs, arranged around three low tables on which were placed the day's newspapers and assorted magazines. An attractive but formidable young lady in her mid-thirties, Ms Swaminathan was elegantly dressed in skirts, stockings and high heels.

She was a bit stiff at first, but after I'd introduced myself she became more relaxed.

'It's such a refreshing change to meet someone from the education field,' she said. 'I'm so tired of meeting rich, uncultured businessmen.'

'I guess they can be a real pain, sometimes,' I said, sitting down.

'They're a big nuisance. I'm sorry to say so, but they think no end of themselves and their little progenies.'

A khaki-uniformed attendant placed two steaming cups of tea on the table. Sipping the tea appreciatively, I spoke to the teacher about Kalyan's family circumstances, how his parents were worried about his falling grades, and how I happened to be a family friend and had felt better placed to approach her. She looked thoughtful after I had finished.

'Now I understand whom you are talking about.' She clapped her hands. 'This boy, Kalyan! He is an intelligent child, but so simple.'

'I know,' I agreed. 'That's what his father believes. He wants to know what can be done to improve his grades.'

'Nothing really needs to be done.' She gave an embarrassed laugh. 'I remember him. Let me give you some background. I started to teach his class only six months' ago. I found that my predecessor had not paid much attention to spelling. There were so many spelling mistakes in what the children were writing that during the half yearly examination I announced that all answers had to be written neatly and without any mistakes. If there was a single spelling mistake, I said I would tear up the entire paper.'

'I see what must have gone wrong, then.' Kalyan would have made a couple of spelling mistakes and the woman must have torn up his answer sheet. 'You think we should concentrate on getting the boy to improve his spelling?'

'No, no!' She brushed aside the suggestion disdainfully. 'I really must be careful about the children taking me too literally. Kalyan had misunderstood me completely. In the half yearly examinations, every time he made a spelling mistake, because I had insisted on neatness, instead of scratching out the mistake and writing down the correct spelling and continuing, Kalyan would take a fresh sheet of paper and start all over again. As a result he couldn't finish the paper in time.'

'How did you get to know this?'

'I found out only last week. During a class test, I saw him coming up again and again for extra sheets. That's when I realised what he was doing. Poor Kalyan.' She shook her head regretfully.

'I suppose all's well that ends well.'

'Would you like to see him?' She glanced at her watch. 'In another ten minutes the music lessons will be over. I have a geography class with his section.'

'I guess not. He is shy, and might feel embarrassed.'

'I'm glad you came so that this misunderstanding could be cleared up.'

'You have been a great help, Miss Swaminathan.' I stood up to leave.

2

It was evening by the time I returned to the village. Diamond was in her room, punching away at the keys of her laptop.

'How did your meeting go?' she asked. 'Successful, I hope?'

'More than I'd expected.'

'Really? What did she say?'

I told her what had happened.

'That's excellent news.' She threw up her hands. 'I'll tell Komal.' She sped off to her house.

I was momentarily tempted to see what she had been typing, then decided against it. Instead I wandered into the kitchen, chopped up vegetables, and boiled some noodles. I was frying rice when she returned.

'Want some coffee?' I said, putting the kettle on to boil.

'I wouldn't mind a cup.'

I poured an extra cup of water for her.

'How's your headache now?'

'Headache?' She blinked. 'What headache?'

I reminded her that she had gone to sleep early the previous evening because of a headache.

'Oh, that! Yes, that's gone now. I think it was Professor Chaudhury and his disciples who were responsible for the headache.'

'I forgot to ask you. How did you get to meet him yesterday?'

'Did I tell you Rehana had asked me to contribute a piece for *The Psychologist*? I would have felt too disoriented trying to work on something else, apart from the dialogue, but I was feeling bad since I'd promised I would do this much for her. It occurred to me that I could reach Summerhill early and talk to some of the professors to see if any of them might be interested in contributing an article. It doesn't necessarily have to be related to psychology, because the journal is loosely structured and has an informal style. It was in this context that I met Professor Chaudhury.'

'What was his reaction?'

'The fellow is unbelievably pompous. It's a pity Rehana never told me about him. He was extremely contemptuous and derisive about the journal.'

'Why am I not surprised?'

'He is prejudiced against the magazine because of an article that appeared on Hindu revivalism in the previous issue.'

'Is that the piece about how certain intellectuals are trying to appropriate Hinduism?'

'Yes, that's the one. Anyhow, I told him I had read several issues of the magazine and had found it very interesting.'

'Where did you have this discussion?'

'He has a private office as the head of the philosophy department. While we were having this conversation, some students came in. They chipped in with their two bits on what constituted "relevant research". One of them wanted to know the subject matter of my research. When Professor Chaudhury heard I was researching "The Aesthetics of the Human Form", he gave a loud guffaw and his three disciples joined in the laughter. They acted as if they had never heard anything so completely irrelevant and nonsensical. Do you remember that young man in the *kurta-pyjama* who seized the mike towards the end of the seminar? He was one of the students. He said, "Madam, in this country people are starving and can't get food to eat. Your research on aesthetics is pure academic speculation, of no benefit to any one." Professor Chaudhury gave him an approving thump on the back. "Was the cost-benefit of research activity to be seen in such crude terms?" I asked the professor. He said, "Now see, madam, your research is neither socially useful nor necessary. It has no relevance at all, even to American society. You Indians who are based in America have no understanding of the ground realities in this country. Why doesn't this magazine include articles about the greatness of our culture and heritage instead?'

The kettle was whistling. I made coffee. We went to sit in the living room.

'How did this conversation finally end?' I said.

'Once it became clear to me that Professor Chaudhury and his gang had extremely rigid views on this, and every other subject, I cut the conversation short. I left the room and decided to wait for you in the canteen.' She took a deep breath. 'I don't envy you their company if you get to join the department.'

'I don't intend to.'

'Isn't that why you've come up to Shimla? I mean, apart from the research with me?'

'That's not the reason. I needed to find out something.'

'I don't understand.'

I looked at her for a long moment. I decided to tell her.

'Yes, it does seem inexplicable,' she said, looking disturbed. She spoke easily, but under the sari her legs were shaking.

'Anyway, forget these characters,' I said. 'How's the dialogue shaping up?'

'I'm making progress. It should take me just another two days to finish the typing.'

'I, too, have a piece of good news for you.'

'Don't sound so mysterious. I know your good news,' she laughed. 'I can smell it. You mean the Chinese food, don't you?'

'No, I don't.'

'It's the sweets, then,' she smiled. 'I've seen those too.'

'You have a one-track mind, and it's on the wrong track, at that.'

'Tell me.'

'It's nothing much, really.' I became cautious. 'Only that I've written a short story which has some psychological aspects to it, so it could qualify to be included in *The Psychologist*.'

'That's great!' She looked taken aback. 'What's it about?'

'You know you can believe in many gods and be a Hindu – like most Hindus. You can also believe in one god and still be a Hindu – like the Arya Samajists.'

'I understand you can also be an atheist and still be a Hindu,' Diamond said. 'There are many sects.'

'Exactly, but it doesn't suit some people – such as your friend Professor Chaudhury – to have Hinduism with so many, often conflicting, beliefs. It is actually one of Hinduism's great strengths and makes it a very liberal religion. There are Hindu extremists, however, who regard this as a weakness and would like Hinduism to be more sharply defined, which would help to counter-pose it against beliefs in other religions and foment trouble. Under the guise of scholarship, you have all these intellectuals writing about what it really means to be a Hindu in an attempt to create a sharper definition of the religion. My story is about a visitor from the Vedic Age who has an encounter with some of these intellectuals.'

'Why didn't you tell me earlier? I wouldn't have wasted my time with this Chaudhury fellow.'

'I wrote it out only last night, after we'd returned from the seminar. Why don't you read it after dinner?'

I went back to the kitchen to add some finishing touches to the meal. An hour later we had finished a Chinese meal: fried rice, vegetable chow mien, and chop suey.

'What are we celebrating?' she said, after the second chocolate pastry.

'The writing of the second chapter.'

'That's slightly premature,' she said. 'Why don't you show me the story now? That's worth celebrating as well.'

I walked across to Asma's room and brought back some papers stapled together, which I handed to Diamond to read.

THE MEANING OF *HINDUTVA*

The time machine raced through the maze of centuries, starting from the period when one of the oldest religions in the world had taken root in the human mind, many thousands of years before the advent of the new religious thinking. I was so preoccupied with my thoughts about the impending meeting that I hadn't realised how much time had elapsed.

With a start I noticed that the time gauge on the dashboard indicated 2010 AD. Hell! We had crossed over. I put my foot on the brake. The machine stopped with a jerk. I quickly put it into reverse gear. Half an hour later we were in 2007.

I stepped out of the machine gingerly, and surveyed my surroundings. It was the Connaught Place area all right, precisely indicated and described by the astronomer Aryabhatt on page 200212 of his Celestial Visions, down to the last detail, which was a car repair shop in the middle circle. I walked across towards Central Park where I had an appointment with a group of relevant researchers.

I walked around the park for some time, trying to locate them. I noticed the fountains were not working.

It was the biologist who first spotted me, and he came running. 'Hullo,' he said, warmly embracing me. 'You are just in time. We were just about to begin discussing the meaning of *Hindutva*.'

'And what, pray, have you been doing up to now?' I asked dreamily. I was still suffering from jet lag.

'Saying prayers,' he said simply.

I was in time for the introductions. The biologist, with whom I had been in correspondence, introduced me to the others as a social anthropologist from the Vedic Age. A pimply researcher enquired hesitantly about the various cultural organisations that existed during the Vedic Age and the possibilities of collaboration.

'What do you think I'm doing?' I asked him arrogantly.

'Sshh,' said all the others.

'Before the discussion begins,' I told them, 'I would like to know your names.'

The stocky individual to my left, who had half a dozen rings on his fingers, said he was Mahinder. The tall, handsome individual opposite me said he was Raminder.

'Are you both from the same tribe?' I said, 'since your names sound so similar.'

'No,' answered the one known as Mahinder. 'We are not related to each other, even distantly.'

Apart from the biologist, present in the august gathering were a journalist, an engineer, a photographer, a chemist, a psychologist, and a psychologist's psychologist.

The conversation proceeded as follows:

Me: Why are your names so similar?

Raminder: Many people have these names. Many people have other similar sounding names, such as Ramesh, Suresh, Dimple, Simple or Sonny, Honey.

Me: It appears to be a healthy trend, indicating the presence of a strong community spirit. It probably also indicates strong family bonds.

Mahinder: No, no. This is not so. In fact, we feel that there is too much individualism and dilution of the Hindu identity. (*suddenly suspicious*) Anyway, who sent you?

Me: The *Hindus*.

The Photographer: Let's light one.

Me: Are you mad?

The group proceeded to ignore me. The engineer took out a cigarette from his shirt pocket, removed the tobacco, threw some of it away, mixed a blackish substance with the remaining tobacco, and refilled the cigarette. He offered it to the journalist.

The Engineer: Will you light the *Hindu*?

The Journalist: (*takes a matchbox from his pocket*) Yes, sure! (*he lights the* Hindu, *and takes a deep drag*) This *Hindu* is very good.

Raminder: (*taking it from him*). Yes. It's very original and fresh. We only rubbed it off the plant this afternoon. We could get only a little because we had to rush to this meeting.

Mahinder: (*after the* Hindu *has circulated and taking the last puff*) Can any of you tell me why a *Hindu* finishes so fast in comparison to an ordinary cigarette? Let this be the first question taken up for discussion today.

The Chemist: Because *cannabis indica* burns faster than tobacco. The refilled cigarette has both substances in it, *cannabis* having replaced some of the tobacco, and therefore the *Hindu* will naturally burn faster.

The Journalist: This is owing to the fact that the refilled cigarette, or *Hindu*, from which some of the tobacco has been removed, is not packed so tightly as the original cigarette. As anyone can see, the *Hindu* is quite loose and can bend very easily. It will naturally burn faster.

The Psychologist: I think it's because each person inhales the *Hindu* more deeply than a cigarette, and once he or she has inhaled, it is passed on almost immediately. Surely you realise that each of us is trying to extract the maximum mileage out of it? The inter puff gap, you see, is much smaller in a *Hindu* than in a cigarette.

The Engineer: I think the main reason is that a cigarette is longer than a *Hindu*. You will notice that the end of the *Hindu* consists of five millimetres of paper that has been twisted round so that the cannabis-tobacco mixture doesn't fall out. The *Hindu* is closed, unlike a cigarette, which is open-ended.

The Psychologist's Psychologist: Surely everyone knows about the studies that have revealed that after taking a puff or two of a *Hindu* a person's sense of time becomes altered? It is this altered sense of time that creates the illusion in our minds that the *Hindu* finishes faster than a cigarette, whereas in fact this is not the case.

During this interesting and illuminating discussion, all of a sudden it began to rain. Perhaps this was why the fountains were deliberately not kept functioning by the municipality. I accompanied the researchers to a nearby coffee house, where they ordered coffee with cooked rice cakes. Several members of the group got up intermittently to go to the toilet. On the fifth such occasion, as I was unfamiliar with the habits of denizens of this time frame, and rather numbed with the quality of the erudition that I had just witnessed, I summoned up all my courage and proceeded to ask a question.

'Why is everybody going for a leak?'

The members of the group smiled benevolently.

The Biologist: It is because there is so much humidity in the air. As a result, waste substances generated in the body cannot be released through perspiration. That's why.

The Psychologist: I think it's because of all these cars and scooters that are going *whish whoosh* on the road. If group members were to recall their childhood, they will remember a parent or an elder trying to persuade them to take a leak by making noises such as *shoo sshh...* which is similar to the sound of flowing water or the sound of traffic on a wet road. It is in fact ultrasound autosuggestion.

The Psychologist's Psychologist: I agree. Also, although we should all, of course, realise that we have all being **seeing** the rain, it is rather our hidden consciousness that has been seeing the rain. Visually, the rain represents millions of leaks taking place. I feel it is visual autosuggestion that is more important.

I wondered if it was jet lag that was making my head spin round and round like a top. After much hesitation, I finally said, 'Don't you think.... maybe.... just maybe... it was also the coffee?'

Members of the group looked at me in disgust. Raminder frowned. Mahinder glared at me. They didn't say anything, however. After all, I would be reporting back to their ancestors. After a few minutes of silent prayer, members of the group began leaving. There was to be a *Bharat Bandh* the following day, for which members had to begin preparations.

Soon, I was left alone in the coffee house. After a moment's thought I decided not to pay the bill. The coffee house might have problems with Vedic age currency conversion. Instead, I stealthily made my way outside. Once outside I ran back to the spot where I had parked the time machine. I was glad to be returning home.

The end

Diamond found it very funny. She was laughing so much there were tears streaming down her cheeks.

'I am sure Rehana will love it,' she said breathlessly.

'We must tell her to mail a complementary copy of the issue of *The Psychologist* that includes the story to Professor Chaudhury.'

'She should, shouldn't she?' Diamond was enthusiastic.

24

Absent-minded Professor

On Sunday afternoon, after a salad bar lunch prepared by Diamond, I was fortunate enough to be able to travel on a bus going directly from Ganahatti to Sanjauli.

Earlier that day, Diamond had been silent and withdrawn, not her usual energetic, bubbly self. 'I have a massive headache,' she explained, after we had eaten a concoction of tomatoes, figs, cabbage and carrots in silence.

I reached the professor's house in the late afternoon. Professor Srinivasan had been due to arrive home at noon, and bearing this in mind I planned to reach the house after he had had time to relax and freshen up.

The professor hadn't arrived, however. The Tamil Nadu Express bound for Chandigarh was running four hours' late.

I sat in the living room, drinking first rate percolated coffee. While I waited for the professor, it struck me how odd it was that he had never written to me about the dialogue. I knew his address from the New Year's greeting cards I'd sent him, a habit I'd acquired from Eliot. The professor had acknowledged my greetings by writing to me twice. These had been short letters: thanking me for my cards, enquiring about my welfare, telling me about the Shimla climate, and providing brief information about developments in the philosophy department.

'What exactly was your work with him?' Mrs Srinivasan asked delicately, pushing a plate of biscuits towards me.

'There is a very important letter written by a friend of mine to the professor, roughly three years' ago. I want to find out if he has still got that letter.'

She accepted my explanation without comment, but shook her head doubtfully. 'You know... I'm sorry... but I think it's terribly unlikely he would still have the letter. He is so forgetful, you know. It isn't only him; everyone in his family is like that. They are famous all over Bangalore for their forgetful habits. I only hope he hasn't forgotten to catch the train. Once my mother in law had this brilliant idea of writing a book in which she would recount various incidents connected with the forgetful traits of the Srinivasan family entitled "The Forgetful Family".'

'Did she manage to get round to writing it?'

'No, she didn't. A relative discouraged her by saying, "Madam, once you begin writing such a book, you are likely to forget where you have kept the manuscript".'

We both laughed. Just then the bell chimed. The professor was at the door, lean, bearded and with round, Gandhian spectacles. He was just the same, with his slight stoop and direct, penetrating regard. He saw me, gave a nod of recognition, and went into the bedroom, a short, stocky coolie trailing behind him with his luggage. Mrs Srinivasan followed him like a mother hen, talking rapidly in Tamil.

He emerged soon after in a spotless white *kurta* and *lungi*, having bathed. Mrs Srinivasan hurried into the kitchen to make more coffee.

'So?' He sat down on the sofa opposite me and gave me a long, penetrating look. 'You want to teach at Summerhill?'

'No,' I said. 'I've come to see you about another matter.'

After I had told him about my reasons for coming to Shimla, he was lost in thought for a considerable time.

'What you say does sound extraordinary,' he conceded. 'I cannot see how it could have happened.'

Mrs Srinivasan came in from the kitchen with coffee and South Indian sweets, and after serving us perched on a cushioned stool next to her husband.

He turned to look at her and said, 'It was a great tragedy. Do you remember Simran, Nityamma? She was that wonderfully intelligent girl who came to our house in the university.' He looked at me and shook his head sadly. 'It was a terrible tragedy. She was so young.'

'Oh yes,' said Mrs Srinivasan, sounding embarrassed. 'Now I remember. I was so stupid not to remember earlier.'

It then occurred to me that I had been insensitive in not having as yet commiserated with the professor about his sister's death. I did so at once.

'No, no.' He waved his hands, now in some distress. 'That was not a tragedy, even though we were very close, you know. She had lived a full life.'

'How did you receive the script?' I said. 'By mail?'

'That's correct. The papers were sent to me by post. I received them nearly a month after we had heard about her death. I remember discussing the subject with other members of the department. We held a condolence meeting in her memory about two months after she died when the university reopened after the summer vacations. At the meeting I mentioned the brilliant dialogue I had received, co authored by you and her. I thought I would discuss it with you, but you weren't around. Later I received your greetings, and knew that you were teaching at Delhi University on a temporary basis. I never wrote to you about the dialogue that I had received in the post, because I took it for granted that you of all people would know about it.'

It all sounded so logical and straightforward.

The Professor was saying, 'I assumed you would have registered for a PhD at Delhi University on the same subject. I thought it was a good idea if the girl who had come with Professor Rehana met you, since she was working on the same subject.'

'Was there any covering letter?'

'There was a brief hand-written note accompanying the script. I remember this, because my interest was aroused as a result of the delay. The letter was undated and the postal stamp on the envelope smudged. Sometimes letters do take a long time to reach places in the hills.'

He fell into a long silence.

Mrs Srinivasan, who had by now understood everything, broke the silence. 'He has been waiting in Shimla for fifteen days now, only to get that letter from you. I told him it wasn't possible you would have kept the letter with you for so long.'

The professor came out of his reverie. He remarked in an irritated tone, 'Of course I have the letter. Why shouldn't I have the letter?'

He must have seen the look of amazement on our faces, because he added by way of explanation, 'I may not remember what day of the week it is, what I ate for breakfast – or even my own birthday.' He smiled at his wife briefly. 'That is because it is not important to remember those things. All important letters and papers are, however, filed immediately. Otherwise I tend to forget or misplace them. This letter would be in one of my personal correspondence files. The same file that I took out the other day so that I could give that girl a photocopy of the script; the girl who is doing research in some American university who had come to meet me with Professor Rehana. What's her name?'

'Diamond.'

'That's correct. How could I have forgotten such a name? Now I will have to search for that particular file all over again. It has to be somewhere in the house.'

Mrs Srinivasan smiled at me conspiratorially.

'In that case I'll come again,' I said politely. 'When would you like me to come?'

'Tomorrow,' said the professor, confidently. 'Come tomorrow.'

I could see Mrs Srinivasan stifling a laugh in the background.

25

Diamond's Story

It was nearing sunset by the time I reached the village. The house was open, yet oddly enough it was dark inside. My room, too, was in shadow. I removed the dark-blue curtain cloth hung between two nails that substituted for pelmets (which would have added to the weight on the mud walls). An orange sun lay ready to be swallowed up at any moment by the vast mountain range.

I assumed that Diamond had gone off somewhere for a short while and had not bothered to lock up the house, but I found her fast asleep in her bedroom in a curled-up foetal position.

In the days following our arrival in Ganahatti, she had kept busy and there was often a bustling air about her. If she wasn't at her laptop, she would be dealing with the houseplants or the ones outside. Over the past few days, though, I had noticed a visible change: she appeared quieter, anxious, withdrawn, and generally out of sorts. Even so, it was unusual to see her like this, lying absolutely inert.

The kitchen was in a mess. The floor hadn't been swept, and piled-up dishes lay unwashed in the sink. After cleaning up, I transferred pulses, rice and various other foodstuffs from paper bags into the labelled tins. Rehana had been kind enough to allow me, a stranger, to live in her house for many days, and I reckoned that the least I could do was to replenish her food stock, which we had been using up so liberally. Afterwards I cooked dinner. There was still not a sound from her room.

After I'd spread out newspapers on the floor of the living room where we habitually ate, and laid out the dishes and plates, I crept into her bedroom to awaken her. She was still lying motionless, though she had turned to one side and had buried her face in a pillow. She hadn't even bothered to wrap a blanket around herself. Sensing a presence, she opened her eyes and turned her face to look at me.

'What's the time?' she asked, sleepily.

'Dinnertime. It's all cooked and waiting for Your Highness.' I became solicitous. 'Are you all right?'

'I'm okay,' she mumbled. 'Sorry about this. Give me a moment. I'll just wash my face and join you.'

A little later she came into the living room, her face freshly scrubbed, but her eyes puffed up and bleary. We ate dinner mostly in silence.

'How did your meeting go?' she asked, breaking the silence.

'I'll find out more tomorrow,' I said laconically, noticing dark circles under her reddened eyes.

After dinner, she offered to make coffee. I stepped out of the house to empty out the rubbish bin at the nearby garbage dump. A tiny, shiny bottle fell out, which I retrieved.

*****

We were drinking coffee in her bedroom when I brought up the subject.

'Since when have you been taking sleeping pills?'

'What do you mean?' Her mouth flew open in surprise.

'It was not so difficult, my dear Watson.' I took out the plastic bottle from my pocket and showed her. 'You should have thrown it outside the window.'

'It wasn't organic matter,' she replied, distractedly.

'Do you mind telling me what's upsetting you?'

She appeared to argue with herself for a while before she said slowly, 'I was sitting here in the afternoon, typing out the dialogue, when I got to thinking about my meeting with Professor Chaudhury and the seminar.'

Was she still thinking of that?

'I would have thought by now that you would have forgotten all about it. After all, the seminar hardly went along the lines it had been planned.'

'I wasn't really thinking of the seminar. I wouldn't even bother with Professor Chaudhury, but the encounter with him and his disciples the other day triggered other memories. Those memories upset me and gave me a migraine. That's why I hurried you home that evening. When we returned, I swallowed some valium to sleep off the headache.'

'What were these memories?'

Diamond looked tired and unhappy. She took a deep breath. 'I was upset because they said that my research was irrelevant. I know how we form strong and heavy prejudices, based entirely on the outward physical appearance of an individual. I know this because I have experienced it personally.' Her eyes brimmed over with tears and before I knew it she was crying.

I sat next to her on the bed and put my arms around her, but she continued to sob. I fetched a glass of water and said confidently, without much inner conviction, 'This will make you feel better.'

But it did help. She took a few sips of water, and said, 'I'm feeling better.'

She appeared to have gained some control over her feelings and continued with her story:

'I haven't told you why my marriage broke up. My husband, Navneet, was a computer engineer in the USA when I married him. A tall, good-looking man, I suppose, most people might describe him as a conservative, though decent, person. That's how I thought of him, too, till his greasiness surfaced and became apparent. He had been working in an American company for five years when he decided he wanted to quit his job and start his own software consultancy firm. For this he needed capital. His own savings weren't enough, so he told me to ask my parents for some money. I refused point blank, shocked that he should have even asked, because I knew that they had enough for themselves but none to spare. His parents were far better off and had fewer liabilities. I pointed out these facts to him. My refusal angered him a great deal. From that day onwards, he began complaining and finding all kinds of faults in me. I was terribly hurt by his attitude, but thought that everything would be all right again in a couple of weeks. When his behaviour continued to be the same for several months, however, I began to see more clearly that he was an individual who valued money more than relationships. Indirectly, he was seeking a dowry. His education hadn't helped him a bit. I began to see that he was crass and mean. I felt devalued, and realised that I was in a loveless marriage.

'I began to understand other things about my marriage, too. Even though he would never admit to it, Navneet actually regarded, and treated, me as his servant. I'd be given pats of approval and presented with the occasional bouquet or dress, or given shopping money, as long as I toed the line and obeyed him completely.

'At that time we were staying in Houston, and had a fairly high standard of living, even by American standards. We stayed in an expensive neighbourhood, kept two cars, ate and lived well. I occasionally earned money from babysitting and working on the computer, but if a calculation had been made, my financial contribution wouldn't have been more than ten per cent of the total expenditure incurred every month.

'But then, I thought to myself, it was mainly he who wanted the high standard of living. For me this wasn't necessary. I could have lived in a one-room tenement and been happy. For me the relationship was everything. And that apparently didn't exist any more.

'After weeks of deliberation, one day I realised I couldn't take it any more, and I told him I wanted out. I said that obviously our marriage wasn't working; he was dissatisfied;

and that I wanted to live by myself for a while and work things out. He couldn't believe his ears. His docile Indian wife, whom he treated like a slave, wanted to live separately?! He threw a fit. When he realised I was serious, he said I could go to hell.

'I moved out of the house and away from the city to nearby Dallas. I sold some of my wedding jewellery, rented a small, one-room apartment in the city, and enrolled in the Fine Arts course at the Southern Methodist University. In the daytime I attended classes, in the evening I did baby sitting and odd jobs. At this time my husband remained in touch with me. He would call me up at the university and even came to visit me several times at my apartment. He apologised for his past conduct and said he had now changed and that I should give him another chance.' She laughed bitterly. 'I think he was finding out that it was cheaper for him to have me as his wife than to stay on his own in a large house.

'Anyhow, it never occurred to me then that this was the real situation. I had deeply ingrained Indian values. His repeated visits, letters and telephone calls softened me. I began to believe what he was telling me. He said he wanted me back. I told him I'd think about it.

'About that time, I switched from fine arts to philosophy, and had to pay my tuition fees all over again. One of my professors, Professor Fowley, who was instrumental in my decision to change subjects, helped me. I received a fifty per cent tuition waiver, but I still had to pay a lot of money – about ten thousand dollars. I had to sell all my remaining jewellery: necklaces, bracelets, anklets and rings. It would take at least six months before I managed to get an Assistantship at the university.

'To tide me over my financial crisis, I took to working in a laundry on the same street where I lived: Wilson's Laundry. It was an easy job. My job was mainly to steam-press clothes. For three hours' work at the laundry I got paid fifty dollars, which took care of the rent of my flat and food.

'One day at the laundry, there was an explosion. The lid of the press I was using flew up. The steam directly hit my face and the upper part of my body. I was very badly burnt.

'They took me screaming with pain in an ambulance to the hospital. I was admitted to the Burns Clinic of the Washington Memorial Hospital.

'During the first four days in the hospital, I had to be given several bottles of glucose and received many blood transfusions. I was in terrible agony.

'Dr Jones, a kind and humane person who was the surgeon in charge of my case, later told me that my husband had come to see me at the hospital twice during the first fifteen days when I was mostly unconscious, taking care to bring the prescribed medicines. He had explained to my husband the severity of my case and the expected length of treatment. Moreover, he was told that if I survived, the cost of treatment would be high. My husband's visits then petered off.

'I was in a semi-coma, barely conscious of what was happening around me. After ten days, the staff at the hospital began to lose hope. They put me on a slow glucose drip. After fifteen days, I was still almost unconscious and delirious, but my body was fighting the onslaught of toxaemia and infection.

'Money was now needed for my treatment. Navneet promptly backed off from any financial commitment. I was covered by health insurance, however, and the insurance company paid for most of the expenses. There were still a few remaining. Professor Fowley met the dean of Students' Welfare and vice chancellor on my behalf, and it was agreed the university would pay for the shortfall.

'After four months of dedicated nursing, dozens of big and small operations, blood transfusions and the administration of costly medicines, my survival was assured. But I had acquired extensive and hideous scars all over my face and the upper part of my body.

'After five months I was sent home to convalesce. Dr Jones said that the second stage of my treatment, which consisted of correcting functional disability and improvement of joint movements, would be undertaken only after a period of six months.

'A black girl, Jessica, who studied in my class, moved into my flat. This, too, was partly Professor Fowley's doing. He was incredibly helpful and sympathetic. I don't think I would have survived without his help. Jessica herself was quite a remarkable person. She took charge of the flat and kitchen, and wouldn't let me move a finger. She was a bright spirit, always wisecracking and tremendously positive.

'My husband came to see me one day at my flat. When he had come to the hospital, my face had been swathed in bandages, but now he saw my face that was horribly scarred, making me look quite grotesque.

'Shock gave way to repulsion. I could see it in his face. He even took care to sit at a distance from me, and I could see that he was thinking of me as a liability and was working out how best to get rid of me. There was not one word of sympathy or concern about how I was managing. He no longer suggested, as he had previously done in his letters, that we should make a new beginning. Rather, he now wanted a divorce, and was concerned that I wouldn't create any more hurdles in his path. By this he meant that he hoped I would not claim any property division or maintenance.

'I couldn't stand the sight of this low life putting on sanctimonious airs in my room, and lecturing me on how I had brought all my troubles on myself. I told him to get out. He could send me the divorce papers any time. I would sign. I didn't want alimony.

'A week later the divorce papers arrived by courien I signed them without hesitation. Jessica, who had herself once been divorced, told me I was being a fool. I told her that as I'd been stupid enough to love this man, I deserved no better.

'It wasn't only my husband who felt revolted at my appearance. At the university it was a similar story. Those who knew me from before sympathised or pitied me, but others felt repulsed or disgusted. Usually people now paid me less attention and generally ignored me. My opinions didn't seem to matter so much. In particular, the men in my class were no longer as helpful as they had been earlier. These were small things, but they mattered. Earlier, if I had been with another woman and male students, the men would never have ignored me, but they did so now. I won't say I was treated like a leper, but there was a great difference in how people treated me. Even when standing in queues, the person standing next to me would take one look at my face and slightly move away in disgust.

'I was the same person – or was I? There had been such a sea change in my life.'

'What about your parents?' I asked. 'Weren't they told about all this? Didn't they come and see you? Your brothers and sisters? Someone from your family could have come and helped you, surely?'

'I'm an only child,' she replied. 'Haven't I told you that before? No, I deliberately didn't tell my parents of my break up with Navneet, or about the accident, till several months after they happened. There was no point. It would only have made them worry unnecessarily. Eventually, however, they did get to know about what had happened.'

'How did they take the news?'

'Rather differently from what I had anticipated.' Her voice sounded sad and far away. 'My father blamed himself for having arranged the marriage. He felt terribly guilty. My mother became very depressed. She died of a heart attack the year before last on *Diwali*. My father also died, barely a month later.'

I thought that this gave us something in common. Or did it? For all I knew, my parents were still alive.

'When did you get plastic surgery?'

'As I've said, the university paid part of my medical bills. Health insurance is compulsory for every student, and although that covered most of my medical expenses, it wasn't enough. The university paid the rest. They asked me to sign certain papers; letters of subrogation, they called them. This meant that if a petition seeking compensation was filed before an American court by me, or on my behalf, against the laundry or the manufacturer of the machine and compensation was awarded, I undertook to repay to the university the amount they had spent on me. I signed all these papers, as well as a power of attorney authorising the university to file a compensation claim on my behalf.

'As things turned out, the matter never reached the courts. After legal notices had been issued by the university, the lawyer representing the university was approached by a lawyer representing the company that had manufactured the steam press in question, and an out-of-court settlement was arrived at. The company undertook to have me flown to Switzerland where plastic surgery would be performed on my face, neck and shoulders by one of the best specialists in the field. There was also a lump sum settlement. If I remember correctly, the lawyer took half, the university took a small portion, which covered all the expenses of hospitalisation incurred by them on my behalf, and the rest came to me.

'I spent six months in Switzerland. Dr Hans Beckerman, one of the best-known specialists in cosmetic surgery, operated on me. I lost an academic year in the process – not that it mattered any more. I now had enough money to pay my tuition fees and live comfortably for a while. They really took care of me at the hospital. It was a small place that specialised in cosmetic surgery located on Fribourgstrasse in Bern, the capital of Switzerland. A beautiful city.

'When I returned to the university, my appearance had been totally transformed. Nobody recognised me. Even Professor Fowley and Jessica didn't. When the time came for me to submit my PhD dissertation, I knew what I wanted to work on. My topic was going to be "The Aesthetics of the Human Form".'

I shook my head in disbelief. 'I would never ever have guessed '

So that's why she was so passionately involved in the subject.

She nodded very seriously. 'It took as many as thirteen operations before the scars could be totally removed.'

'It's incredible!'

'I have a new face now,' she said, wryly. 'Different from the original, you know.'

'Really?'

How had she looked earlier?

'My lawyer told me that I would probably receive greater compensation had I chosen to file a case instead of settling out of court. The case would have gone for trial before a jury, and juries have been known to be extremely generous under the American legal system. Yet like all judicial verdicts, there would have been an element of uncertainty, and the case would have taken some time to be decided. The success of the operation depended on it being done without any delay.'

'Do you have any photographs showing what you looked like earlier?'

'Yes, of course, but I'm not carrying any with me.'

'You've had a terrible experience.'

'It was horrible. I don't like to think about it. The day I met Professor Chaudhury and he ridiculed my thesis I thought of all this, and that set off my migraine. Again today, while I was typing out the second chapter in the afternoon, I began to think of that terrible traumatic period in my life, so I took a valium.' She saw the expression on my face. 'Don't look so worried, for God's sake. I promise not to take any more. But now I'm feeling sleepy, so please excuse me...'

After she'd left, in a little while I went to Asma's room. Before I fell asleep, I remembered a section of a comic strip I'd found a few days earlier. Charlie Brown is depicted on a steamer and there is someone, probably Lucy, who tells him that on the ship there are two kinds of people. Passengers gathered on the front side of the ship want to see where they are going to, while others are looking behind because they want to see where they are coming from. 'On the ship of life, Charlie Brown,' she asks, 'where are you standing?'

26

A Strange Resemblance

The next day I woke up at eight a.m., later than usual. As was now my routine, I went to the kitchen and put the kettle on to boil. While my initial feelings on seeing the note left by Diamond at my flat in Delhi had been grief and anger, subsequently I began to wonder if there was more to Simran's death than I had supposed. A small flame of hope began to burn inside me. Perhaps her death was a fiction. A pack of lies invented by her family.

I had also had some misgivings about coming to Shimla with Diamond, as this particular piece of research had been such a deeply personal venture. But yesterday's revelations about why and how Diamond had felt compelled to research the issue had dissolved all such reservations. Her involvement was as personal as mine.

I went into her room to see if she wanted any coffee.

She was sleeping soundly under the quilt, possibly as a result of the valium. I decided not to wake her.

I suddenly noticed something. The shape of her ears; they were noticeably tilted to one side, though not completely cauliflower. I hadn't noticed them before now, because usually her hair fell over them. *They were exactly like Simran's.* Momentarily, I was confused about the identity of the person lying on the bed. I lifted the quilt gently to take a closer look.

Convincing myself I wasn't losing my mind, I drank some coffee. By the time I had showered and dressed, Diamond had woken up and was in the kitchen making breakfast.

'How are you feeling today?' I said, laying the table.

'I'm all right now. Sorry about last night.' She sounded embarrassed. Changing the subject she added, 'I will probably finish typing out the second chapter today.'

'That's great! By the way, what are your plans?'

'I need to be back in the US in ten days' time if I want to retain my Assistantship. Rehana arrives the day after tomorrow. There was a telegram from her yesterday. Asma is on the fast track to recovery now. I would like to spend a day with her and then leave for Delhi. What about you?'

'I'm not sure,' I buttered some toast. 'Much depends on what happens today.'

'I was going to ask you. How did your meeting go?'

I told her what had happened when I met the professor the previous day.

'Is he sure he has the letter?'

'That's what he says.'

'That might explain something,' she said thoughtfully. 'What are you planning to do after you get hold of it?'

'That, too, might explain something,' I said slowly. 'I don't know exactly what, though. I may go to Gurdaspur to meet her parents.'

'Have you met them before?'

'Yes and no. I've been to her house and seen her parents, but I haven't spoken to either of them.'

'Are you sure they're still living there?'

'No, I'm not, but they own agricultural land there and are well known in the town.'

'So even if they have moved elsewhere, someone in the neighbourhood would be bound to know their whereabouts?'

'That's right,' I said, pushing my plate away.

I looked at her carefully. Had I been imagining things in the morning? The resemblance had been uncanny. Unlike Simran, who had kept her hair long and uncut in the Sikh tradition, and had tied it in a single knot so that her ears were very visible, Diamond had short hair that fell over her shoulders.

'Tell me something,' I said, thinking about what I had seen in the morning.

'Yes...?'

'Those plastic surgery operations you underwent....'

'What about them?'

'Did they do something to your ears?'

'My ears?' She lifted her eyebrows. 'What do you mean?'

'Did they shape or design your ears differently?'

'No, my ears were not affected at all,' she said. 'But why do you ask?'

'Nothing in particular,' I said, watching her closely now.

'It was fortunate that my ears weren't burnt,' she said. 'It might have affected my hearing.'

I could see her legs shaking underneath the table. There was something wrong. I perceived a strange anxiety in her expression. She caught me staring at her, and I looked away embarrassed.

Putting on an expression of false brightness, she said, 'Anyway, best of luck for your meeting with the professor,' and rather abruptly began to clear up the breakfast table.

On the way to the bus stop, I thought about the coincidence. The coincidence of two women doing research on roughly the same topic in aesthetics, at different times, unknown to each other, both having practically identically shaped ears. That I, a third party, should know both these women compounded the coincidence further. Yet in a way, wasn't everything in life a coincidence?

27

Breakthrough

1

The sound of an approaching bus interrupted my reverie, and I cleared my mind of such philosophical absurdities. The conductor rattled off the names of various small towns the vehicle would stop at. I listened attentively till Sanjauli was mentioned. It was my lucky day, I thought. Perhaps I would learn something from my meeting with the professor.

For most of the journey we had little traffic on the road. Despite the ramshackle and noisy nature of the vehicle, the ride was a pleasurable experience. It could no longer be argued that large populations inhibited a country's economic development as India was now doing very well in terms of its annual growth. I reflected, though, that there was little doubt that population growth diminished the serenity of natural environments, and on this sparsely travelled road this seemed particularly evident.

The sun was hidden somewhere behind the clouds, so far from being a bright and cheery morning the atmosphere was one of gloom and foreboding. The mist was rising.

An hour later, the State Roadways bus approached the small suburban town. Mrs Srinivasan had spoken about lapses in the professor's memory. It was more than likely that my former teacher would have forgotten where he had kept the file, and it would take him a week or even two to find it.

A short while later I was sitting in the professor's study, drinking excellent filtered coffee prepared by his wife. He had taken out a file, from which he withdrew a thick, white paper that he handed over to me.

'It's an exceedingly short letter,' he said, 'and as you will see it is undated.'

I read the note in silence. It was brief, handwritten, and formal, as befitted a research scholar writing to her guide.

'Dear Professor Srinivasan,

I am enclosing a typed copy of some ideas written with regard to the thesis.

Regards,

Simran'

That was all. It disturbed me to see this letter written by her, and for a few minutes I was too choked with emotion to speak. My face must have betrayed my feelings, since the professor, and his wife who had joined us silently, were quiet for a while. I begged to be excused.

The professor came out of the house to see me off. Before turning back, he said, 'I heard about what happened the other day at the seminar. I'm very glad you spoke out. As things stand at the moment, I'm not sure whether I would even suggest you apply for posts in the department that are shortly to be advertised. The new vice chancellor and Professor Chaudhury are certain to be on the interviewing panel. You will almost certainly be blackballed.'

I didn't want to tell him that in all likelihood even my temporary employment at Delhi University would be discontinued as a result of my intervention during the seminar. I thanked him for his help and advice.

I walked a short distance away from the house and turned to wave to the professor and his wife who had come out on to the porch to see me off. I heard the Professor shout,

'Do come to see an old man whenever you next come to Shimla.'

2

From the professor's house I went to Shimla. I purchased milk cake from a bakery on the Mall and walked across to the YMCA, a deep ache within me.

Prakash was in his office reading a file. There were several other files stacked on his table. He seemed to be busy wading through what must have seemed to his Bombay scriptwriter's mind to be endless pages of trivia.

'I'm feeling dead tired, Prakash,' I said without any preliminaries. 'Could I have a room for a few hours to sleep and relax in?'

'No problem,' he said. 'There are a couple of vacant rooms always kept on hand for an emergency. The trouble is I have to attend to some urgent files and then rush to Chandigarh, so I won't be able to come across and chat with you.'

'It's not a problem. In any case, I'm feeling too tired to talk.'

Prakash pressed the buzzer on his table. A young Nepali boy in a grey uniform came in. Addressing the young boy as 'Major', Prakash instructed him to give me a room on the first floor of the building.

Prakash returned to his files. I followed the boy to the room. The furnishings were more extravagant compared to the room where I had spent the night on the day I had first arrived in Shimla: a blue carpet on the floor, an extra dressing table, and framed photographs of various Himalayan peaks hanging on the walls.

'Major,' I said, 'will you get me half a bottle of Old Monk rum or whatever good whisky is available?' I handed the boy some money.

'Major' understood. Drinking was strictly prohibited at the YMCA, but then wasn't I the assistant manager's friend?

A short while later he reappeared, carrying a tray containing a bottle of the designated spirit hidden surreptitiously under a tea cosy.

After he had left, I poured rum into a glass. I drank it quickly in two or three large gulps, and immediately felt better. I poured myself another drink and put it on the small table by the side of the large wooden bed. I lay down on the bed in a half sitting posture, my back leaning against pillows propped up against the wall, and sipped my drink slowly. I now had to decide what to do. I took the letter out of my pocket and read it once again. There was something wrong, although I couldn't put my finger on what it was.

28

Simiran Simran

I was haunted by the memory of that fateful day when she had returned to our room at the hotel in Rishikesh, having made a long-distance call to Radha in Shimla from the post office.

We had arrived in Rishikesh only a few days earlier from Haridwar. Already ten days had passed since we had attended the office of the Registrar of Marriage with Radha and Salim, and in another three weeks' time we would be returning to Shimla to complete the marriage formalities. Radha was checking Simran's mail in our absence. We would periodically ring her up during our travels to keep abreast of possible developments.

It was her second call to Radha since the day we had left Shimla. She had gone to the local post office at Rishikesh to make the call. I had stayed behind in the hotel room. When she returned, she looked badly shaken.

'What's happened?' I asked. 'Did you get through?'

'I spoke to Radha,' she said tensely. 'She says there are two letters and a telegram.'

'What do they say?' I said impatiently.

'The first letter is an ordinary, routine letter written by Mummy. My father wrote the second one that reached Shimla a weak ago. It appears that he has somehow learnt of our plans to get married and has asked me to come home immediately.'

'And what does the telegram say?'

'Radha received the telegram only this morning. It reads: 'MOTHER SERIOUS, COME IMMEDIATELY.'

After a long moment, I said, 'What does Radha think?'

'She's sure that it's a trick to get me home and lock me up in my room in true *filmi* style.'

'That's what it looks like,' I agreed. 'What about you? What do you think?'

She took a deep breath.

'It's probably a ruse,' she admitted, 'but can I afford to take a chance?'

There wasn't much I could say to that.

'I think I shall have to leave at once,' she said.

'You will have to take a taxi,' I said. 'I'll come with you.'

'No,' she said. 'Let me go alone.'

'Let's wait for tomorrow. Buses are not ploughing through Punjab at night, as yet. It's not safe for you to go by taxi at night all alone.'

'I suppose you're right,' she said listlessly. 'I'll catch the early morning bus, then.'

Later, I cursed myself a thousand times for not letting her leave that same night by taxi.

The next day at six in the morning I put her on to a bus bound for Chandigarh, there being no direct bus to Gurdaspur. She would need to catch another bus from Chandigarh.

The explosion took place at two in the afternoon, according to the news report published in the *Tribune* (which I read later for details of the accident). Barely five minutes before the explosion took place, the conductor had gone to the front of the bus to chat with the driver. He had stated in his interview that after the bus had left Chandigarh, it made a brief stop at Roop Nagar at a quarter to two. Two bearded youths, later identified as members of the Khalistan Commando Force, had got off the bus at this point. In the rear of the bus, under a seat, they had left behind a medium-sized transistor concealed inside a cloth bag.

The bomb had been crude but powerful, and exploded shortly after the bus left Roop Nagar. In all, there were fifteen passengers who died. Those who received the full impact of the blast died instantly, their body parts scattered in the debris, but others succumbed to their injuries in hospital. Many more were seriously injured. The dead and the injured were taken to the Roop Nagar Civil Hospital in ambulances, and police jeeps rushed to the spot.

Later at the *Bhog* ceremony, her uncle told me that she had been sitting in the rear section of the bus. Being close to where the bomb had been placed, she was one of those who had stood absolutely no chance of survival. There would have been no pain.

*****

The police managed to identify her by the student identity card kept in her handbag that was found in the wreckage. They sent a message by wireless to the police station at Summerhill, and asked them to run a check at the university on a woman named Simran Kaur. A press release was published in the following day's newspaper that gave out the names of various identified persons who had been killed or seriously injured in the bomb blast.

I remember tossing and turning that night in the hotel room. A queer anxiety oppressed me. The more I thought about it, the more convinced I became that her mother was not really ill.

Before she had left, we discussed how she would let me know about the true state of affairs that existed at her parents' house. Had there been a phone in the house, I could have called, pretending to be one of her professors. I could even have managed a female voice impersonation. But there was no phone in the house, thus ruling out this option.

We decided to use Radha as an intermediary. On the day she reached Gurdaspur, Simran would ring up Radha and let her know if her mother was actually ill, and the following day I would call Radha up to find out what had happened; and the subsequent day Simran would telephone Radha to find out what I had said and to apprise her of any further developments, and so on and forth.

On the fixed day, I couldn't get through to Shimla. The lines were badly clogged. Finally, late in the evening, I got through after trying to phone the whole day.

Radha was on the line at once. In a trembling voice she told me what had happened in a few short, broken sentences.

It couldn't be true. Dear God, let it not be true.

Half an hour later I was on my way to Gurdaspur in a black yellow taxi, a big, burly Sikh behind the wheel.

My atheism dissolved during the crisis, and I kept making prayers throughout the eight-hour journey. 'Dear God, please don't let it be true. Take me instead, please. Don't let it be true.'

Periodically I would bury my face in my arms and sob. It must have been distressing for Sukhdev Singh, the middle-aged taxi driver, but he maintained a sympathetic silence throughout.

We reached Gurdaspur the following day. Dawn had just broken and there was a chill in the air. As the ambassador wound its way through the town area, we saw little figures huddled together, still asleep, some on string beds while others lay coiled up on the pavement, outside shops still to open.

We found Rang Mahal or the Coloured Palace, without any difficulty: a large old-style building where Simran's parents lived. The family, as well as the house, was well known in the town; the postal address was simply Gurbux Singh, Rang Mahal, Gurdaspur. 'You mean the people whose daughter got killed in the bomb blast, don't you?' queried a turbaned youth on an early morning jog as he paused to give us directions.

The car made its way slowly through the narrow lanes of the bazaar till we finally reached the house. The last building at the end of a lane, it was a tall, pink-coloured building of imposing proportions. It was, however, poorly maintained, with plaster peeling off in sections. A few labourers were busy rigging up a tent in the open space in front of the house.

I directed Sukhdev Singh to turn round and go back to the *bazaar* area, where I checked into a nearby lodging house I had spotted in our meanderings through the town. I freshened up inside the hotel room, drank some tea, and then walked back towards Rang Mahal.

By the time I reached the house, the tent had been put up and strains of melodious cooling music were pouring out of it. A hundred odd men and women squatted on rugs spread out on the floor inside the tented enclosure. Most of the men were Sikhs, with a visibly rural appearance, but several were clean-shaven like me. I placed a white handkerchief on my head, folded the edges behind my ears, and went inside.

At one end of the enclosure sat three turbaned men on a raised platform of thick mattresses, chanting sacred hymns from religious texts of the Sikhs. It was soothing music. I sat down unobtrusively and unnoticed in a corner. There wasn't a single person I knew in the gathering or for that matter anyone who knew me.

After a while, a lean, elderly Sikh gentleman with an aquiline nose joined me. He was evidently from an affluent, urban setting; the only one in the gathering to be dressed in an immaculately tailored, white, safari suit.

Squatting next to me, he whispered, 'Are you from Summerhill?'

I nodded.

'I'm her maternal uncle,' he introduced himself. 'I've heard about you, but only recently. If I'd known about the two of you earlier, I would have tried to help. I'm sorry. It's terrible that this should have happened.' In a flash of anger, he muttered, 'The bastards!' referring to the militants, and then fell silent.

'What's this ceremony?' I asked, fighting back the tears.

'It is *Bhog*,' he said. 'The cremation was performed yesterday. There was no point in waiting for anyone, you understand. I arrived in India only last mouth, in connection with the sale of our ancestral land in Punjab. I am a professor of economics at George Washington University, and have been settled in the US for more than twenty years now. I came down to Gurdaspur a week ago to meet my sister and her family before returning to the States. I heard about the two of you from my sister, and decided to stay on for a few more days.' He paused before adding cautiously, 'Have you met her parents?'

I shook my head.

'That's her father.' He pointed to a short man with a snowy-white beard sitting in the front, his face cupped between his hands. 'And that lady, in the white salwar kameez, is my sister, Simran's mother.' He gestured towards a portly woman, with a large face made red by crying, sitting ahead where the women were gathered.

She looked as healthy as a butcher's dog.

'I heard she was ill...'

'It was to bring Simran home,' he said shortly, 'so we could discuss everything...'

If they hadn't called her back, none of this would have happened.

The uncle was telling me about the accident. I couldn't bear to hear him. I felt sick and disgusted with the whole show, the lies and deceit, all the planning and cleverness of these petty-minded people and all their stupid games that had cost a life. I now knew I wanted to leave, to get away from this place. There was no point in my staying any longer. She was not present. She had gone.

Brushing aside the feeble protests of her uncle, I left the gathering and returned to the hotel. I paid off an embarrassed hotel manager, found the taxi parked nearby, and shook the driver awake. We could start back for Rishikesh, whenever he felt up to it. The driver had slept for only a couple of hours but he claimed it was enough for him and we left at once.

I got off at Haridwar and paid off the taxi driver. I spent one month there, reliving the time we had spent together and trying to come to terms with what had happened.

It was unbearable for me to even think of staying on in Shimla. The town was unimaginable without her. She would be there indelibly, in every place we had ever visited, every person we had both known. Even a tree or rock would evoke memories too painful to bear.

When I finally returned to Summerhill, it was to gather my belongings and say goodbye to the few people who mattered.

*****

Meanwhile Salim had taken up a job with a TV company in Lucknow. A distraught Radha had abandoned or restyled her activism, and begun preparations for the examinations held annually by the Union Public Service Commission for entry into the civil services. It was she who told me about the condolence meeting held in the department in Simran's memory. We met briefly before I returned to Delhi, and I saw that she still looked miserable and in shock. We couldn't talk about what had happened, and any other conversation seemed stilted, forced and unnatural. Despite both of us being intimate with Simran, we were ourselves not close enough to have comforted each other.

Later she qualified, and from the greetings she and her husband Sitaram regularly sent me I learnt she had been posted as a district magistrate at Bhagalpur in Bihar, discharging her duties in her usual efficient manner.

When I returned to Delhi, I had barely enough savings to last me a few months. The city felt empty and desolate. I was drinking with friends every evening, and sinking deeper and deeper into depression.

A researcher friend, Ranjan, a drinking companion recovering from a divorce, pinned me down one day during such a session. 'What are you doing these days?'

'I'm thinking,' I said.

'What do you mean?'

'Just that. I'm thinking.'

'Do you realise you've lost a great deal of weight?'

'Isn't it better to ponder without being ponderous?'

'Are you interested in doing some work for the embassies?' he persisted

'How do you mean?'

'Research work, you know. A Syrian diplomat needs some help. I would have done it myself, but I'm tied up right now. Are you interested?'

'I guess so.'

The following week, Ranjan told me he had spoken to the diplomat. The Syrian was throwing a party at his residence and was keen that I came and met him. He would even send his CD number-plated car to pick me up and drop me home.

I was running out of money and didn't have a job. My former employers at the publishing house told me I could have my old job back, but I felt I couldn't take the strain of a nine to five routine any more.

I noticed an advertisement in the *Hindustan Times*. Delhi University was looking for ad hoc lecturers in philosophy. Two weeks later, I passed an informal interview and began teaching logic and aesthetics.

A month later I bagged my first research assignment. I had to ghost-write a PhD on 'The Scientific Basis of Reincarnation' for the Mauritian ambassador, a devout Hindu.

The clink of the empty Old Monk bottle falling off the small table interrupted my reverie. I got up from the bed, feeling high though not drunk. The rum had succeeded in calming me down. I locked the room, left the keys at the YMCA reception, and caught a bus to Ganahatti.

29

A Sudden Departure

It was dusk by the time I returned to Ganahatti. As I climbed up the pathway leading up to the village, I could see the mist rising below. The streets in the village seemed deserted. Smoke was rising from several of the mud houses in the village. Food was cooking slowly over smouldering *chullahs*. Rehana was the only person in the village who used gas. An old Standard Herald, in which she had driven down to Chandigarh, enabled her to fetch and return gas cylinders from Shimla. The gas company hadn't extended its supply so far out of Shimla because as yet there wasn't enough demand.

I reached the house. A large, forbidding lock stared me in the face. Where could Diamond have gone? A slip inside the grey metal lock read: 'The key is with Komal,' reminding me of a game I had played at school.

Somewhat mystified, I walked ahead to Komal's house and knocked on the door. A red-eyed Komal opened the door. My first thought was that Bahadur had been beating her up again.

'Diamond *didi* has gone away,' she wailed. She repeated this statement twice, all the while dabbing at her eyes with a handkerchief.

'Where has she gone?' I asked, trying to be patient.

Instead of providing an intelligible answer, she burst into tears.

Kalyan heard the sound of our voices and came out of an adjoining room. 'She has left a letter for you,' he said. He dug into his shorts and pulled out a white piece of paper that he solemnly handed over to me. It was a typed letter.

'Dear John,

'At noon today, I received a call from friends at SMU that my friend Jessica, who now lives in New Jersey, has been declared HIV positive. I am therefore leaving for Delhi at once. I'll ask my travel agent to put me on the first available flight to New York.

'I'll write to you from the US about the possibilities, as I see them, of getting an expanded and more detailed version of the two chapters published in book form. This morning I finished typing out the second chapter. I've left a copy for you on the writing table. I think we should also have a lot of illustrations. What do you think?

'I've also typed out the short story you wrote for Rehana's magazine. I'm positive she'll enjoy it hugely. I have left it together with a thank you note from both of us.

'I'll be waiting for your comments on the second chapter, especially suggestions on how it could be improved. We could also discuss the need for working on a third chapter, via letters and email. That was your original plan.

'I'm confident that the university press would want to publish the material if it were put into an academic format, but that wouldn't really serve our purpose, would it? Yet like you I'm convinced this is something that has a market potential and can be brought out by mainstream publishing houses. I'll begin approaching American publishers once we are both agreed on what the final shape of the dialogue is to be.

'You have my address. I hope to hear from you soon.

'With love,

'Diamond.'

Komal had by now re remerged from some corner she had disappeared into. Still sniffing loudly, she handed me the keys to the house.

Back in the house, I tried to rearrange everything the way we had found it when we had arrived. It was a pity I wouldn't meet Rehana.

I packed my luggage, locked the house and returned to Komal's house. I gave her the keys and said goodbye to her and Kalyan. I planned on taking the night bus to Delhi.

*****

At the Shimla bus terminus I purchased a ticket for the air-conditioned coach leaving for Delhi. I wanted to travel comfortably, and temperatures in Delhi would now be fairly high.

I drank tea at a nearby stall whilst waiting for the coach to fill up. As I waited, I reflected that the situation was not bereft of irony. Simran, who had left for Rishikesh urgently because of her mother's pretended illness, had left behind – or had at any rate posted – a first chapter on aesthetics. Now, after all this time, another woman had written me a letter; again the excuse was one of illness, and the said person had disappeared in similar fashion – leaving behind a second chapter on aesthetics. Was it Karl Marx who had said that history repeats itself twice, the first time as a tragedy, the second time as a farce?

I was feeling sad, aware that I was on the verge of becoming depressed. After Eliot's death, and then Simran's, I had become fearful of depressions. They were like phantoms, always close at hand, never very far away, and would sink their claws into you if you weren't careful. Eliot used to say that one couldn't help but be normal; abnormality was an artificial human construct for what people did not understand. Madness was often simply a consequence of being more sensitive than others. I drew strength from that observation, but had developed my own psychological 'mad tactics to counter these ghosts of gloom. My antennae were sharply tuned to pick up signals. They tried to close in on you undiscovered, but with the precautions that I exercised it was more difficult for them to do this. My hearing was now so sharp that I could detect the softest footfall.

The bus made its way slowly through the winding roads, making a couple of stops on the way to pick up passengers. It began to rain. Lightning streaked across the sky, momentarily displaying flashes of green vegetation that grew on the hillside. I caught a whiff of the rain inside the coach even with all of its windows closed.

Sitting next to me at the end of the bus was a flashily dressed Sikh, and matching him in attire an overdressed woman in salwar kameez, both engaged in rapid-fire conversation in Punjabi. From the way they spoke to each other I judged them to be a younger brother and elder sister.

It was ten o'clock by the time we reached Kalka. It was completely dry there, and fairly warm. The air-conditioning was switched on. I took out Simran's letter from my shirt pocket and once again examined it. I felt it was trying to tell me something.

It was past midnight by the time the bus crossed Chandigarh. Most passengers in the bus had gone off to sleep; there was something not quite right with its alignment, because the machine bore us past the starry skies as if it were a large horse, and the sleeping passengers swayed with its motions. The Sikh sitting next to me had fallen asleep, and his head was resting on the woman's shoulder. She was still awake, a tall, dark handsome woman in her thirties. Eventually, though, she, too, succumbed to the alternately smooth and lurching motions of the bus and fell asleep, her head slumped against his. It was an interesting posture, with a comic element to it.

Around five thirty it grew brighter outside, and passengers started waking up. A passing milestone showed we were now on the outskirts of the capital. Bright sodium lights and fluorescent signboards whizzed past, indicating that we were approaching a big city.

The flashily dressed Sikh woke up and resumed his conversation with the woman.

He was saying, '*Bahenji*, do you know what I will do when I reach Berlin tomorrow morning?' Without waiting for her reply, he carried on, 'From the airport, I will take a taxi to my house. I'll rest the whole day to recover from jet lag. In the evening, when I'm feeling refreshed, I'll remove my turban and go for a bath. I'll shampoo my hair thoroughly and dry it out completely with an electric dryer. I'll ask a woman friend who lives next door to help me comb it properly, and let it hang loose over my shoulders. Afterwards, I'll call a couple of my German girl friends and fix up to meet them at a disco. These German girls go absolutely wild about my long hair and beard. They simply love it! At the disco, I'll dance away till the early hours of the morning.'

He had returned from foreign parts ... and she **was** his sister.

His talk was amusing, part of the much-touted cultural adaptability of the North Indian. I was reminded of Kumari who also switched roles with ease, though differently. Only two months earlier, she had gone to her village, in the Guntur district of Andhra Pradesh, as a male. It was to attend her elder sister's daughter's wedding, for which she had contributed three thousand rupees towards the expenses.

According to Kumari, she had been born with both male and female genital organs, unlike most *hijras*. Her father, a village blacksmith, had met with a fatal accident during his wife's pregnancy. His mother knew of the baby's dual sexual organs, but had somehow managed to keep this a closely guarded secret from relatives, people in the village, and for many years even from Kumari's father's elder sister. In later years too, it had been possible for her sexual identity to remain concealed because she had a unisex face, with small breasts that were easily concealed by wearing a thick vest under a loose shirt. Thus, whenever Kumari went to her village in Andhra, she switched from saris and salwar kameez to shirts and trousers, from *hijra* to man. Her physical structure and apparent sexual characteristics were such that she could easily pass as a male. She reverted to her *hijra* status when she returned to Delhi, or when she visited other cities and towns where she had friends among the community.

When I first came to know her, I often wondered why Kumari, with her education and her ability to pass herself off as a male, didn't try to secure a regular job in mainstream society. Most *hijras* were men who suffered from gender diaspora and had undergone castration. They were the equivalent of male-to-female transsexuals in the West. Kumari was so talented that if she had put her mind to it, she would probably have succeeded in any profession, business or job. Whenever I asked her about the possibility of her becoming a 'full timer', she would shake her head and say, 'No, no. That's impossible.' Eventually I understood. The smaller and more oppressed the community, the more difficult it is to walk away.

The bus reached the Inter State Bus Terminal. There was the usual scramble by passengers to get out of the bus. After most of the bus had emptied, I took the little baggage that I had – a suitcase and a sling bag – and walked with it to the *auto* stand nearby.

*****

I was still thinking of Kumari as I climbed the steps to my flat and found her note written on the message pad outside.

30

Lost Jobs, People and Causes

1

Kumari had such beautiful handwriting, I always found it a pleasure to read what she had written. In her brief note, she politely asked if I had had an enjoyable stay in Shimla and told me that she had prepared a charter of demands in the form of a petition and had placed a typed copy of it in my mailbox.

The flat was in a mess. A kitchen window had been left open inadvertently, and a lot of dust had come inside.

I found the petition inside my mailbox: ten neatly typed sheets in Hindi. It was a well-drafted Charter of Demands, highlighting the plight of the *hijras*, and suggesting welfare measures that ought to be introduced. There were also five or six letters, but only two that were relatively important – one from the Embassy of the Republic of Iraq, and the other from the Department.

According to Eliot, Napoleon was once reported to have instructed one of his aides with the following: 'If it's bad news, give it to me at once. If it's good news it can wait.' In the present instance, both these letters could only mean bad news and, following the order of priority observed by Napoleon, I decided to read them before turning to the rest. I first reac the letter from Professor Mahan.

'Dear Colleague,

'This is to inform you that the department no longer has any need of your services, which are hereby terminated with effect from 31 August.

'Yours sincerely,

Professor J. P. Mahan'

It was short, to the point, and without any frills. I noted, without any bitterness, that the letter did not convey any appreciation or state, as was usually appropriate, even for form's sake, that I was being thanked for already-rendered services. The Department did not regret anything; it only sought to tell me that it no longer employed me.

It was now mid-May. My contract with the university was due to expire in three-and-a-half months. I had been teaching for two-and-a-half years now, but held no lien on my job. Every six months I would receive a fresh letter of appointment after an informal interview; sometimes the appointment was extended even without an interview. It depended more or less on the professor in charge. This letter meant that the Department was positively not extending my services. Technically though, I was still employed with the university and would be able to draw a salary for another three-and-a-half months.

The letter was dated three days' ago. It must have one of the first letters Mahan had written on his return to Delhi. On the journey, Milan would have added fuel to the fire raging inside him with graphic descriptions of my various misdeeds.

Bastard. Though in spite of myself I had to admire his 'don't waste a minute' direct action policy.

I went into the kitchen, made some black coffee and sipped it thoughtfully as I plotted out a possible course of action with regard to this missive – actually, it felt more like a missile.

The embossed lettering on the second envelope, which was made of fancier and superior quality paper, indicated that the Embassy of Iraq had sent it. Was the ambassador asking for his money back? But I didn't have a money back policy.

Fortunately, it was nothing so drastic; just a polite letter, tinged with anxiety, enquiring about my progress with 'the task', and requesting me to meet the ambassador at my earliest convenience.

*****

An hour later as I was leaving the house, I met Ram Lok Uncle at the gate.

'Someone came to see you yesterday evening,' he remarked, after we had exchanged greetings.

'Who was it?'

'I don't know. I didn't speak to him, but I did see him go up to your flat. He came in a red Mercedes.'

I nodded. There weren't many people I knew who possessed a red Mercedes. It could have either been an emissary or the Iraqi ambassador himself. I realised my social standing had gone up several notches in Ram Lok Uncle's estimation.

2

I dialled the number of the guest house, where Diamond had been staying earlier. The phone rang, but no one picked up the receiver. I tried a second time, but it was still the same story.

I rang Sonia. She was hopping mad, as I had anticipated.

'Why do you go off so abruptly, *yaar*, without letting your friends know?' she demanded, after I'd explained that the reason I'd been out of touch was because I only just returned from Shimla.

'I'm sorry,' I said. 'I had an extremely rushed programme. I tried calling you up twice from Shimla, but no one picked up the phone.'

'Yes,' she admitted, sounding mollified. 'The bloody phone was out of order. I gave the area manager a big rollicking yesterday. Anyhow, what's been happening?'

Briefly, I narrated the entire sequence of events: the journey to Ganahatti, the meeting with Professr Srinivasan, Simran's letter, and the final disappearing act of my research collaborator.

She listened attentively to the story. 'Listen, why don't you come over? I'm planning to cook some Italian food for lunch.'

'Sounds tempting,' I said, 'but I can't make it today. Right now I'm going to a guest house in south Delhi. Afterwards I have to see a bureaucrat at the Welfare Ministry. I'll come over as soon as I'm back from Gurdaspur.'

'Listen,' she repeated softly.

'I'm listening, Sonia.'

'Are you all right?'

'Why shouldn't I be?' She could be infuriating, I thought.

After a slight pause she said, 'Then all these things you have been telling me, including your stay in Ganahatti with this girl with the crazy name, really happened?'

'Your name sounds equally weird,' I said. 'People don't know if it's Italian or Indian. My God, what do you think's been happening, Sonia? Do you think I've gone mad?'

She was silent, but I could hear the wheels of her mind turning round.

'No,' she said defensively. 'I was only making sure. Tell me something. Do you have that letter Simran wrote to the professor with you?'

'Yes.'

'Is it in her handwriting?'

'Yes, it is.'

'It all sounds funny.'

It did but it wasn't. I hung up, after promising to look her up the day I was back from Gurdaspur.

I tried phoning the guest house number a third time. Once again the phone kept on ringing.

I hailed a passing *auto-rickshaw* and told the driver to take me to Defence Colony.

*****

I found Block F without any difficulty. It was a double-storey bungalow, painted white with a sloping red-tiled roof, reminding me of cakes I had seen at the bakery at Shimla. On the roof, a big neon sign read 'Bon Bon Guest House'.

The black iron gate in front of the huge lawn on the front of the building was locked. There were no signs of any life or activity inside. I strolled across to the rear side of the building to see if there was an entrance from there. A dark young man with long hair in a white uniform sat outside on the steps below the door leading to the house with a mournful, hangdog expression on his face. Sitting next to him on the steps was another, older, man, with white, grizzled hair, who appeared to be lecturing him on some subject or other.

'*Bhaisahab*, is the guest house closed?' I directed my question to the younger man.

'Yes,' he replied, in a heavy South Indian accent. 'The guest house is closed. It will open after ten days.'

'No, no *Apparaju*,' said the other man. 'It will open after two days. Don't worry my friend; you will get your wages in a day or two. Just wait and watch. Madam will be back by then.' He looked at me penetratingly, and repeated, 'Come after two days. It will be open.'

'I've come looking for my sister in law. She was to have come from Agra and should have stayed here last night,' I said, trying to win their sympathy. 'I don't know where she is staying. Has she left any message at the guest house? Since when has it been closed? What's the reason?'

They looked at each other. The younger one said craftily, 'Your sister in law could have stayed at your house.'

'You don't understand. I don't live in Delhi,' I said. 'I've only today come from Rohtak. She said she would be here.'

Seeing that they were not going to get rid of me so easily, the older one finally said, '*Bhaisahab*, there has been a raid conducted here.'

An income tax raid?

The younger man added, 'Not everyone is virtuous like your sister in law.'

It was a brothel raid. I questioned them more closely, but beyond letting on that there had been a police raid of the premises, and that three women, including the proprietors of the guest house, had been arrested, they had no other information. According to the younger man with the long hair, two women of ill-repute had got into the premises pretending to be tourists and had besmirched the reputation of an otherwise respectable guest house.

3

From Defence Colony, I went to Shastri Bhawan. At the reception I asked the attendant to connect me to Roshan Lal, the joint secretary, whom I had met earlier. I would be permitted to climb the staircase leading up to his office only after he had approved my entry.

A voice on the other end of a phone said, 'the Joint Secretary Sahib has not come to the office today.'

I decided that I would try to meet the joint secretary's superior, the deputy secretary, directly.

'In that case, can I be connected to the Deputy Secretary Mr M. M. Gupta?'

'What is your business with him?'

'I have to speak to him regarding some welfare measures.'

There was a click, following which I was connected to another voice.

'Yass,' The new voice hissed.

'Am I speaking to Mr Gupta, the Deputy Secretary?'

'Yass,' The voice hissed once more.

'I want to submit a petition listing certain demands of an underprivileged group. Mr Lal, the joint secretary, suggested I meet you.'

'All right,' said the deputy secretary. 'You can leave the petition in the box.'

'In which box?'

'There is a box marked 'Ministry of Welfare' kept near the reception desk. Just put your petition in the box.'

'I would like to meet you.'

'What for?'

'To discuss what happens next. What does the ministry do after receiving such petitions?' *Put them in the waste paper basket or sell them to the recycling factory?*

Have you put the name of your organisation and its address on the petition?'

'I've done that, but can't I come up and see you?'

'No. That's not the correct procedure.'

'The petition may get lost.'

'It will not get lost. I don't have time to talk to people. Everything you want to say should be written down. Your petition will automatically reach me in an hour's time. There is mail clearance every hour.'

'When do I check with you?'

'Check what?'

Check what you have done with the petition, bloody idiot.

'Check what you have done with the petition.'

'You don't have to check. We will write to you.'

The phone went dead in my hands. He had disconnected.

I stepped out of the building, simmering with rage at how government bureaucracy functioned. Damn him. I would not put the petition in the box but come another day to meet the deputy secretary's subordinate, who had been slightly more helpful. This was Roshan Lal, the lean and hungry bearded bureaucrat, who could have easily played Cassius in *Julius Caesar* that had been directed by Eliot in my school. Was he disloyal to the bureaucracy or to the people, though?

I would hand over the petition to him, even though it was now becoming clear to me that in all probability the ministry would just write a polite letter after some four months stating that they had received the petition and were considering its proposals. After sending off this letter they would regard their duty as done, and promptly toss the file into some obscure corner.

31

The Quest for Beauty

I spent the next four hours in the Connaught Place and Paharganj areas, entering and then rapidly leaving various hotels and lodgings popular with tourists with a medium-sized budget, but their registers revealed no entry with the distinctive name of Diamond. It wasn't the most efficient way to look for someone, I realised, as she could have been in any one of several hundred hotels in the city – assuming that she hadn't already boarded a flight for the US.

It was half past ten by the time I got back to my flat. A second message from Kumari on the note pad stated that she would be coming to see me in the morning on some urgent matter, and for me to keep my day free if possible.

I remembered that I had the second chapter in my suitcase that I had been unable to read on the bus owing to poor lighting. I took out the typed pages from my bag, stepped on to the balcony, and switched on the tube-light so that I could read.

The Second Chapter

Rishikesh was the starting point for thousands of pilgrims who would make their ascent into the mountains. At the riverfront, however, the two friends did not see a single pilgrim, except for an old *sadhu* who sat in a corner, quietly smoking a *chillum*. It was just before dawn and too early for most pilgrims.

Far away, in the upper reaches of the Himalayas, the summer sun was melting the snows, releasing a torrent of swirling, grey waters that flowed through the holy town. As they waited, the orange sun rose behind the blue mountains.

AFFECTION: Tell me Confusion, why is there a need to analyse so much about the nature of beauty? Isn't it completely pointless?

CONFUSION: I hope I don't sound sanctimonious or moralising, but don't you think that our perception of beauty with regard to the human form tends to obscure and distort our perception of the inner beauty of a person? By inner beauty I mean, of course, his or her feelings, sensitivities, sensibilities, etc. Isn't it clear that we connect even 'goodness' with outward physical appearance? Most of our gods, goddesses, prophets, saints, etc, have a physically attractive appearance. At the same time, we have ugly, repulsive-looking villains and devils. I remember reading somewhere about the court trial of a woman in Ancient Greece who had been accused of murdering her husband. After the prosecution had closed its evidence, her defence council got her to disrobe completely and displayed her totally naked form to the judges. He didn't offer any other argument in her defence. By a unanimous verdict she was acquitted of the charge against her. In the judgement it was observed that no woman who possessed such a beautiful body could ever have committed the heinous act of murder.

AFFECTION: Yet don't you find that criminals more often than not tend to look like criminals?

CONFUSION: How many criminals have you known? In the previous century, Lombroso propounded a theory of criminality whereby he drew a direct connection between various types of criminal behaviour with the presence or absence of various physical characteristics held by the criminal concerned. His theory became very popular, and was widely accepted for a very long time. Even today,

Lombroso is regarded as the father of modern criminology, because he succeeded in shifting the focus from the crime to the criminal.

AFFECTION: All the same, don't you find people with 'strong' chins or jaws to be very determined or stubborn? And that people with thin lips and hawkish eyes tend to be very cruel and sadistic?

CONFUSION: No, I don't think so at all. Unfortunately, many of us do tend to form opinions about others at 'face value'. A combination of certain facial and physical characteristics might suggest to an impressionable observer that the person concerned had a certain mental make up and psychology. The reality, however, might be totally different.

AFFECTION: Why should such an impression be created? What is the reason why certain physical characteristics are connected in our minds with certain psychological attributes?

CONFUSION: An anthropologist might possibly provide a comprehensive explanation for this. But consider the following two examples. You know how all of us wrinkle our noses as an expression of disgust? This facial mannerism is connected with the experience of a certain human emotion. Now there may quite conceivably be someone who has a naturally wrinkled-up nose. This may create an impression in the mind of an observer that this person is always disgusted (with life?). Alternatively, consider the case of a woman with very small lips, which, because of their shape and structure, are physically incapable of ever conveying the impression of a 'wide' smile. Such a person may appear to be less welcoming than others when you meet her. Thus physical attributes often create assumptions in our mind that are totally false and baseless.

AFFECTION: All the same, I personally have observed a strong correlation between the physical appearance and mental make-up of a person.

CONFUSION: How can this be, Affection? The medical specialisation of cosmetic surgery has given the deathblow to all theories of criminality or personality based on physical characteristics. Now the human face can be re-fashioned by cosmetic surgery. This will surely reform criminals! The hawkish nose you spoke of can now only too easily be remodelled. The repair or modification of the nose is medically referred to as rhinoplasty. Reduction rhinoplasty – that is to say, treatment to reduce the size and prominence of a nose – is one of the most common nose operations plastic surgeons are called upon to perform. Next, let us consider the large, prominent chin you mentioned. A small, 'weak' chin can be successfully augmented by a plastic surgeon. Some patients request their surgeon to provide them with high cheekbones. Implanting custom-designed silicone implants into pockets cut out from the skin over the cheekbones can create these, and so on and forth. The possibilities are endless.

AFFECTION: (*sounding a little depressed*). You are right, of course. There is no question that facial and other physical characteristics can now be remodelled. A corresponding change in the psyche of the person can hardly be expected. Therefore, physical appearance cannot conclusively be said to be an indicator of personality or behaviour. I follow your line of reasoning. I still cannot rid myself of the impression that such a correlation exists, however.

CONFUSION: What you are saying is true for most of us. Our intellectual recognition of the impossibility of such a correlation is often weak and ineffectual. Such a correlation continues to remain in our conscious mind and in the unconscious, irrespective of its absurdity. It exists in the mind of even the most sensible and level-headed people.

The only association that can exist will be there because of the effect the outside world's prejudices will have on the individual concerned. A particular individual with, say, a prominent chin from childhood onwards will receive 'first sight' responses from others. Gradually such a person will come to realise that he or she is perceived as stubborn or determined. Could it not be that such large-scale perceptions might actually foster the growth of a stubborn quality in an individual?

AFFECTION: Aren't you perhaps imagining all this?

CONFUSION: Yes, I am imagining it all, but I do think it has some basis in reality.

AFFECTION: Perhaps we do misjudge people on the basis of their appearance. Yet what would life be without a sense of beauty? After all, as you yourself admitted in Haridwar, our aesthetic perceptions with regard to the human form have a democratic character about them. Perhaps it is the best compromise.

CONFUSION: Yes, the narcissism of our species is not peculiar to us. It is probably true of others species as well, although to a lesser extent. I am not suggesting that it is completely undesirable. After all, human beings would start coupling with dogs and cats if this self love were totally absent. It is natural that we will find forms resembling us, that is, other humans, more attractive, and to a certain extent this is desirable.

There is, however, another side to the coin. What about the feelings of ugly and deformed people, in terms of the psychological repercussions of our aesthetic perceptions of them?

Ugly people are criticised and made fun of because of their appearance. It may be that they are not overall ugly, but have a particular physical characteristic that invites comment. Such persons become extremely self-conscious and develop a complex about their appearance. It so happens that observers often reach totally false conclusions on the basis of certain physical characteristics. A young woman with extremely large breasts might be thought to be sexually promiscuous (even if desirable otherwise), just as a person with thin lips, together with a hawkish nose, might be thought of as a sadist. This self-consciousness about people's physical appearance may result in certain behaviour patterns.

AFFECTION: Aren't you exaggerating our reaction to physical appearance?

CONFUSION: Am I? Take a look at the spate of magazines on glamour and beauty care. The beauty industry is huge. There are hundreds of lotions, creams, skin preparations, etc, which are guaranteed to make you look younger and more beautiful: hot packs, cold packs, mud packs. With technological advancement, you have facelifts, laser therapy and cosmetic surgery. Hair dyes and even hair transplants are now commonly advertised in newspapers.

It is not only in consumerist Western societies that people are obsessed with their physical appearance. Even in poorer or less-developed countries, there is a big demand amongst the middle classes and affluent sections of society for what the beauty industry has to offer.

In certain cities in the West and South East Asia, cosmetic surgeons have undergone cosmetic surgery to alter and/or beautify certain physical features. They know that there is a beauty bias that exists in these societies, and the idea seems to be that with an improved physical appearance they will be able to attract more clients.

AFFECTION: People should take care of their physical appearance. What's wrong with that? You are being too didactic, if that's the word I want. After all, not everyone can be a hermit like you and go and live in a forest. It's a purely personal matter.

CONFUSION: To use a modern day cliché, Affection, the 'personal is also political'. Take apartheid as it existed in South Africa. Political discrimination based on physical appearance! Simply that.

AFFECTION: (*thoughtfully*) If aesthetic perceptions of the human form are actually so illusory and flexible, from region to region, culture to culture, how is it that blacks are universally perceived as belonging to an aesthetically inferior type? Are you certain, Confusion, that your theory does not fit in with your wish of how things *ought* to be? It occurs to me that you believe that no race ought to be regarded as inferior in aesthetic terms, and are therefore looking for arguments in favour of this position.

CONFUSION: I am not doing that, Affection. Don't forget that historically blacks have been dominated for a long time. Worldwide, it is the majority culture of the whites that is ascendant. In the US blacks are in a minority and the majority culture of whites is dominant. In other regions, where blacks are in a majority numerically speaking, nonetheless until now the whites have been dominant in cultural and economic terms. It is quite possible, indeed likely, that in a society where blacks ruled over whites they, that is, the blacks, would not be perceived to be aesthetically inferior – neither by themselves nor by the others.

AFFECTION: I know for a fact that cosmetic surgeons are often requested by patients to convert broad, flat noses, which are common amongst blacks, into narrower, more prominent, noses. I feel certain that no person would ever request a reversal of this. I don't think it's the cultural dominance of the whites that is responsible for this.

CONFUSION: Don't be so sure. The impact of culture cannot be underestimated. In the US, people of Japanese origin surgically change the shape of their eyes from Mongoloid to European. In South East Asia, on the other hand, such an operation is practically unheard of.

AFFECTION: How can it be that perception of beauty with respect to the human form is biased, whereas, according to you, beauty does exist with regard to nature, for example, in the perception of rivers, mountains, birds, etc?

CONFUSION: Beauty does exist with respect to the human form as well, but our existing perceptions are mostly sheer bias, nothing else. For example, a very fat woman might be beautiful, but our existing biases prevent us from seeing that beauty. It is our obsessive narcissism and ideas of what is 'normal' that prevent us from seeing this beauty. Even geometric shapes are beautiful, and in the context of the human form these would be relevant. A certain sharpness (triangles), a sense of proportion (circles, squares), or clarity of outline conveys a sense of beauty. Also, in the architecture of cities you will find geometry pleasing to the eye, but when the particular geometry becomes monotonous and swamps everything else, it becomes aesthetically repulsive.

AFFECTION: Why should our sense of what is 'normal' distort our perception of beauty in the human form? Don't we extend this notion of normality to the outside world?

CONFUSION: Possibly, but not to the same extent. You find flowers of so many different shapes and colours beautiful, don't you? But as regards the human form, we tend to be extremely rigid in deciding what is beautiful. With respect to flowers, we do not insist on any particular classificatory system, such that a flower must conform to a maximum or minimum size, or that flowers that are closer to a 'normal' size are more beautiful.

You will find fewer regional or cultural variations in the perception of beauty in nature. A sunrise (*Confusion points to the rising sun*) is perceived as beautiful everywhere in the world, in all cultures and civilisations. Such a perception is almost as old as the human psyche. The presence of human variation in the perception of beauty, as is the case with respect to the aesthetics of the human form, is indicative of the falsity of such a perception.

AFFECTION: I think you have become horribly logical and scientific in your thinking. It all sounds terribly antiseptic and dry.

CONFUSION: I could say the same thing about you. You go about scientifically and methodically slugging an axe, aesthetically classifying human beings. Unthinkingly, you throw millions of human beings into the category of ugliness. Additionally, you then seize upon individual features, classify them and throw several million human features into the same category. With the rising sun, we have no such strict categories. Our perception of beauty in nature is relatively spontaneous, even though in certain cultures there may be a fear of natural phenomenon such as lightning and floods or of huge, powerful-looking mountains that may distort the perception of beauty. But perception as regards the human form is largely man-made and socially engineered.

32

Poonam's Story

'Why did they arrest her? Was it begging?' I handed Kumari a glass of milky tea, which was how she preferred it.

We were sitting in my flat, and she had just told me the shocking news of Poonam's arrest three days previously by the Paharganj police.

'No, *babu*.' She shook her head regretfully. 'That's what I'd also thought to start with. In fact I went to the wrong courthouse and couldn't be at the Children's Court, when she was first produced. Had she been accused of begging, she would have been out by now. Matters are far more complicated than that. They have charged her with theft.'

'She's only a child,' I said. 'What do they say she has stolen?'

'They have charged her with stealing twenty rupees from a cigarette shop near the railway station.' She laughed bitterly. 'Some *hijras* had gone to the railway station to buy train tickets and had taken her along. She was sent to a shop to buy some cigarettes. According to Poonam, she found a twenty-rupee note lying on the road, just outside the shop. It must have accidentally dropped out of a customer's pocket. She innocently picked it up. The shop keeper saw the note in her hand, and came to the conclusion that she had picked it out from the tin box in which he kept his money, while he had his back turned to her to collect the cigarettes she had asked for. He grabbed the note from her and started shouting loudly that she was a thief. A beat constable picked her up and took her to the police station.'

'What happens now?'

'What can happen, *babu*? They will produce her today before the magistrate in charge of the Juvenile's Court at Kingsway Camp.'

'Can the Kingsway Camp Station House Officer be of any help?' I asked.

'Not directly, since the case is being handled by the Paharganj police station. Perhaps later he can put in a word to the Paharganj SHO if we find it necessary. I want you to come to the court today. You look respectable and speak English. That makes a lot of difference. They will let people like me enter the courtroom only as someone accused of some crime, not otherwise.' She looked at me anxiously. 'Will you come?'

'Yeah, sure I can come,' I said easily, 'but I want you to brief me on what I have to do.'

'Nothing, *babu*. Your presence will be enough. You will see. I met the girl yesterday. She is being kept in a Special Home near the Sikh temple next to the Tibetan market. She will be produced in court today by a female warder, who will say that she wants to plead guilty...'

'Plead guilty?' I couldn't conceal my astonishment. 'Why on earth are you making her plead guilty if she hasn't committed the theft?'

'It's very simple. If Poonam pleads guilty, all that the magistrate will do will be to admonish her, and she will be released immediately. If she doesn't plead guilty she will continue to remain in the children's home for the duration of her trial, unless she gets bail. Even if she does somehow get bail, she will have to keep going to the court to attend various hearings. That would be very traumatic for her.'

It all sounded fairly insane to me, yet this was the legal position, Kumari assured me. She had checked it out with a lawyer who occasionally represented the community. I didn't doubt that she had done so and that she had the correct facts; she was generally very thorough.

'What happened to her parents?' I asked.

She said in a low voice, 'It's not known who her father was. Her mother either didn't know or wouldn't tell. I asked her several times.' She sipped her tea slowly. 'Poonam's mother, Rani, was a woman who lived and slept on the pavements of Connaught Place. A professional beggar, she got pregnant and had a baby. After the child was born she left the Connaught Place area, and went to live with a relation of hers, a man called Jagdeep who lived with his wife in a slum at Shakarpur. She gave up begging and started doing odd jobs here and there. She was quarrelsome and eccentric, and couldn't get along with people. When Poonam was four years old, she was forced to leave the slum and return to the Connaught Place area to resume begging, her earlier vocation. This was because of problems with Jagdeep's wife, as well as several other people who didn't want her to stay in the slum. She wasn't liked very much. People easily turned hostile to her. She was always fighting. She wasn't attractive, would never take a bath, would always look filthy, with skin infections, lice, etc. The slum people didn't like to have such a person live with them, so when the child was a little older, they forced her to leave. Yet for all her quarrelsome nature, Rani loved the child and didn't get her to beg when she returned to the Connaught Place area.'

'How did Poonam come to live with you?'

'I knew her mother, you see,' she said sadly. 'We got along together. She had a wonderful sense of humour, you know, and I enjoyed chatting with her. Also, she was a tremendous fighter and I admired her for her spirit. When Rani returned to the Connaught Place area, she had contracted tuberculosis. The disease had reached the last stage by the time she began taking medicines, and the Connaught Place pollution must have aggravated the disease further. It was perhaps too late for the anti tubercular medicines to have any effect, and she continued to have a terrible hacking cough, occasionally vomiting blood. One day she came to meet me with Poonam and asked if I could keep her for a while. I took the child with me to our section in the slum. I would have taken Rani there, too, but the others would not have allowed it. There was some consternation in the community at my bringing a female child to stay with us, but I managed to convince the others that the Goddess would be pleased if we let her stay with us till she got a little older. Moreover, I argued that Poonam could run errands and occasionally get tea and cigarettes for us. She would stay with me in my *hutment*.'

'When did her mother die?'

Her face clouded over. 'She died two months ago. Not from tuberculosis. Around ten o'clock at night, a speeding car hit her from behind while she was crossing the road in Connaught Place. She died on the spot. It was a hit-and-run case. No one managed to note down the number of the vehicle. It was a red Maruti. I learnt about it the next day from our beggar friends who operate in the Connaught Place area.'

'Does Poonam know about this?'

'No,' she replied. She appeared to think for a while. 'There was no need to tell her. I think she was scared of Rani. She doesn't ask for her any more.'

'If she gets released today and goes back with you, how long can she continue to stay with you?'

'I don't know,' she admitted. 'As I told you, there has been some opposition to her presence in the community. In any case, when she is a little older, we won't be able to stay together. Perhaps it is better that she leaves now, but I don't trust any of the government orphanages. The children are really badly abused in them. At the same time, I think she should start going to school now. Do you know of a good family, a childless couple, perhaps, who might want to adopt her?'

I tried not to look depressed, but it was difficult. I knew how orphanages functioned and what the atmosphere inside them was like. I felt a dull ache inside me.

Kumari was looking at me, waiting for an answer.

At length I said, 'I'll find out.'

One question was bothering me. 'Kumari,' I said, 'who will the court grant custody of the child to? For obvious reasons you couldn't be her parent, and the court will hesitate to appoint you as her guardian. Are you suggesting that I pretend to be her father?'

'No,' she laughed. 'That won't be necessary. Initially it did cross my mind that I could dress up as a male and pretend to be her father, but then I thought better of it. The police recognise me by now. I have, however, managed to contact Rani's cousin Jagdeep who lives in Shakarpur. This is the same cousin in whose *hutment* she lived for four years. He is very attached to the child and didn't want Rani to leave, but ultimately he was forced to give in to the wishes of his wife. He has agreed to come to the court today and take custody of her.'

'So the judge will hand over custody to Jagdeep inside the court room, and a little later you will both meet when Poonam will then go back with you?'

'Yes, *babu*. That's the idea.'

'What does Jagdeep do for a living? Why didn't he come with you?'

'Jagdeep drives an auto these days. He didn't come here because he wants to be seen around with me as little as possible. He is afraid he may get into some kind of trouble with the police. He will go straight to the Juvenile Court.' Kumari finished her tea. In a sad voice, she said reflectively, 'Sometimes I do think of becoming a full-time male because of her. Society does not accept a *hijra* living with a young girl. When she came to stay with me, I made a conscious effort not to become too emotionally attached to her. Even more important, I tried to ensure that she did not become overly attached to me. I have failed in both respects. What can you do with a six-year-old girl? In the five months we have lived together, we have become close, although she still feels very insecure and gets scared easily. Such a beautiful child. Is it possible for anyone not to love her? Yet for her own sake, she must leave.'

It was time for us to leave. The judge would start sitting at ten o'clock. We stepped out of the building. I could see someone inside my landlord's house pull a curtain. Ram Lok Uncle and his gang were watching us.

Outside on the main road people stopped to look and stare. Kumari was wearing a salwar kameez instead of a sari. It made us look less incongruous, but we were still unusual enough to attract attention. Still, neither of us cared. We were used to it by now.

'Should we take a bus?' I said.

'Not necessary. The place is close by. We can walk it.'

It took us barely fifteen minutes to reach the Juvenile Court, barely two hundred yards away from the Kingsway Camp market crossing, within a complex of buildings, which also housed a school for the blind and some probation officers.

The court itself was a medium-sized hall, fifteen feet by fifteen feet, with extremely sparse furnishings. I had the impression that one of the classrooms used earlier by the blind school had been cleared to accommodate it. The judge, who had not yet arrived, was supposed to sit opposite a long table at one end of the room. On one side of the judge's table sat a young, overdressed stenographer, and on the other side an elderly person in a white bush-shirt, grey trousers and sandals, whom everybody referred to as the reader. At the other end of the room, behind some small tables, sat a few other court clerks and two policemen exclusively assigned to the court.

I managed to ascertain from the reader that the judge had gone to Tihar Jail to conduct an identification parade, and that he would be back at noon.

Outside the courtroom Kumari introduced me to Jagdeep, a short, paunchy man with a Marxist beard that suggested union activity and leadership of some kind, possibly with the *auto-rickshaw* unions. Something about his demeanour suggested that Jagdeep was a professional unionist, and that he carried his philosophy to whatever job he happened to be doing currently. Introductions complete, Kumari then moved away, keeping her distance. I briefly chatted with Jagdeep, sensing that he was uncomfortable and did not want to prolong our conversation.

Kumari and I went out into the open towards the *pipal* tree, outside the red-bricked court building. Under its large, sprawling branches, there were a couple of benches to sit on. Someone had also set up a makeshift teashop near by. The shop served tea along with buns, rusks, *mathis*, *fains* and assorted biscuits. We sat down on one of the benches.

I asked the thin, middle-aged tea stall owner to bring us two teas and some *mathis*. On the other bench sat a scruffy-looking lawyer wearing a white collar and a badly faded, ancient black coat, which had visible tears in it. He was with a client who looked even more impoverished and scruffy. They, too, were waiting for the judge to turn up.

We finished the tea and after a while ordered a second round, but even after that had been consumed there was still no sign of the judge. It was now the lunch hour, and the court would sit again at two o'clock.

'Have you managed to convince members of the community in Sadar bazaar and Paharganj to join the association?'

I was curious to learn from Kumari about her progress in bringing all *hijras* in the city under a common platform, so that they could ventilate their grievances collectively and take some joint action.

'There hasn't been much progress on that front,' she said ruefully. 'We call ourselves an All India association, but so far we haven't got sufficient members to join us, even in Delhi. I do have one or two friends in the Sadar bazaar area, but most *hijras* who live there don't trust me because I am from Andhra while they are mostly from Kerala. Many of them are devotees of a crooked saint, who holds a religious meeting on Sunday near the New Delhi Railway Station. This charlatan charges them for attending the prayer ceremony and fleeces them in various other ways as well, but they pay up willingly because they are all so much under his influence. Two members of the community from the Sadar bazaar area asked permission from him for them to join the association, but he was naturally opposed to the idea.'

'They and the others must join,' I said soberly, 'if any progress is to be made.'

'Yes,' said Kumari. 'The problems are caste, language and region. Big obstacles to overcome.'

This was the tragedy. Even though the *hijras* were one of the most oppressed minorities, they were far from being united.

'You will have to convince them,' I repeated. 'Unless we can add to the strength of the association and take some visible collective action by organising a demonstration or protest march, nothing will happen. Government machinery is too insensitive to take any positive action on its own on the basis of written representations.'

'That's true.'

I told Kumari about my encounter with the bureaucrat the previous day at Shastri Bhawan.

'Did you abuse him, *babu*?'

'No,' I said, 'although it did cross my mind to do just that.'

'It was only natural that you wanted to do that,' she commented. 'You should have roundly abused the fellow. In any case, he would be of no help. Tell me something: these government servants are supposed to be public servants, isn't that so?'

'Yes,' I said. 'That's right.'

'Then as members of the public we are their conceptual masters', she argued. 'If he is a public servant with the Ministry of Welfare and he is not doing his job, he deserves to be abused.'

'I'll do that now,' I said. 'You've convinced me. I'll call him up today and abuse him on the phone.'

'You are joking, perhaps. You are too decent to abuse anyone.'

The scruffy-looking lawyer sitting on the other bench said something to his client and stood up. We turned to look. A police jeep had driven up. There were some policemen inside the jeep and the judge had finally arrived. It was two thirty now, past the usual time for the start of the afternoon session, yet Poonam had still to be brought to the court from the children's home, although several others were now present. Among those who were there, some were on bail and had come on their own, while others had arrived in a van from the special homes.

The judge promptly disappeared into a cabin next to the court that served as his private office.

'Excuse me, *bhai sahab*.' I addressed the court usher, a thin, balding man with a pencil-thin moustache. 'Can I have a word with you?'

'What is it?' he said. 'I'm very busy right now.'

I knew just what he wanted. I took out a fifty-rupee note from my wallet, folded it conspicuously, and slipped it into my shirt pocket.

He got the message.

'What do you want to know, Sahib?'

'There is a juvenile by the name of Poonam who has not been produced in court. What's the reason for this?'

'Which police station is in charge of the case?'

'Ajmeri Gate, I think.'

'I will find out.' He conferred briefly with a clerk sitting near the judge's seat.

'Nothing to worry about, Sahib. You have been waiting quite unnecessarily. On the previous occasion when she had been brought to court, Judge Sahib passed an order directing the girl and her parents to be present at two o'clock today. That's the reason she has not been brought to court so far.'

'But it's past two now,' I said.

'She will be coming any time now,' he insisted.

I gave him the money.

True to the usher's words, a few minutes later a van from the welfare home arrived, carrying Poonam and several other children assessed as neglected or delinquent. Apparently the vehicle had broken down on the way to the court, which is why there had been a delay.

A female warder in blue uniform helped Poonam climb out of the van. The warder was an attractive girl in her early twenties, with a kindly expression on her face. Despite her reassuring presence, Poonam looked lost and confused. Dressed in a grey frock suit, she was without doubt the youngest child in the van.

33

Courtroom Drama

1

The Judge took his seat opposite a long wooden table with a pale green cloth spread over it. Poonam and the other children gathered outside the courtroom waited their turn as their cases were called out one by one by the usher.

Poonam looked relieved when she saw Jagdeep. He gave her a reassuring smile, and made a gesture with his hand to indicate that everything was going to be all right. He had visited her at the children's home the previous evening with Kumari, who had explained to her that Jagdeep would come to the court to get her released and bring her back to the slum area.

Kumari had left. She had explained it was better she went away so that Poonam would not see her. Otherwise, she would reach out to Kumari who would be unable to respond because of the visible police presence.

I stepped inside the courtroom get a proper look at the judge. He was a greying, bespectacled man in his early forties, with a very forthright manner of speech. Yet, as I watched him dispose of several cases that were called out by the court usher, I observed that while his manner was in the main inquisitorial and geared towards seeking explanations, he was also exercising restraint.

It was almost four o'clock by the time Poonam's case was called. Only a couple of cases remained to be heard. The blue uniformed warder stepped into the courtroom, holding Poonam, who looked scared, by the hand. Jagdeep also came in and stood alongside. I stood at the extreme end of the room; it had been agreed that I would step forward only if the need arose.

The Judge scanned the file placed before him by the reader and then looked up. He didn't seem surprised to see such a small girl in front of him.

He gave Jagdeep a piercing stare. Jagdeep stood in a placatory posture, his hands folded behind his back.

'Are you her father?' the judge demanded in a belligerent tone.

Jagdeep looked down at the floor respectfully and said softly, 'I am her uncle.'

'Where are her parents?'

'They are dead,' he replied. 'Her mother died six months' ago.'

'Does she live with you?' The Judge's voice was gentler.

'Yes.'

'Where do you stay?'

'Shakurpur.'

The female warder ventured a step further. In a low voice, she said, 'Judge Sahib, she wants to plead guilty.'

The Judge ignored her. Instead he looked directly at Poonam now, who was looking extremely apprehensive. In a stern voice, he asked, 'Did you steal the money?'

She shook her head slowly.

'A twenty-rupee note was found on you,' said the judge. `If you didn't steal it, where did you get the money from?'

The female warder was nudging Poonam, trying to remind her to say she had stolen the money.

But Poonam wasn't listening to her. She was looking straight at the judge.

In a piteous voice she said, 'I found it on the road.'

The Judge looked pleased. He triumphantly exclaimed, 'See, she says she is not guilty!' He shifted his gaze to Jagdeep and asked accusingly, 'What did you think? That if she pleaded guilty, I would give her an admonition and discharge her? You think you can fool me in this fashion? No you cannot. She does not plead guilty. The trial will have to take place.' He turned to the reader. 'Call out the next case.'

The female warder and Jagdeep were both looking distressed about what had happened. It was time for me to do my bit.

'Your Honour,' I said, stepping forward, 'since a trial is now going to be held, I request that the court direct that in the meanwhile the girl might be released on bail and custody be given to her uncle.'

The Judge looked at me. 'Who are you?' he enquired rudely. 'Why haven't you come forward until now?'

I said evenly, 'I have come to stand surety in this case. If the trial is to proceed, in the meanwhile the girl might be released on bail.'

'Are you a relative of the delinquent?'

'No,' I admitted, 'but the girl and her uncle are known to me.'

'Why did you ask her to plead guilty?' asked the judge, who now understood that I had not come forward earlier on because I knew that Poonam was going to plead guilty and assumed that she would be admonished and released after doing so.

'It was because trials take several months, even years, to conclude.'

He appeared satisfied with this answer and grew thoughtful. 'Yes, sometimes they do,' he agreed. He removed his spectacles and cleaned them before putting them on again. 'Do you realise that if she pleads guilty today I may admonish her and direct her be released, but that if some months later she is again brought before me charged with having committed some other crime, her previous record of having pleaded guilty will go against her?'

He did have a point there. It hadn't occurred to me.

'I agree with that, Your Honour,' I said. 'Let the trial proceed, but meanwhile may she be released on bail?'

'She may be better off in the children's home,' said the judge.

'I am standing surety for her,' I said. 'She will be better off outside.' I added something I had read somewhere. 'The Supreme Court has repeatedly held that bail, not jail, is the rule.'

'The special home is not a jail.'

'It could be worse,' I said evenly. 'In any case, she is entitled under the law to be released on bail.'

The judge looked taken aback. 'Is the offence bailable?'

'Yes,' I said, wildly.

'Are you a lawyer?'

'No, but I teach philosophy of law at the university.'

I showed him my identity card and salary slip. Technically, I was still teaching at the university till the end of August. The judge scrutinised the documents carefully. He looked suitably impressed.

'All right,' he said finally. 'On your agreeing to stand surety, she can be released on bail.' In a more sympathetic tone he added, 'In my court, cases don't take that long. I will finish the trial in two or three weeks' time.' He dictated a short order to the stenographer sitting next to him. 'Juvenile present in court. She is hereby released on bail on her guardian furnishing a personal bond to the sum of Rs. 3000/ , with one surety in the like amount. During the course of the trial, she will remain in the custody of her guardian, her uncle, Mr Jagdeep Pershad, whose place of residence shall be verified by the police before the next date of hearing. The police shall also confirm that the delinquent is staying with him.' He gave a date in the coming week for the hearing of the case.

We stepped out of the courtroom. I felt a load off my shoulders. Relief was writ large on the faces of Jagdeep, Poonam, and even the female warder.

In a room adjacent to the courtroom, I filled up the bail bond, and then signed it together with Jagdeep. We both followed up with other necessary signatures on various other forms and registers, and then it was over. We were free to go. More important, **she** was free. The female warder patted Poonam's head affectionately. She accompanied us outside, after I had been persuaded to disburse a further hundred rupees as unofficial payment for services rendered by the court usher, the reader and other court clerks.

2

From the Kingsway Camp market, the three of us boarded an *auto-rickshaw* for Golcha cinema in Daryaganj. It had been decided that Kumari would meet us outside the cinema whenever we happened to arrive, but we couldn't find her.

The evening performance was about to begin. A crowd had gathered outside the cinema gate waiting to go in.

The movie running was something called '36, China Gate'.

'Have you seen this movie?' asked Jagdeep, lighting a cigarette.

'No,' I said. 'It doesn't sound particularly interesting.'

'It's third rate.' He puffed at his cigarette. 'Don't make the mistake of going to see it. It's going to be a big flop.'

'It seems to be a hit.' I pointed to a big board outside the hall, which boldly stated in capital letters: 'HOUSE FULL'.

'All matinee shows at Golcha run house full,' said Jagdeep, 'irrespective of what they are showing. It's the best place to black market.'

Kumari came across from the other side of the road, wearing a big grin on her face. She had changed into a sari and looked her usual self. Poonam's eyes lit up and she rushed towards her.

'Where the hell were you?' I said sourly.

'I'd gone to my favourite shop at Ansari road to get a *paan.*' Kumari spat some betel juice on the pavement, taking care not to splatter passers by. 'What happened in court?'

I gave her a summary of what had happened: the judge had ordered the trial to continue; Poonam was on bail; and Jagdeep had been entrusted with her custody. The police would verify whether or not Jagdeep was actually staying with his niece at the residential address he'd provided.

'What do you think, *babu*?' said Kumari, looking worried.

'I don't think she should go with you,' I said. 'It would be better for Poonam to accompany Jagdeep and stay with him till the trial is over. Or at least until the police verification has taken place.'

Kumari nodded. She addressed the child, 'Poonam, you will have to go with Jagdeep *mama* today.'

The girl shook her head sullenly. She was upset, wanting to go with Kumari.

'I'll come to see you everyday, my dear,' she said patiently. 'It's only a matter of a few days.'

She wasn't satisfied with the consolation she was being offered.

Suddenly, with all the strain of the past two days, Poonam broke down and began sobbing uncontrollably.

'Why don't you come with me and Poonam?' suggested Jagdeep, addressing Kumari. 'You can go back later tonight.'

'I'll do that,' said Kumari, putting her arms around the girl, who was now wiping her eyes with her elbow.

We crossed over to the other side of the main road where there was a bus stop. I watched them board a Green Line bus for Shakurpur. My entire day had been spent waiting for a juvenile judge, and although barely two minutes of verbal exchange had taken place in the courtroom, the tension had taken its toll on me. I was exhausted, needed a drink badly, and didn't have the patience to wait till I got home.

Broadway Hotel on Asaf Ali Road boasted an expensive restaurant, a popular watering hole with the executive crowd that was close by. Fortunately, the bar wasn't crowded. I ordered a single, chilled bottle of strong Indian beer, and when that did not have the desired impact I followed it up with two large whiskies.

*****

At nine o'clock I stepped out of the bar. Outside, the night was cool. A 'Use AT&T' girl gave me a welcoming smile from the hoarding opposite the hotel. I thought of America and Diamond. Had she left for New York?

When I returned to my flat I realised I hadn't eaten either lunch or dinner, but I was feeling too hot and tired to eat or cook.

34

Dreaming the Past

The sound of someone sobbing woke me up. For a few brief moments I wondered who was crying. With a start I realised I was alone. It had been a dream, a peculiar kind of dream – and someone had been crying in that dream. I searched for my watch under the pillow. It was two o'clock.

I pulled a chair to the balcony and sat outside. It was pitch dark outside. A peacock screeched. I could barely remember the hazy outlines of a dream in which there had been a number of people: Eliot, Simran, Professor Srinivasan and Poonam.

I sat outside looking at the stars, tormented by memories of the past. I repeatedly saw Poonam's sobbing face.

I thought of Eliot as he had been when he had first come to the orphanage: Chetna Orphanage, Nirala Nagar, Lucknow. He was young then, tall, only a few years older than I was now, with long, black hair falling over his shoulders. He rarely smiled, even then, but his eyes were warm and his voice was deep. I later learnt that it was not his natural voice. He had acquired the ability to speak like that through months of practice, till it became effortless.

Once I had lost my initial fear of him and had gained some confidence Eliot one day said to me, 'I want to be your friend. Come and stay with me.'

He never mollycoddled me. Even so, as a child I felt his presence around me like an invisible shield, providing me with security, warmth and comfort.

He was both father and mother to me. He could have been either actually, literally speaking, because, like Kumari, he was not a castrated male, or a eunuch, but a hermaphrodite, one of those rare accidents of birth.

However I thought of him as a man, and in that sense more as a father, and that is how he would also have wished it.

In this sense he was different from Kumari, who maintained that while *hijras* were neither men nor women, if it came to a choice, most of them preferred a female identity, and accordingly, like her, kept a woman's name.

I learnt the truth about him after many years of living with him; it was Eliot himself who told me one day.

On Sundays at home there were many people who came to meet Eliot. He had studied homeopathy and was qualified to practise, but preferred to teach for a living and diagnosed and prescribed medicine free of charge. There were schoolteachers who visited, but also leprosy patients and other people who were sick, and also members of the most despised community of all: the *hijras* of Lucknow.

The coming and goings of this last category of people were viewed with disapproval by other residents of the school's staff quarters. Boys at the hostel had spread a malicious rumour that Eliot was a frustrated old bachelor and was having sex with the *hijras*.

Even though he knew it to be false, when he heard about the rumour, Eliot was suffused with impotent anger. He knew that there was no easy way to quell such suggestions. A day after the rumour started, I tried to convince Eliot not to allow them to come. He simply laughed.

'Shall I tell you something?' he said, 'I, too, am a *hijra*.' He stunned me with his words.

I listened, at first with disbelief and then with growing fear and horror, when Eliot explained to me that, no, he wasn't joking; he really was both man and woman. It was suddenly clear why he would always remain heavily attired, even in the heat of summer. He wouldn't play games or go swimming.

'Don't look so horrified,' he said. 'If I have an operation, I can become a man.'

'Why don't you have the operation then?'

'When I was young, the operation was little heard of. Later on I felt it wasn't necessary,' he replied briefly. 'It doesn't really matter any more.'

'Why does it matter to other people, then?' I persisted. 'And why do you hide what you are?'

'That's the whole point,' he said. 'Our vision is so narrow that we condemn anyone who is not like us.'

His last statement set me thinking, long and hard. After a week I felt suffused with shame and guilt.

We never discussed the subject again, but as an adolescent I made a vow that, if I did nothing else, I would somehow in my life pay my greatest benefactor a tribute that would honour his own life in some way.

It was a long while before I managed to get sleep again. I had barely dozed off when I was woken up by the sound of my door bell. It was Salim.

35

Photo-finish to the Airport

1

I was in the black Ambassador car coming from Karnal, confidently misdirecting the driver away from Delhi University. That's where the elderly couple sitting behind him wanted to go to, but instead, with an increasing sense of guilt, I was directing the driver towards the India Gandhi International Airport.

Amazing coincidences: Salim's early morning arrival owing to a delay in the flight from Calcutta and his unexpected encounter with Diamond in the airport lobby.

I was sure that if I managed to meet her, it would resolve all the doubts and questions that had been plaguing my mind. It was therefore tremendously important that I had a face-to-face encounter with her before she boarded her flight.

From Mall Road I directed the car straight down the Ring Road to Pragati Maidan, and then on to Aurangzeb Road. It was early morning and as yet there was little traffic. The driver drove fast and reached the Ashoka Hotel tri-section in good time.

We were now approaching the motorway that led directly to the airport. No matter how trusting my co passengers were, I knew I couldn't possibly take them right up to the airport without their realising that they had been taken on a wild goose chase.

'What subject do you teach Professor?' A polite question from the red-faced elderly gentleman in the brown safari suit, sitting in the rear of the car, interrupted my thoughts.

'Philosophy,' I replied briefly, thinking of what I should do.

'That is very interesting,' he said politely. 'My son has been admitted to Delhi University this year to take an MA in History. He is staying at the Jubilee Hall Hostel. Would you know the location of this hostel?'

'Oh, it's in the campus area,' I said. *Jubilee hall in Delhi University was at least twenty-five kilometres behind us now.*

'How far is the university now?' asked the thin, grey haired woman sitting next to the gentleman.

'Hardly ten minutes.' I was getting a headache with all these questions.

'We were lucky to have met you,' said the old man, 'and that just by chance. It would have been a real problem for us to find the university without any help.'

'Please don't mention it.' I kept my face expressionless.

All at once the solution to the twin problems I was faced with – on the one hand the moral dilemma of betraying someone's trust and on the other hand the practical problem of reaching the airport with the public transport system at a standstill – presented itself to me.

I could go to Sonia's house and take her car. Her fancy clientele was the kind who ate breakfast in bed at half past eleven. It was far too early for her to step out to meet any of them. She would certainly be at home. It was very possible this elderly trusting couple might smell something fishy before we reached the airport. There would now be a great many signboards on the way giving the direction and distance to the airport.

I guided the driver towards Munirka Enclave, and stopped the Ambassador near her house. Stepping outside the car, I addressed the elderly gentleman: 'You will have to take this road and turn right after two hundred yards.' I pointed towards Jawaharlal Nehru University, the other big university in the city and major rival to Delhi University. 'That road goes straight to the university. You will have to excuse me. I need to visit a colleague who lives here.'

I watched the car speed away. While it wasn't Delhi University, it was, after all, a university in Delhi I had guided them to. Perhaps they might now believe that I had guided them to Jawaharlal Nehru University in good faith. I smiled at the thought and shook my head. *Who was I kidding*?

*****

I sprinted across to Sonia's house. Her Fiat was parked on the lane outside her flat, which meant she was at home. I pressed the bell and let it ring.

She opened the door a moment later, having first identified me through the glass eye embedded in the wooden door.

'What the hell, *yaar*!? You nearly blasted my eardrums,' she exclaimed.

'I don't have any time,' I said urgently. 'Just hand me your car keys now. I have got to reach the airport fast.'

She didn't waste time asking questions. She simply picked up a bunch of keys hanging on the wall and, pointing out the ignition key, handed it over to me without uttering a word.

I was inside the car, when she came out of her flat and yelled, 'Who's leaving?'

'Diamond.' I shouted back.

2

I drove the Fiat past the guards posted at the security gate, outside the colony on to the main road, and raced the car towards the airport. I was at the airport in fifteen minutes flat. Inside the parking area, I tried to manoeuvre the car into a parking slot pointed out by the parking attendant, but all of a sudden the engine went completely dead. I handed the car keys together with a fifty-rupee note to the attendant as payment for him to get help from someone and physically push the car into the slot, or sort out the problem some other way. Not bothering to collect the change I ran to the International Departure section.

Inside the hall, the display charts on the computer screens listed a United Airlines flight leaving for New York via Paris at 10.05. It was almost 8.30 now. She might already have gone through the security check and be about to board the aircraft. My eyes searched the hall desperately. There were many Indians, some Europeans and a large group of Japanese. She was nowhere to be seen.

Then I saw her. I hadn't noticed her, because all the while, without realising it, I had been looking for a woman in a cotton sari wearing glass bangles on her arms. She was there all right, but wearing a dark blue T shirt and faded jeans, sitting in a corner, smoking a cigarette, looking just like she had when she had come to my flat the first time. Only this time she wasn't blowing smoke rings.

*****

As I moved towards her, a diminutive, bald man with a drooping moustache blocked my way.

'Please take some *prasad*,' he cried, proffering a large steel plate with two *ladoos* on it.

'Where's it from?' I asked, stretching out a hand.

'Tirupati.'

I had seen *ladoos* from the holy temple at Tirupati. They were very large, the size of a tennis ball, and were stuffed with dry fruits. These *ladoos* were tiny in comparison, and looked like something available locally. I somehow thought it unlikely that this man had transported *lodoos* all the way from

Tirupati. Why would they abandon their traditional preparations and adopt a less impressive product? The fellow himself seemed fake to me, not unlike the sweets he was distributing. But I hadn't eaten any breakfast and so after a mental shrug I took one of the *ladoos*, ate half of it, thanked the little man, and walked ahead.

I stood directly in front of her, put my hand out and imitated the small man's refrain. 'Please take some *prasad.*'

'No, thank you,' she said firmly, her eyes downcast. She even didn't bother to look up to see who it was.

I didn't move away, just kept standing there, with my arm outstretched. Seconds later she lifted her face angrily to see who it was. Her anger gave way to bewilderment.

'No,' she said, in a low voice. 'It can't be. How on earth...?'

I sat down on the hard, brown plastic chair next to her. Briefly I explained the sequence of events that had led to my being with her.

'I've been looking for you all over Delhi,' I said. 'Where did you stay this time? I checked the Defence Colony guest house yesterday. You weren't there.'

'I didn't stay there. There was something fishy about that place, you know. A lot of rough-mannered people kept coming in and out. This time I stayed at the Broadway Hotel; some passengers on the Himalayan Queen had recommended it to me. Why are you laughing?'

I was laughing at the absurdity of it all. I had spent several hours unsuccessfully checking out more than a hundred hotels in the city before giving up the search for Diamond, but yesterday in the evening, after the day at the court, I had gone across to the Broadway Hotel bar for a couple of drinks. It had never occurred to me to check if she was there; she had probably been just a few yards away in her hotel room, packing her suitcases for today's journey.

'How could you refuse a *ladoo*?' Half the sweet was still in my hand, and I offered it to her once again.

'No, thanks. I refused one earlier. Was it a short man with a Hercule Poirot moustache who offered it to you?'

'Yes,' I admitted, taken aback. 'Have you taken to being clairvoyant these days?'

'Clairvoyant, nothing. He came to me hardly five minutes ago with the same *ladoos*.'

'Oh, I see. But why?'

'I stuffed myself silly with sweets last night,' she said, 'and early today finished what was left. Unbelievable as it might sound right now, I'm sick of even the thought of sweets. I refused to take one from this fellow, even though he was very insistent. Don't even mention the word '*ladoo*' to me again for the next six hours.'

'I couldn't do that in any case,' I said dryly, 'because in a short while from now, you'll board your flight.'

'There was no need to leave right away as I'd thought at the time. I want to apologise. Last night I spoke to Jessica on the phone. She has recovered from the initial shock of being diagnosed as HIV positive. All the same, I'd like to be with her soon. I have to be back at the university in a week's time, so I might as well catch this flight.'

All at once, I felt giddy. I was certain that if I tried to get up from the chair, I would fall. Controlling the sensation, I said, 'Yes, there is no point in missing the flight, but do employ your powers of deduction once more before you leave.'

'My powers of deduction?' she repeated blankly.

I took out Simran's letter addressed to Professor Srinivasan from my hip pocket, and handed it over to her. 'I had a hunch that if I managed to meet you, it would solve something.'

As she bent her head to read what was written in the note, I noticed a strange, worried expression in her eyes that I had seen on the morning of the day that she had left Ganahatti.

I glanced at the letter once again, and it then dawned on me what was wrong with it. How could I have missed it? That handwriting...

Everything now became clear to me. *And I knew that she knew.*

Her face suddenly became less focused and then blurred. The waiting area of the airport started spinning round and round. I fell into darkness.

36

The Denouement

1

I was first conscious of the whirring sound of the ceiling fan. I knew then that I wasn't in my flat at Banarsi Das Estate.

I tried opening my eyes, but my eyelashes seemed to be glued together and wouldn't open. *Where was I? No, a better question was where could I be? Where was I living these days? Was I in Shimla at the university hostel, or was I at Ganahatti or some other place?* I remembered all these places, but couldn't recall much else. It was as though my memory was a tape recording that had suffered a partial rupture, and parts of it that related to recent events in my life had been completely erased.

I rubbed my eyes with the palms of my hands. Eventually, with some difficulty, I managed to open them.

I was in a square room full of whiteness. Everything in the room was white: the walls, the ceiling, the floor, the iron bed, the white-painted wooden armchairs, the sheets and even the white dressing table in the corner. All it needed to complete the picture was the Indian screen villain Ajit sitting in one of the armchairs, wearing his immaculately white, tailored three-piece suit and pointed white shoes. Obviously a hospital.

I attempted to sit up in bed, found the effort too great, and slumped down again. I realised I was in a very weak condition. Too weak to move.

All right, then. I would simply have to wait for someone to find out what had happened.

After what must have been an hour, I heard the sound of footsteps. Someone was walking in the corridor outside the room. The sound of the footsteps became louder. Whoever it was was probably heading towards where I was. The footsteps stopped outside the room.

2

She came inside and stood quietly in a corner.

'I'm glad you're awake now,' she said. 'I was hoping to be able to talk to you before I left for the US. I have a flight to catch in a little while.'

Her mentioning the word 'flight' triggered something. The past came flooding back. I was remembering. At the airport I had been sitting next to her in the lounge, when I had abruptly begun to experience a terrible sensation of dizziness and nausea.

'Why am I in hospital?' I said.

'Eating too many sweets.'

'No, seriously.'

'Seriously! Apparently, that dinky fellow with the drooping moustache had put some drug in the *ladoo* you consumed.'

'Why did he pick on me?'

'That's an easy one,' she grinned. 'He obviously picks on people travelling unaccompanied. He must have been observing me for quite some time and realised I was alone. When I refused the sweets he said it was *prasad* and tried to convince me, but I was adamant. He must have then picked on you, because he noticed that you, too, were alone.'

'Whoever eats the *ladoo* will, in a matter of minutes, fall unconscious. This fellow must have some accomplice who pretends to be a friend or relative – and then they clean up.'

'Exactly.'

'What time is it now?'

'It's about six in the evening. You've been asleep for more than ten hours. The drug knocked you out cold. They had to get your stomach washed out.'

'What hospital is this?'

'It's a private nursing home in Vasant Vihar. Sonia suggested it.'

'Sorry, my mind isn't very clear as yet. How does Sonia come into the picture? I was at the airport with you when I lost consciousness, right?'

'She arrived at the airport within minutes of your passing out. After you left her house, she realised there wasn't enough petrol in the fuel tank for you to reach the airport. You were in such a tearing hurry that she gave you the keys immediately, forgetting to tell you to fill up with petrol on the way.'

That explained why the engine had gone dead after I'd reached the airport.

Diamond was saying, 'It's only after you had left that she remembered. She borrowed her neighbour's Gypsy and drove to the airport, thinking she might find you stranded somewhere on the way. At the airport she spotted her Fiat at the parking lot and assumed you were inside the airport. She came to find you and found you collapsed on the floor with a number of people crowding around you. She immediately realised that I was Diamond and managed to get everyone else to move away. With the help of another man, both of us managed to carry you to the car Sonia had borrowed. It was she who suggested this particular nursing home.'

'I see.'

'Today, when Sonia went to the airport to collect her car, she found out that the police had managed to arrest the fellow. He's a crook from Banaras.'

Banaras! That figured. I was reminded of a visit to Banaras many years ago with Eliot. At the railway station I'd heard an announcement being made repeatedly on loudspeakers: 'Kindly do not accept any sweets or *prasad* from any *sadhu* or other person. Certain criminals pretend to be holy men, and mix drugs and poisonous substances in the *prasad*. After consuming them, you will fall unconscious, and they will then run away with your cash, valuables and luggage.'

'Where is Sonia?' I asked.

'She headed off for the Sudanese Embassy for some try outs. She was here almost the whole day. In between, she had to go back to the airport in her neighbour's car with some petrol for her own car, take it home, then go back to the airport in a taxi to collect her neighbour's car. She also helped me to get a ticket on the flight leaving tonight at ten o'clock.'

'I'm sorry to have put you both to so much trouble,' I said. 'Did missing that flight cost you?'

'No, it didn't. I would, however, like to meet Jessica as soon as possible, now, so I decided to leave tonight. Sonia fixed everything. She left this letter for you.'

I took the envelope from Diamond, tore it open, and read the brief note inside.

'*Dear John,*

'*I hope you wake up in time to have a long chat with your friend. I have some urgent business to attend to. See you in the evening.*

'*Incidentally, this place is costing seven hundred and fifty bucks a day. I reckon that information will help you to recover fast.*

'*Love*

'*Sonia*'

I put the note down on the bed. I looked at her directly, not saying anything.

'You are her sister, aren't you?'

'Yes,' she replied, softly.

Everything was clear now. There was a terrible feeling of let-down and hollowness. A deep disappointment that after all there was no mistake.

'Why did you have to give me this long spiel about your being a researcher in aesthetics from the Southern Methodist University, and how you met Rehana and then Professor Srinivasan who asked you to meet me?'

'It's all true,' she replied earnestly. 'Everything. It's all true.'

'What isn't true, then?' I let my anger show. 'Suppose you begin by telling me that?'

She drew a deep breath and began speaking in a low voice.

'Simran was my elder sister. There was a four-year difference. When we were young we were close, had the same likes and tastes, and were friends. Later, differences developed and surfaced; I'm not sure how or when.

'My father was in government service and hadn't had an easy time when he was young. His family, being Sikhs, didn't want to stay on in Pakistan and risk their lives and therefore had moved to India from Lahore during the partition of the country, leaving everything they had. He struggled to make a living, somehow managed to get to college, and eventually got a job. Perhaps for this reason he was always thinking 'money'. At the same time, he wasn't career-minded for his daughters. He thought that a job or a lot of education would interfere with their marriages. He belonged to a school of thought that believed that women should be married off at an early age, and that their primary task was to raise a family and look after the home. When Simran turned twenty-four, having finished her BA in Psychology from Chandigarh, he felt it was time for her to get married.'

'How did she feel about this?'

'She was dead set against the idea. A conventional marriage was a trap, according to her. My parents felt that she had already become far too self willed and independent. She had ambition, a desire to **do** something. And that something definitely didn't mean making money, since as I've said, making money was something of an obsession with my father, and she didn't want to be like him. In many ways I think Simran's personality developed as a reaction to the way my father behaved, even though emotionally she was quite attached to him.'

'I remember her once telling me that she really had to fight to be allowed to do her Master's.'

'Yes, that's true. My father tried to persuade her to get married, but only succeeded in making her take an even more rigid stance on the matter. At that time, because of all the tensions and daily arguments that used to take place regarding this issue, she moved away from him emotionally and became closer to my mother.'

'What were you like, then?'

'I was different. At that time, I saw nothing wrong in not studying, or in getting married early. I didn't want a job. I thought I would be happy looking after a home and raising children, which was in accordance with my father's wishes. At that time, I identified completely with my father's point of view, and didn't understand why Simran thought or acted as she did. This created a gap between us.'

'So instead of Simran, your father got you married off?'

'Yes. My father wanted at least one of his daughters to get married before he retired. As I've told you, I wasn't averse to marriage at all. At the same time, Simran was adamant that she wouldn't get married till she had at least finished her Master's degree. Finally it was agreed that I would be the one to marry first. After all, my father reasoned, there wasn't that much of an age gap between the two of us.

'When I first met Navneet, I was impressed with how he dressed. I thought he looked like a film star. He was always saying things that made me laugh. After two or three meetings, I said yes. He liked me too, although in hindsight I now realise that even then he had expectations of a fat dowry from my father.

'Simran was the only one in the family who was opposed to the idea of my marriage, and insisted I should do a Master's, at the very least. "She can do so after her marriage," argued my father. "If you yourself aren't going to get married, at least don't stop others from doing so." Simran was naturally overruled, because, in addition to being good-looking and dashing, Navneet was also, in my parents' eyes, a successful Non Resident Indian to boot. And at that time I was foolishly happy at the idea of getting married to this fellow.

'I got married and joined my husband in the States. Simran went to do her Master's in Philosophy at Shimla. It was only when cracks began to appear in my marriage that I remembered what Simran had said. I couldn't write to anyone at home about my problems, least of all to her, because I had gone into the marriage against her wishes. The rest of my story you already know: the stint at art school, my changing over to philosophy, the accident, and my divorce.'

'You were the one who got Simran's handwritten notes typed on to a computer and mailed to Professor Srinivasan?'

'Yes, it happened like this. Barely a week after my divorce came through, I received a telegram from home saying that Simran had died in a bomb blast. I couldn't believe what had happened.

'Before my divorce, I had agreed with Navneet that I would claim no maintenance and that I would grant him a divorce by mutual consent, but I had put in a condition that everything be kept a secret till the divorce was final. He kept his part of the bargain. My parents had no idea either about my accident or my divorce.

'There was a reason for not letting them know. I knew my father would not easily agree to the idea of one of his daughter's getting divorced. He would move heaven and earth to make us become reconciled and agree to live together. I didn't doubt that he would sell all his ancestral land, even the house, and donate all the proceeds to Navneet to help him start a business. He would do anything to appease his son-in-law.

'I, however, wasn't prepared for any such reconciliation. I had troubles enough on my head without wanting to compound them with the strain that would inevitably occur were I to try and explain my position and views to a father who stuck firmly to the idea that marriage was for keeps and wouldn't really be listening to me. It would surely be better, I thought, to present the divorce as a fait accompli.'

I smiled sadly. 'So the resemblance between the sisters extends to other things as well...?'

'Yes...' She gave a sad smile. There was so much pain in her eyes. 'After I received news of Simran's death, I caught the first flight home. I didn't arrive in time for the *Bhog,* the day you came. I arrived the next day. I was together with my parents for a month. We shared our grief. I found out about you from my mother, who told me about Simran's involvement with a college friend, some six or seven years older than her. They learnt about my accident as soon as I arrived home. It couldn't be hidden any more, since my face had changed after the operation. I told them about my divorce from Navneet.

'Simran's Air India air-bag had been recovered. Inside it, I found her notes and a neatly written conversation between two people called Confusion and Affection. I found the conversation fascinating, more so perhaps because of my accident and studies in philosophy.

'I did think of trying to meet you even then, since you had been such an important person in Simran's life. My uncle from Canada, however, who had met you during the *Bhog,* dissuaded me. He was certain that you wouldn't want to meet me since I was part of her family.

'I realised that the strange conversation Simran had written out related to a research project for which she ought to get credit. I typed it out on my laptop while in Gurdaspur and, together with a handwritten note, mailed it to the Head of the Philosophy Department, Summerhill University.'

'It's odd that your handwriting should be so like your sister's.'

'It's not unusual at all. It's in fact common for two members of the same family to have similar handwriting. This is not owing to personality traits or any similar reason – do we need to conduct a PhD thesis on this now? – but because a younger member in a family often tries to copy the handwriting of a senior member. As a child I had tried to copy Simran's handwriting. It was a conscious and deliberate effort on my part, so the resemblance was bound to be there.'

'When did you decide to meet me?'

'As I told you, I met Rehana at a conference. When I learnt that she was from Summerhill University I was naturally curious to know if she had known my sister. She had known her, though not very well. Rehana and I became good friends, and when I came to India I went to Shimla especially to see her. Before she introduced me to Professor Srinivasan we had agreed not to tell him about my relationship with Simran. When the topic of my PhD came up he grew excited. He told me that two of his brightest student had been doing research on the same topic. He went to his study and came back holding a copy of the very same dialogue I had mailed to him a few years earlier. He had, of course, no idea of my relationship with Simran.

'He began talking of the tragic accident that had happened to her and then he spoke about you. How you were someone genuinely interested in the subject. At that point I decided I would meet you. I knew how hostile you felt towards my family. In spite of being the only surviving member – as I told you, both my parents have died – I decided to tell you only part of the truth and to conceal my relationship with Simran.'

'I might never have guessed, if it hadn't been for the letter. When you first came to my flat and left a note, I was shocked to read it because it so closely resembled Simran's handwriting. I even compared it with some old letters I had of hers, and then saw there was a difference. When the Professor gave me the handwritten note received with the dialogue, I didn't realise that it wasn't Simran's handwriting because of the resemblance. There was something odd about it, though, but I couldn't put my finger on what that was. It was only when I was next to you in the airport lounge that the pieces fell together.'

'When you told me about the letter, I was very worried that you would find out that it was written not in Simran's but in my handwriting. Rehana was the only one in Shimla who knew, but you wouldn't have got anything from her since I had sworn her to secrecy.'

I was quiet. After a while I said, 'What time does your flight leave?'

She looked at her watch. 'I should be leaving now.'

'Where's your luggage?'

'It's at the reception. I'll go now.'

I tried to get up, but she stopped me with a gesture.

We shook hands.

She left.

Epilogue

Having told them to carry on ahead, I went to sit on a huge, black boulder, below the steep cliffs. I watched the mist clearing, displaying magnificent snow-capped peaks all around us.

Simran was to have been here with me. Our agreement had been to explore, through discussion, if a beauty existed that transcended physical manifestations, but only once we had reached Gangotri, the source of the Ganges. This was a third, personal dimension to the thesis, which now perhaps would never be written. Still, there was good news. In a recent letter, Diamond had mentioned a publisher in New York who was willing to publish the material, after getting an artist to illustrate several points made in the dialogues. This was necessary to make it more 'reader friendly' (she had quoted the expression used by the publisher).

At this height, beside powerful mountains, I felt I had left behind city life, a world full of mean and petty politics, and that I would never return.

At length, I went back to the path and once again started walking towards the gigantic green glacier, which was now close by.

I was walking well above the tree line on a narrow four-feet-wide path. It had been a hard climb to reach this point, from where I could now hear the roar of huge blocks of ice tumbling down from the glacier into the river.

It didn't take me long to cover the remaining distance up to Gaumukh, the massive green glacier that was the ultimate source of the Ganges. I saw both of them laughing and smiling at the edge of the mountain path. I was curious to learn what made them so upbeat, and turned to see that their excitement was caused by the extraordinary sight of a *sadhu* taking his bath in the ice-cold, melted waters of the glacier. I came and stood next to them.

'What do you think?' I said.

'It's magnificent,' replied Kumari.

'Not going for a dip?'

'Not really,' she said, then added mischievously, 'but **she** wants to go.'

Poonam turned around, her eyes bright with excitement and gave me a smile.